# ReSHONDA TATE BILLINGSLEY

**Her bestselling novels of family and faith have been hailed as**

"Emotionally charged . . . not easily forgotten."
—*Romantic Times*

"Steamy, sassy, sexy." —*Ebony*

"Compelling, heartfelt." —*Booklist*

"Full of palpable joy, grief, and soulful characters."
—*The Jacksonville Free Press*

"Poignant and captivating, humorous and heart-wrenching."
—*The Mississippi Link*

**Don't miss these wonderful novels**

## *THE SECRET SHE KEPT*

"Entertaining and riveting. . . . A heartfelt and realistic look at the damaging effects of mental illness on those who suffer from it and the ones who bear the burden along with them. . . . Jaw-dropping, a drama-filled story. . . . Definitely a must-read."

—AAM Book Club

## *SAY AMEN, AGAIN*

**Winner of the NAACP Image Award for Outstanding Literary Work**

"Heartfelt. . . . A fast-paced story filled with vivid characters."

—*Publishers Weekly*

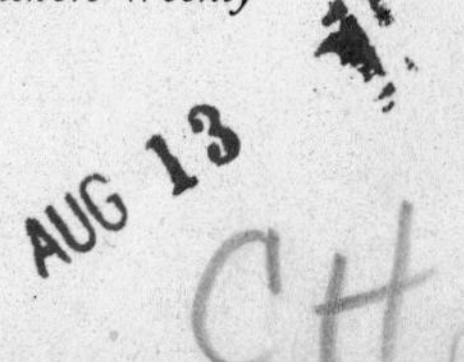

## *EVERYBODY SAY AMEN*

**A *USA Today* Top Ten Summer Sizzler!**

"A fun, redemptive book, packed with colorful characters, drama, and scandal."

—*RT Book Reviews*

***Soon to be a BET original movie!***

## *LET THE CHURCH SAY AMEN*

**#1 *Essence* magazine bestseller**

**One of *Library Journal*'s Best Christian Books**

"Billingsley infuses her text with just the right dose of humor to balance the novel's serious events.

—*Library Journal* (starred review)

"Amen to *Let the Church Say Amen*. . . . [A] well-written novel."

—*Indianapolis Recorder*

"Her community of very human saints will win readers over with their humor and verve."

—*Booklist*

## *A GOOD MAN IS HARD TO FIND*

"Billingsley's engaging voice will keep readers turning the pages and savoring each scandalous revelation."

—*Publishers Weekly* (starred review)

## *HOLY ROLLERS*

"Sensational. . . . [Billingsley] makes you fall in love with these characters."

—*RT Book Reviews*

## *THE DEVIL IS A LIE*

"An entertaining dramedy."

—*Ebony*

"A romantic page-turner dipped in heavenly goodness."

—*Romantic Times* (4½ stars)

"Fast moving and hilarious."

—*Publishers Weekly*

## *CAN I GET A WITNESS?*

**A *USA Today* 2007 Summer Sizzler**

"An emotional ride."

—*Ebony*

"Billingsley serves up a humdinger of a plot."

—*Essence*

## *THE PASTOR'S WIFE*

"Billingsley has done it again. . . . A true page-turner."

—*Urban Reviews*

## *I KNOW I'VE BEEN CHANGED*

**#1 *Dallas Morning News* bestseller**

"Grabs you from the first page and never lets go. . . . Bravo!"

—Victoria Christopher Murray

"An excellent novel with a moral lesson to boot."

—Zane, *New York Times* bestselling author

## Also by ReShonda Tate Billingsley

*Friends & Foes*
(with Victoria Christopher Murray)
*Sinners & Saints*
(with Victoria Christopher Murray)
*The Secret She Kept*
*Say Amen, Again*
*A Good Man Is Hard to Find*
*Holy Rollers*
*The Devil Is a Lie*
*Can I Get a Witness?*
*The Pastor's Wife*
*Everybody Say Amen*
*I Know I've Been Changed*
*Let the Church Say Amen*
*My Brother's Keeper*
*Have a Little Faith*
(with Jacquelin Thomas, J. D. Mason, and Sandra Kitt)

## And Check Out ReShonda's Young Adult Titles

*Drama Queens*
*Caught Up in the Drama*
*Friends 'til the End*
*Fair-Weather Friends*
*Getting Even*
*With Friends Like These*
*Blessings in Disguise*
*Nothing but Drama*

# a family affair

ReShonda Tate Billingsley

G

GALLERY BOOKS

New York London Toronto Sydney New Delhi

Gallery Books
A Division of Simon & Schuster, Inc.
1230 Avenue of the Americas
New York, NY 10020



First Gallery Books trade paperback edition July 2013



Manufactured in the United States of America

10 9 8 7 6 5 4 3 2 1

Library of Congress Cataloging-in-Publication Data

Billingsley, ReShonda Tate.
A family affair / ReShonda Tate Billingsley. — First Gallery Books trade paperback edition.
pages cm
1. Young women—Fiction. 2. Family secrets—Fiction. 3. Self-realization in women—Fiction. I. Title.
PS3602.I445F36 2013
813'.6—dc23 2012051385

ISBN 978-1-4516-3969-8
ISBN 978-1-4516-3971-1 (ebook)

*Dedicated*
*To The Hicks and The Tates*

# a family affair

# Prologue

Everyone that had ever crossed paths with Adele Wells knew that she was not a woman to be crossed. In the nine years that Lorraine Dawson had worked for her regal employer, she'd seen her fury on numerous occasions. But never had she seen an eruption like this.

"You disgraceful, low-life cheat! You disgust me," Adele spat at her trembling husband.

While the living room of the Wellses' twenty-two-thousand-square-foot mansion was bigger than the average person's house, it felt like the walls were closing in. Lorraine stood off in a corner, her head bowed, like a scolded child. She wanted to protest, speak up in her defense, but truthfully, no words could excuse what she'd done.

"And you," Adele said, spinning around to face Lorraine.

Fury filled her pale face. “I took you into my home!” Her hazel eyes burned with rage. “I cared for you and that little nappy-headed mongrel of yours. I treated you like part of my family!”

Again, Lorraine wanted to say something. Yes, she was paid a nice salary as the Wellses’ nanny, but she earned every dime. Their son, Kendall, thought she was more his mother than Adele. Still, Lorraine remained silent, her eyes downcast.

“Look at me when I talk to you!” Adele snapped, grabbing Lorraine by the chin and raising her head. At five foot nine, she towered over Lorraine’s petite frame. Lorraine feared the matron was about to slam her head into the wall. Instead, Adele glared at her. “If you’re woman enough to sleep with my husband, you should be woman enough to look me in the eye.”

“I’m s-sorry,” Lorraine managed, her voice weak with fear.

“Shut up!” Adele commanded, and Lorraine immediately clamped her mouth closed. She kept telling herself that Adele had every right to be furious. What she’d done had been the ultimate betrayal. “I don’t want to hear your tired apologies.” Adele took a deep breath, composing herself, in a vain attempt to return to the classy demeanor she usually exhibited.

“Sweetheart, please don’t blame her,” Bernard said, finally speaking up for himself. He hadn’t said much since Adele had summoned them both into the living room and confronted them with the evidence they’d tried to keep hidden for the past four years.

“Did I tell you to speak?” she hissed at her husband. She’d been domineering in the past—being the daughter of one of the wealthiest men in the country had given her the right as far

as she was concerned. But she'd always allowed her
to hang on to some dignity. But now that consideratio
gone out the window and Bernard was in no position to ar
otherwise.

"I'm just saying, it's not her fault," he said, albeit with not as much conviction as before. He was taller than his wife, but right now he appeared shrunken.

"Did you drug her?"

His shoulders sank in defeat. "No, I did not."

"Did you put a gun to her head and make her have an affair with you?"

"No, but it's not—"

Adele turned her attention back to Lorraine. "Then she was fully aware of what she did when she crawled into bed with my husband. And on top of that betrayal—" Adele's voice cracked for the first time. She'd shown no emotion other than rage since they'd stepped into the living room. "On top of that, this other deception is unforgivable." She waved the piece of paper that had sent their worlds spiraling into this horrible abyss. "What does that filthy TV show say? *You are the father!*"

"Adele, please . . ."

"Is this a lie?" She shook the paper at him. "According to this, the probability that you're that child's father is ninety-nine point nine percent. Is it a lie?" she screamed again. The vulnerability in Adele's teary eyes dared him to deny it.

"No, it's not a lie," he reluctantly admitted.

She flung the paper at her husband, then released a maniacal laugh. "My husband, the esteemed Bernard Wells, CEO of

England Enterprises, pillar of the community, philanthropist, and all-around good guy," she said, her tone a mixture of sarcasm and pain. "You *are* the father of that little bastard child."

Lorraine winced at Adele's slanderous words against the little girl that was her heart and soul, the joy of her life. She was just grateful that Olivia wasn't here to witness this nightmare. The little girl was asleep out back in the maid's quarters, the place Lorraine had called home for the past nine years.

"And to think, I doted over that little girl. I spent thousands of dollars buying her the cutest clothes and taking her places. I loved her! And all along you both knew that was my husband's child?" Adele screamed.

Neither Lorraine or Bernard said a word. They stood as if they were frozen in place.

Silence filled the room as Adele gathered herself. The time for venting was over. Now she had to make some decisions.

"Let me tell you how this is going to work," Adele said, spinning back around to face Lorraine. Adele was now eerily calm. "You are going to get your belongings and get the hell out of my house."

She walked over, picked up her checkbook off the imported marble coffee table, and tore out a check. "You will take this." She scribbled on it, then flung the check at Lorraine, who couldn't move as it fluttered side over side to the floor.

"Pick it up!" Adele commanded.

Lorraine stooped down and obeyed. She gasped when she saw the zeros. The amount was $250,000.

"The child shouldn't have to suffer because she has two

lying, deceitful parents. So take this and provide for her." Adele fought back a wave of tears before continuing, "But you are never to contact us again."

It was Bernard's turn to gasp. Adele was ordering him to stay away from his flesh and blood? Lorraine just knew he was about to put his foot down—for once. He loved Olivia, and even though they'd kept his parentage a secret, he had never been shy about letting Lorraine, or the little girl, know. No way would he go for a total ban.

"Adele, can't we talk about this?"

She ignored her husband as her eyes shot daggers at Lorraine. "You know firsthand what I'm capable of. I will destroy you, that unfaithful ingrate I call my husband, and then have your little princess sent to a foster home."

Lorraine didn't have to wonder if Adele would make good on her threats. She'd watched the woman single-handedly ruin the business, marriage, and finances of a former friend who had double-crossed her. *Ruthless* could've been her middle name.

"So, what is it going to be?" Adele asked.

Lorraine directed a silent plea to Bernard, but his crestfallen expression told her that they—that she—had no other choice. He looked away, helpless to intervene. At that moment Lorraine realized she was in this all alone. And once again, Lorraine felt herself despising the man she'd loved for so long. Even now he could not choose her.

"We'll leave tonight," she said quietly, pushing the check down into her apron pocket. "I'll just go pack my things and get Olivia."

"Your things are packed," Adele hissed, motioning toward the front door, where Logan, the Wellses' family driver, magically appeared with two black garbage bags. Next to him, Lorraine's beloved three-year-old girl stood, wide-eyed and innocent, sucking her thumb and clutching her stuffed white rabbit, her very first gift from Bernard.

Lorraine fought back tears. "Fine. I'll just go say good-bye to Kendall."

"You'll do no such thing."

Lorraine raised her hand to her mouth in shock. Kendall was like her son. She'd raised him since he was two months old. He took his first steps with her, said his first words with her, and made no secret that he preferred Lorraine to his mother.

"I-I can't say good-bye?" Lorraine said, clutching her chest. It felt like someone was taking a thousand pins and sticking them into her heart.

"What part of *you are to never come near my family again* do you not understand?"

"But—"

"Get out!"

The noise made Olivia jump and she called out for her mother. "Mommy! Why Miss Adele mad at you?"

Lorraine raced over to her daughter and scooped her up. "Shhh, it's okay, pumpkin."

"It's not okay, pumpkin." Adele tried to smile through her tears as she knelt down to stroke Olivia's hair. "Listen, we won't get to have our teatime anymore or go shopping for pretty clothes."

"Why not?" Olivia whined.

Faced with the girl she had loved so much, Adele could not reply. She just continued staring at her and rubbing her hair.

"Why not?" Olivia repeated.

Lorraine knew Olivia would not stop asking why. She took her daughter's hand and tugged it lightly. "Come on, sweetie, Mama will—"

"Tell her," Adele said, turning the little girl around to face her mother. "Tell your daughter why Miss Adele is so mad. Tell her why she has to leave the only home she's known." Adele rose to her full height, her anger returning. "Tell your daughter what a whore you are."

"Adele!" Bernard cried as Lorraine covered Olivia's ears.

"Shut up, Bernard!" Adele's unbridled fury returned as she gave Lorraine a hard push. "You're lucky I'm a classy woman, because I should beat the hell out of you right here in front of your child. Get out!" Adele pushed Lorraine hard again. She had to struggle to keep from falling. She clutched her daughter's hand tighter.

"Mommy!" Olivia cried.

"Get out and don't ever come back!" Adele pushed Lorraine again toward the door.

Olivia screamed louder as Lorraine fought back her own tears.

"Nana, where you going?"

Everyone stopped and turned toward the voice coming from the bottom of the spiral, wrought-iron staircase. Seven-year-old Kendall stood in his baseball pajamas, looking confused. Just seeing him opened up the river of tears Lorraine had been trying to hold back.

"I have to go," Lorraine called out. "But please know that I love you. I always will love you. I'm sorry!"

"Go? Go where?" Kendall said, sprinting toward her.

"Kendall, go back to your room!" Adele snapped, snatching the boy by the arm as he passed her. "For the last time, get out of my house!" she shouted at Lorraine.

Logan, who had gone to put the bags in the car, gently swooped Olivia up. "Come on, Miss Lorraine. Let's go," he said softly.

Kendall broke free from his mother and darted toward Lorraine. "Please don't go. Don't leave me. I promise I'll be good," he cried, throwing his arms around her waist and holding on tight.

Lorraine sobbed as Adele yanked her son away. With her other hand flailing madly, she pushed Lorraine out and slammed the door. Lorraine fell to her knees outside on the front stoop, crying uncontrollably. At long last Logan helped her to her feet and led her down the steps.

As Lorraine climbed into the car, she glanced up at the living-room window. Kendall stood in the window, tears streaming down his face. Behind him stood Bernard, and Lorraine could see the endless sorrow in his eyes. Then Adele appeared and whipped the curtains closed.

# Chapter 1

*Seventeen years later*

"Hey, girl, when are you gonna come get with some of this?"

Olivia Dawson kept walking, ignoring the catcalls and jeers from the group of men that had taken up their usual posts outside her apartment building. It was unseasonably cold for November. Houston usually didn't see these frigid temperatures until January or February. Still, the group hung out, smoking, talking, and seeing what kind of trouble they could create.

"You know you want this," someone else yelled.

She was used to the attention—and the disparaging remarks. Many of the guys in her neighborhood were attracted to her, not only for her all-American-girl looks but her toned dancer's body. Yet Olivia never gave any of those guys the time of day.

She struggled to open the front door of the building, shifting her oversize purse on her shoulder and then humping the two bags of groceries around to one side. Not one of those idiots offered to help.

"Maybe if you weren't so stuck-up we'd do the gentlemanly thing and help you with those bags," the leader of their little pack, Danny, said. "But since you're such a bitch, carry on." They all busted out laughing. She cut her eyes at them as she got the door open.

Olivia hated this filthy place. Everything about it—from the dilapidated units to the graffiti-laden walls to the pissy-smelling hallway—made her stomach turn. But sadly, this had been home since she was twelve years old. Before that, they'd lived in several apartments not much better than this, but at least she didn't have to worry about the riffraff or getting shot by a stray bullet. No, this had been a step down, even in a life already sunk in poverty.

Before moving here, her mother, Lorraine, had worked serving food in Olivia's school cafeteria. That had been so embarrassing for Olivia. Then Lorraine had overheard some kids teasing Olivia, and the very next day she'd transferred Olivia to another school.

That was just one of the many selfless things her mother had done over the years. Her mother had *always* been selfless. Olivia couldn't imagine her world without her mother. All her life it had been just the two of them against the world.

Olivia jabbed the elevator button, then cursed when she saw the OUT OF ORDER sign hanging lopsided on the door. "When is the stupid contraption ever *in* order?" she mumbled as she began the six-flight trek up the stairs.

Olivia made herself a promise for the thousandth time: she would get her mother out of this place if it was the last thing she did.

The thought of Juilliard, the world-famous performing arts school in New York City, popped into her mind, and she swallowed a lump that formed in her throat. That had initially been her ticket out of the hood. She had excelled as a ballet dancer since she was eight years old. Her ballet instructor said she was a natural, and she'd even let Olivia continue coming to the classes when her mother could no longer afford to pay. The same instructor had made sure Olivia participated in—and often won—area competitions all throughout high school. Her first-place honor in a citywide competition had caught the eye of a teacher from Juilliard, who'd encouraged Olivia to apply to the school. Olivia had gotten accepted, and she'd planned to become a famous dancer with a ballet company or on Broadway—a profession that would garner her a lot of money.

But Juilliard was a distant dream now.

"Mama," Olivia called out once she'd finally reached their tiny apartment. The main lock hung slightly askew, as always, a victim of a long-ago attempted robbery. "I'm home." She walked in to see her mother sitting at the kitchen table, clutching a folded piece of paper. "How are you feeling?"

Lorraine had been sick over the past few months, even passing out a few times. She'd blamed the problem on exhaustion and had even quit her second job. But Olivia was sure that the cause was simply years of working too hard and stressing as she tried desperately to make ends meet. Olivia vowed that somehow she would make good so that her mother could sit back and enjoy her golden years.

Lorraine looked up, but her normally pleasant smile was gone. "Well, I was feeling okay until I saw this." Lorraine held up the creased paper and Olivia's heart dropped.

"Wh-where did you get that?"

"From your hiding place. Under your mattress."

Olivia wanted to ask her mother what she was doing snooping under her mattress, but that was a moot point. Lorraine felt that anything that went on in her house was her business.

"You told me you didn't get into Juilliard."

Olivia set down her purse and the bags of groceries and slid into the seat across from her mother. "Mama, it doesn't matter."

Tears were brimming in her mother's eyes. "Yes, it does!" She waved the paper. "This was your dream! Why didn't you tell me?"

"For what, Mama? What difference would it have made? Juilliard costs forty thousand dollars a year. Even with a scholarship, which I didn't get, how was I supposed to pay for that?"

*"We would've found a way,"* Lorraine cried.

Olivia so wished this conversation had never happened. "That would've been one more thing for you to worry about."

"We would've found a way," her mother repeated with conviction. Since her mother had gotten sick, they depended largely on Olivia's meager paycheck from her job as a salesclerk at Eden's, a local high-end clothing store.

Olivia looked at her mother flatly. "Mama, we can barely find a way to eat."

Lorraine slammed the paper on the table so hard, Olivia jumped. "We. Would've. Found. A. Way!"

This was exactly why Olivia didn't want her mother to know she had been accepted to Juilliard. Olivia knew her mother would stress herself out trying to figure out a way to pay for an impossible dream.

Olivia went to her mother's side, kneeling next to her. "Okay, Mama, calm down. It's not that big of a deal."

"Yes, it is." But Lorraine was calming down. Her voice turned solemn as she gently stroked her daughter's cheek. "This was your dream, baby. You never asked me for anything. All you talked about since you were ten years old was going to Juilliard."

Her mother was right about that. The late-night and early-morning practices, the nonstop practicing of routines in her tiny room, catching the bus downtown in the blazing heat to dance in the Ensemble Theatre's summer musicals—all of that had been designed to ensure Olivia's acceptance into Juilliard.

"Why did you lie to me?" her mother asked, turning her attention back to the acceptance letter.

"I didn't get the scholarship, Mama. There was no way we could've come up with that kind of money." When her mother started shaking her head, Olivia continued, "But it's not like it's forever. I can still save up the money and go later."

"You and I both know how hard it is to get in." Tears began to trickle down Lorraine's face. "And you got in."

That had been both the happiest and the saddest day of Olivia's life. She'd been so excited when she got the acceptance letter. Yet that very evening her mother had come home and announced that she'd had to quit her second job for health reasons. How in the world was Olivia then going to say to her, "Sorry about the job, Mom, but I need forty grand for school"?

Olivia had remained hopeful that she could get a scholarship, and she had been devastated when she'd learned that because of a decrease in funding, that wouldn't happen. A counselor had told her she could get some financial aid, but the sums were nowhere near enough. Olivia couldn't bear the disappointment. Her dance instructor had wanted Olivia to continue dancing, even teach a couple of classes. But when the Juilliard dream died, so did her desire to dance. So she'd hung up her ballet shoes and focused on getting a job.

Lorraine dabbed her eyes. "You missed out on so much in your life. You go over there to that store and deal with all those snobby rich folks. You should be on their same level—shopping in that store, not waiting on them." Lorraine was almost talking to herself, getting angrier with each word she spoke.

"Mama, the job isn't that bad," Olivia protested.

Lorraine grabbed Olivia's arm, startling her. "You are destined for greatness. You deserve better. You should have better than this!" Lorraine motioned wildly around the apartment.

"It's just a stepping-stone." To what, Olivia didn't know. She liked working in fashion, but her true passion was dance, and she wasn't making any progress toward her dream now.

"No." Lorraine fell silent, struck by an idea, before she finally stood up and announced, "I'll be back."

"Mama, where are you going? It's cold out there."

"I'm going where I should've gone a long time ago," she muttered, grabbing her coat.

"You shouldn't be going out in this weather." Not only was the temperature in the thirties, but at the store Olivia had heard reports of a brewing ice storm.

"I'll be back," Lorraine said with conviction. She had a determined look on her face, and Olivia couldn't imagine why.

"Mama, it's too cold for you to go out."

"Don't you worry about me. You just get to writing those folks—because you're going to that school."

Olivia wanted to be honest with her mother as she watched her leave. She should tell her that it was too late now. Not only had she not laced up a pair of slippers since she found out she wouldn't be going to Juilliard, the chances of her being able to get back in after two years were slim to none. And even if she did, unless her mother was going to rob a bank, Olivia would have to save up for a hundred years before she had the money to go.

# Chapter 2

The long hand on the clock hanging on their yellowed kitchen wall seemed to be revolving in slow motion. With each tick, Olivia's heart quickened.

Her mother had been gone for three hours now, and with the raging winds and blistering sleet coming down, Olivia was beyond worried. They weren't used to this kind of weather in Houston, so her mother couldn't be faring well in it.

They had no house phone, and Olivia's cell phone was cut off because she couldn't pay the bill until the first of the month, so she had no way to call around and check on her mother.

Olivia was about to put on her coat and go searching herself when she heard a tap on the door. Maybe, in her rush to leave for her mysterious destination, her mother had forgotten her keys.

"Mama?" Olivia said, swinging the door open. She frowned at the sight of her landlord and neighbor, Mrs. Worthy. The old, meddlesome woman could be a nuisance sometimes, but Olivia smiled anyway. "Hi, Mrs. Worthy. How are you?"

The landlady didn't return the smile. Her weathered skin hung from her face as worry filled her eyes. "Baby, I'm okay, but, ummm"—she wrung her hands nervously—"I just got a phone call. It's about your mother."

Olivia stiffened. "Who called you and why?"

Mrs. Worthy shrugged like she hated to be the one delivering this message. "Well, I don't know. They said they looked up my address."

"For what?" Olivia felt like the breath was slowly being let out of her. "Where's my mother?"

"I guess they called me because I live next to your mama, and, ummm"—Mrs. Worthy took a deep breath—"they got your mama's address off her license."

"What? Where is she?" Olivia's heart was racing now.

"Honey, your mama is at Memorial Hermann Hospital. She had a heart attack."

Olivia gasped as she fell back against the wall. "Oh, my God. Is"—she had to pause before she could say the words—"is she dead?"

Mrs. Worthy looked unsure. "I don't think so, but they need you to get down there right away."

A flash of panic swept over Olivia. The buses had stopped running, and even if she could contact her best friend, Mona, she would take at least an hour to get here from her apartment on the other side of town. Olivia didn't know what she was going to do.

"My nephew Thomas is here," Mrs. Worthy said, anticipating Olivia's dilemma. "I already told him to get the car. He's waiting downstairs for you. He'll take you to the hospital."

"Oh, thank you so much." Olivia hurriedly grabbed her coat and purse and followed Mrs. Worthy down the stairs.

Twenty minutes later, Olivia burst through the lobby doors of Memorial Hermann. "Yes, I'm here to see Lorraine Dawson," she told the woman sitting at the front desk.

The desk clerk took her time as she pulled out a piece of paper and slowly scanned the list. "Dawson . . . Dawson . . ." She ran her finger down the page.

"Please, hurry." Olivia's heart was about to jump through her skin. On the drive over, she had pushed away thoughts of life without her mother. She'd prayed desperately for God to pull her mother through.

The woman narrowed her eyes as if she didn't appreciate being rushed. "Are you family?"

"Yes, I'm her daughter."

The clerk pointed down the hall. "Okay, she's in Room 407. You can go through those doors and take the elevator up to the fourth level."

"Thank you."

Olivia raced down the hall. Outside Room 407, she took a deep breath before she went in. She had to brace herself for the worst, she told herself. She slowly opened the door. She didn't know what she would find, but she definitely hadn't expected this. Her mother lay in a hospital bed, tubes seemingly coming from every part of her body. The slow hum of a light-blinking machine was the only sound in the room. The sight of her mother so pathetic was heartbreaking.

"Mama, are you okay?" Olivia eased to her mother's side and took her hand.

"Sorry, baby, she can't hear you." Olivia hadn't noticed the heavyset nurse working in the corner of the room. "She be resting. They've sedated her, so she'll be out for a minute," the nurse said in a thick West Indies accent. "I'm Anya, and don't worry. I'm taking good care of your mother."

"Is she okay?"

Anya flashed a warm smile as she headed toward the door. "Let me get the doctor. He should be able to tell you more."

After what seemed like forever, the doctor finally appeared in the doorway. He was a giant of a man and his face was devoid of any compassion as he scanned the chart he picked up from the end of the bed. "Are you Ms. Dawson's daughter?"

"I am." Olivia tightened her hold on her mother's lifeless hand. "What's going on with my mom?"

"Your mother suffered a massive coronary heart failure," he said without looking up.

"What? Is she going to pull through?"

The doctor continued scribbling on his paper. He was an older man, which meant he'd probably been telling patients and their relatives awful news for years. In that case, someone needed to teach him some people skills.

"Well, we've stabilized her, but that's all we can do for now." He stopped writing and glanced at Lorraine. "We will monitor her over the next twenty-four hours. Then we should get a better idea of what we're dealing with."

Olivia hated the coldness of his voice, as if he were talking about the weather. She wasn't normally outspoken, but a part of her wanted to remind him forcefully that this woman was more than just a name on a chart. She was all Olivia had. He needed to show some serious compassion and do everything possible to make sure her mother was okay.

But before Olivia could say the first word, the doctor dropped the file in the slot at the end of Lorraine's bed. "Sorry, I gotta go. Gotta check on other patients." He marched out before Olivia could ask any more questions. She was no closer to figuring out what had happened to her mother, and one step closer to having a serious heart attack herself. She was definitely feeling like she was about to pass out.

The hospital-room door eased open, and her best friend, Mona, stuck her head through. Olivia had used Thomas's cell phone to call Mona and let her know what had happened.

"Hey, can I come in?" Mona didn't wait for a reply as she walked in the room. She let out a gasp at the sight of the woman who'd become her second mother.

"I know, she looks so frail." Olivia turned back to her mother and stroked her hand.

Mona took slow steps toward the bed. "Is she going to be okay?" she whispered.

Olivia nodded as she fought back tears. "She has to be. She just has to be."

Mona, who was always the bubbly life of the party, squeezed Olivia's shoulder and said solemnly, "We just have to pray."

Normally, Mona's being serious would've scared the crap out of Olivia, but right now she knew her friend was right. As she gazed down at her mother's slack expression, Olivia knew that prayer was the only thing that could save her now.

# Chapter 3

This had been the longest forty-eight hours of Olivia's life, and she had yet to leave her mother's side. Lorraine had briefly fluttered her eyes this morning, but other than that, she'd been completely unresponsive. Olivia had never been as religious as her mother, but as a devout Christian surely her mother had some get-well credits stocked up. Olivia was praying that she could cash them in. But so far, nothing. The doctor had returned a few times, but he had pretty much given the same report. Seeing how a person recovered from a coronary was a waiting game.

"Hey, Olivia," Mona said, easing into the room. "Sorry I'm late. I had the hardest time getting someone to cover me at work."

Olivia tried to smile at her best friend. Mona had been Olivia's saving grace over the last two days, keeping her from completely collapsing under the stress of worrying about her mother. Mona hadn't left Olivia's side the first day and only went home this morning to change and call in to work.

"So, Mama Lorraine ain't up and bossing these poor nurses around?" Mona tried to joke.

Olivia stroked her mother's hand. She would give anything to have that right now.

Mona didn't say another word as she walked up behind Olivia and rubbed her back. Olivia knew she looked a mess—her hair was disheveled and she could feel the weight of the bags under her eyes.

Mona said quietly, "You really should go home and get some sleep."

*Home?* That was laughable. Home was the place made by the people that lived there. If her mother wasn't there, then Olivia didn't really have a home. She had a sudden thought: Where would she live if her mother died? Her great-aunt Betty lived in a nearby senior center, but other than that, Olivia had no other family. She was old enough to live on her own, but she couldn't imagine staying in that apartment if something happened to her mother.

Olivia shook off that thought. Mona had been telling her to think only positive thoughts, and that's what she'd been trying to do.

Trying. Most of the time, to no avail.

The door to the hospital room opened, and a woman wearing a navy business suit, her hair pulled back in a tight bun, appeared.

"Miss Dawson?"

"Yes?" Olivia eyed the woman. Something about her officious demeanor didn't feel right.

"I'm Mrs. Markham from the business affairs office." She glanced down at her folder. "Ummm, I need to talk to you about your mother's financial situation."

Olivia didn't respond as she waited for the woman to continue. If she was about to ask for money, she was wasting her breath.

Mrs. Markham stopped at the end of the bed. She had a sympathetic expression across her face, but the condolence felt contrived. "I'm not sure if you're aware, but your mother doesn't have insurance."

"I know." They hadn't had insurance since her mother lost her job.

"Well, that is problematic."

Olivia held up her hand to cut the woman off. "Whoa. Didn't the president make it that you can't deny medical coverage?"

"We're a private facility, ma'am."

"So? What does that have to do with anything?"

Mrs. Markham took a step back, as if she didn't know how this hostile relative was going to react. "I'm sorry, but your mother owes a bill from the last time she was here. We can't treat her any longer. We are going to have to move her to a public facility."

Olivia shook her head in disbelief, but before she could say anything, Mona stepped forward. "Are you freakin' kidding me? You're going to deny her mother medical attention?"

"It's not that we're denying her." Mrs. Markham fidgeted nervously. "Ms. Dawson is stable enough to move."

"Are you kidding me?" Mona asked again. "Look at her. She's not awake. But you're just gonna up and move her?" Mona moved closer to Mrs. Markham, who backed up even farther.

"Olivia?"

Olivia gasped at the sound of her mother's frail voice. "Oh, my God, Mama," she said, rushing to her mother's side.

"Mama Lorraine!" Mona said, rushing to the other side.

"I'll get the doctor," Mrs. Markham said, heading toward the door. But she stopped and added in a firm voice, "Miss Dawson, I'll come back later, but we're still going to have to move her. So please be advised."

Ignoring the woman, Olivia smothered her mother's face with kisses. "Mama, you had us so scared."

"Wh-what's going on?" Lorraine's voice was weak and her eyelids looked heavy, but she was conscious.

"You had a heart attack, Mama. But you're gonna be okay."

Lorraine was trying to get her bearings. She glanced around the room, then settled her gaze on Olivia. She eased her hand up and wiped Olivia's cheek with a calloused finger.

Olivia didn't even realize she was crying. Before she could tell her mother how glad she was, the doctor walked in. She didn't want to release her mother's hand, but she took a step back so that he could examine her.

"How are you feeling, Ms. Dawson?" he asked, pulling out a device and peering into her eyes.

"Not good," she mumbled.

"You've been through a lot." He stood, checked the heart monitor, and frowned.

"What?" Olivia said, panicked.

"Hmmm, her heart rate concerns me. It was up, but now it's abnormally slow." He turned to the nurse, who had walked in behind him. "I need to get an EKG right away." Then he turned his sights on Olivia. "You and your friend probably should wait outside and let your mother rest."

"I'm not leaving," Olivia said.

"This room is small. We can't have this many people in here."

"Fine," Mona said. "I'll leave. But she's staying." Mona walked over, kissed Lorraine on the forehead, then squeezed Olivia's hand. "I'll be right outside."

Olivia nodded. "Okay." As soon as Mona walked off, she asked the doctor, "So, Doc, what's going on?"

"Uhhhh," Lorraine said, trying to sit up.

"Mama, don't move," Olivia said, darting over to help her mother lie back down.

"Stay still," the doctor said, patting Lorraine's shoulder gently. "Just rest until we get those tests done." This was the first sign of compassion that he'd shown since Olivia had arrived.

"Doctor, what's going on?" Olivia asked as her mother closed her eyes and inhaled deeply.

"We'll know more in about an hour. Just make sure your mother takes it easy." He headed out the door.

"It's okay, you're gonna be fine, Mama," Olivia said,

squeezing her mother's hand. With her other hand she brushed a wave of fine, salt-and-pepper hair out of her face.

"Olivia . . . I-I need to tell . . . tell you something before I die." Her voice was strained and she wore an agonized expression on her face.

The words made Olivia's heart drop into the pit of her stomach. "You're not dying, Mama."

Lorraine smiled wearily. "Yeah. Yeah, baby, I am." She weakly patted Olivia's hand. Olivia had never noticed how worn-out her mother looked. She was only fifty-four, but in that hospital bed she looked twenty years older.

"Mama, what were you doing out in that weather?" Olivia didn't want to get her mother worked up, but she'd been trying to make sense of what would drive her mother out into the blistering cold.

A lone tear fell down her face. "Trying to get you money for school."

"Getting money, on a street corner?" Olivia asked, horrified.

Her mother tried to smile as she sat up, but the attempt was cut short as she grimaced in pain.

"Never mind, Mama. We can talk later," Olivia said, stroking her mother's hair. Any answers she needed could wait. Right now her mother's health was first and foremost.

Lorraine slumped back against the bed. "No . . . I . . . I have to say this. I was trying to call someone."

"Call who?"

Suddenly, the lone tear was accompanied by a stream of others. The sight of her mother crying scared Olivia to no end.

"Mama, what's going on?" Olivia fell into the seat next to her mother's bed. "What's wrong?"

Lorraine closed her eyes and became so still that if not for the steady beep of the machine, Olivia would've sworn she had just peacefully died. Finally Lorraine said, "I should've told you . . . a long time ago, and the only reason I'm telling you now . . . the only reason I'm saying something now . . ." She took a deep breath, then forced herself to finish. ". . . is because I don't want to leave you in this world all alone. I've denied you what's rightfully yours for too long."

"What do you mean?" Olivia had never seen her mother so worked up, and the distraught tone of her voice was frightening.

"You deserve it . . . just like Kendall," she finally said before closing her eyes and beginning a series of guttural moans.

Who was Kendall? Was her mother delirious? Olivia leaned in closer to her mother. Beads of sweat dotted Lorraine's forehead. "Mama, just get some rest. Don't talk, okay?"

Lorraine ignored her and went on, "It's not fair that your brother gets everything and you get nothing."

That made Olivia sit straight up. *"Brother?"*

Lorraine was shaking her head, like she was preparing herself for a journey. "I am so sorry, baby, but she promised to have you taken away from me if I ever uttered a word to anyone." Lorraine shook her head faster and faster as she began sobbing harder and harder. The beeping of the machine sped up.

"Mama, you need to stop talking. Just rest. You're talking crazy."

"No, I'm not!" she exclaimed, and the beeping intensified.

"He's your f-father and I should've never let them make me leave."

That stopped Olivia cold. Lorraine had never talked about Olivia's father, saying it was too painful. All Olivia knew was that he had died when she was a little girl. "My father?" Olivia whispered. "You said he was dead."

"I'm sorry. I'm so-o sorry. I hope"—Lorraine took a breath—"I hope you can forgive me." The machine seemed to be beeping out of control. As bad as Olivia wanted answers, she hugged her mother and said, "Shhhh, Mama. Of course I forgive you. I love you. You are my life. That's why I need you to get better."

She held her mother tightly, rocking her. She breathed a sigh of relief as the beeping slowed down . . . and down . . .

Not until she felt her mother's body sag limply did Olivia realize the beeping had stopped altogether.

# Chapter 4

"So what time can we expect a shipment in? . . . Well, do what you have to do to make it happen."

Bernard Wells hung up the phone in his home office, where he conducted almost half of his business as CEO of England Enterprises, the company founded by his wife's father. Bernard discovered his son was standing in the doorway. A pair of expensive Dr. Dre Beats earphones was around his neck, and rap music was blaring from the earpieces.

"Yes, Kendall?" Bernard said, not bothering to say anything about the music.

"Yo, Pops, I need four hundred dollars."

"Kendall—"

He held up a hand, cutting Bernard off. "Hold up before you start the lecture. It's just until payday."

"Kendall, you got fired, remember? You don't have a payday."

Kendall flashed a crooked smile. "Oh, yeah."

Bernard shook his head in disappointment. Kendall was always getting fired from somewhere. He was always trying to get by on his boyish good looks and charismatic personality. But he was the most trifling young man Bernard had ever seen. Kendall came from a long line of people who worked from sunup to sundown, who valued hard work. But if Kendall thought any work had to be done, he could always be found going in the opposite direction. He had worked everywhere—from a pizza joint to a nightclub. He kept no job longer than a month. He didn't necessarily feel entitled—like many rich kids. He was just lazy and would rather go without than have to work hard for something. Luckily for him, Adele didn't believe in letting him go without, so he had everything his heart desired—at least material things.

Bernard had tried to bring his son into the family business. But after he made several lewd comments to secretaries, botched up a major shipment, and insulted a client, Bernard had decided his heir wasn't ready to take on the Wells family business.

Judging from his saggy Sean John pants, plaid, button-down shirt, and Timberland boots, he wouldn't be ready anytime soon either.

"Speaking of jobs," Bernard said, "we really need to talk about your future."

Kendall rolled his eyes and groaned.

"You can get exasperated all you want, but this is ridiculous. You had me spend all that money for UCLA, and what happened? You dropped out. Then the Art Institute, and what happened? You dropped out."

Kendall had an answer ready. "That's because all that stuff was for you guys. It was your idea, your dream. I want to be in the music business."

"Oh, here we go again." Bernard threw his hands up in the air.

"How many young thugs want to be a rapper?" his wife said, walking into the office. Adele seemed to magically appear wherever she went, which was surprising since she had such a dominant persona. "You're too old for this foolishness, Kendall."

The sight of his mother instantly soured Kendall's kidding mood. He rolled his eyes at his mother, but she continued her rant. "It is high time you do something with your life. How we raised such a worthless child is beyond me. Your father and I are so disappointed in you." She dropped a manila folder on Bernard's desk.

Kendall lifted the earphones from around his neck and cupped them over his ears. "Yeah, I know. I'm the scum of the earth, you remind me every day." He walked toward the door. "Forget the four hundred. I'll find another way."

Bernard unhappily watched his son go. "Must you berate him every chance you get?"

"Somebody needs to," she snapped, folding her arms. "You raised a wimp of a son, you know that, right?"

Bernard didn't bother to engage in the argument. It was useless anyway. Sometimes he didn't understand why he stayed married to Adele. Yet he was a sensible man. He loved his lifestyle—at least outside his home. He loved the *things* in his life. The power, the prestige. The money. Sure, he'd made the England empire into what it was today, but Adele never hesitated to remind him that it was all built on the backs of her family. And she'd been clear from the beginning—and in writing—that if he ever decided to leave, the company stayed under her control. Bernard was confident that he could build another business just as successful as England Enterprises, but at fifty-nine he had no desire to start over. So, he endured.

Over the course of their twenty-five-year marriage, Bernard had learned how to tune Adele out, nod when appropriate, and agree to disagree. Most of the time he just let her have her way, since most of her issues didn't matter to him. Every now and then she could even be sweet. They slept in separate bedrooms, had obligatory sex every other month—neither of them had any desire to be intimate with the other—and made all the social appearances. The sex, when it happened, was laughable. It was mechanical and lacked any passion, an item checked off on her to-do list. But he'd learned to live with that as well.

Keeping a mistress cost him plenty, but Alyssa kept that itch scratched when he needed it. He smiled as he thought of Alyssa's sexy lips, her perfectly toned body. He'd bought the breasts, but everything else on her was natural. Best of all, Alyssa stayed in her place. Bernard hated that she worked for his company, but at least she was in the public relations department and he didn't have to see her every day. That would've been torture because every time he caught sight of her, his body craved her more.

Alyssa was the perfect mistress. She never begged for more time, and she had no delusions of marriage. As long as Bernard came over when he could, she was happy. And when she was happy, she made him happy. Just not happy enough to leave his wife. For as much as he adored Alyssa, relished their time together, he didn't love her. He couldn't love her. Bernard had long ago given up any grand ideas of "happily ever after."

When he was younger, Bernard fell in love, but then he met Adele and got a taste of money and power. And money and power trumped true love. Bernard thought that he'd grow to love Adele, but over the years he had come to the conclusion that she just wasn't lovable. She didn't know how to let go of the past, forgive, and move on. Things would've been so different with his one true love—

"So, did you fire Walter and Jerry?" Adele's raspy voice interrupted his thoughts before Bernard could travel too far down memory lane. She wanted to make sure he didn't get any pleasure whatsoever—not even with his thoughts.

Bernard sighed as he removed his reading glasses and set them on the desk. He wished Adele would be like all his colleagues' wives and bury herself in her charitable organizations, but since business was in her blood, Adele wouldn't go away that easily. She still held a VP oversight position, and she came into the office at least twice a week to make sure everything was flowing smoothly, which simply meant to be a pain in Bernard's backside.

"Adele, how many times have I asked you to let me handle the business operations?"

"And how many times have I told you that you have a soft spot for these people and that doesn't mix well with business?"

He looked at her, exasperated. Underneath all that hardness, and stone-cold demeanor, Adele was actually a beautiful woman. But she no longer cared to let that part of herself show.

"You want me to fire a father of six a month before Christmas, Adele?"

"I don't care if Walter's the father of sixteen," she snapped. "He got the order wrong and it cost us a lot of money."

"So then we write him up, we suspend him, we don't fire him."

"And we create an environment that says we tolerate ineffectiveness. And this is Jerry's third screwup. How many more chances should he get, Bernard?"

Bernard knew that arguing on Jerry Cooper's behalf was futile. He had missed so many days of work it was ridiculous. Bernard understood that Jerry took the time off because his eight-year-old daughter had leukemia and he was spending so much time at the hospital, but Adele was willing to be only so patient.

"Adele, please let me handle this." Jerry, that was borderline, but firing Walter simply wasn't an option for Bernard. Walter knew too much. Besides, Bernard liked him. And running this company was the only place Bernard was able to put his foot down with his wife. It was the only place he felt like a man. He didn't want her coming in and taking that from him as well.

"Fine," Adele said, acquiescing. She still looked at him like he was some pitiful specimen. "But one more screwup from either of them and I'm not waiting on you to act. My father, God rest his soul, worked too hard to let this company be run into the ground because you have a bleeding heart."

Enough was getting to be enough. "Don't you have some foundation work or something you can attend to?" he asked when she continued to stand over his desk.

"Don't I always? These sorority members are once again coming to me, like I'm the only one with any money," she barked.

Bernard couldn't understand, with all of her griping about her charitable organizations and sorority, why she continued to be such a vigorous part of them. It must be because his wife relished having everyone place her on a pedestal.

"Can you let Vianessa know I will take my dinner here in the study?" he said, hoping Adele would get the message and leave him alone.

Adele narrowed her eyes at him, her displeasure evident. "So another evening that you expect me to dine alone?"

"I have a lot of work to do," he lied, immediately turning his attention to the folder she'd dropped on his large mahogany desk.

Adele huffed, spun around, and exited his office.

Usually, he would force himself to sit through cold and impersonal dinners with his wife—Kendall had long ago stopped joining them. But today Bernard simply wasn't in the mood. The run-in with Adele had him once again wondering the what-ifs. Feeling a familiar wave of loneliness coming on, he reached under his desk, into a secret compartment, and pulled out a worn and tattered photo.

He gently fingered the picture. Even after all these years he still thought about her every day. He could still remember how soft her skin was, her contagious laugh—and how her touch sent shivers up his spine. He remembered how incredibly in love with her he'd been.

"And can you not forget that we have the Russos' dinner party tomorrow?" Adele said, sticking her head back in the door.

Startled, Bernard eased the photo back into its compartment. "Yes, dear," he mumbled. Not only did his wife put a damper on his day, she was notorious for messing up his daydreams as well.

Bernard sat, watching the closed door for a full minute. He wanted to pull the picture back out, stare at it as he'd done countless times over the years. But then he decided he couldn't stand the torture, so he picked up the phone instead and punched in the number that had been his salvation.

"Hey, Daddy," Alyssa purred, picking up the phone on the first ring.

"Hey, beautiful. What are you doing?"

"Thinking about you while I sit all alone in this bubble bath. You know, I have a spot on my back I can't reach. I wish you were here to get it for me."

He released a throaty moan as he felt the bulge in his pants rise. He imagined her smooth, youthful skin covered with bubbles. Her long auburn curls were probably pinned up with just a few cascading down over her face. "I wish I was there, too, baby."

"Well, you know I'm always here for you, Daddy. And I have a special surprise to thank you for the beautiful diamond earrings." He'd left the gift on her desk with a note that said, "Love, Clark," which was their code name for him at the office.

"So you liked them?"

"I loved them." Her voice lowered into a sexy whisper. "And I want to show you how much I appreciate all that you do for me."

Bernard swallowed, adjusted himself. "I'm on my way." He hung up the phone, trying to figure out what lie he would tell to sneak out.

He still hadn't come up with anything as he walked by the dining room ten minutes later. He expected to be greeted with Adele's scowl, but instead she said, "Are you sure you don't want to join me?" She motioned at the long, antique hickory dining-room table. "It gets kind of lonely," she admitted with a smile.

That rare admission made him feel a twinge of guilt. But then images of Alyssa in the bathtub, waiting on him, and the surprise she had in store, made him say, "Sorry, left some papers at the office."

She lost her smile, her glare cutting through his lie.

"I won't be long," he said, heading out the door. At least, he told himself, not all night long.

# Chapter 5

"Babe, you've got to eat something."

Olivia's ex-boyfriend, Stephon, was standing over her with a plate. Thank God, her great-aunt Betty had stepped in and helped her make funeral arrangements, since Olivia had been completely incapable of doing anything. Betty had contacted the funeral home, arranged everything, and even put together the program.

Although the service had passed in a blur, Olivia remembered how relieved she'd been to see Stephon. Mona had called him, and the two of them had stayed by Olivia's side the entire service.

"I'm not hungry," Olivia finally said. Seeing Stephon had reminded her of their plans to go away together. She was supposed to attend Juilliard and he was heading to NYU. Once she didn't go, Olivia had thought it was only fair to him that they break up. Stephon had wanted to keep their relationship going, but Olivia had heard too many horror stories about long-distance relationships and had "set him free." Now, seeing him again brought back all the memories.

"Eat," he commanded.

She sighed but accepted the paper plate stacked with fresh fruit. "Thank you."

"You know you don't have to thank me." He sat down next to her on the sofa and brushed a piece of lint off her black dress. "Mona is so upset that she had to leave. Besides, her job barely gave her the time off to attend the funeral."

"It's okay." Truthfully, Olivia was no longer in the mood for people—not even her best friend or ex-boyfriend. Now that she was back home, she just wanted to be left alone. "When are you going back?"

"I have to return and take finals, but I don't want to go back. I want to stay here to help you through this. I know how close you were to your mother."

That warmed her heart—and saddened her at the same time. "No, I'll be fine."

"Yeah, but if I'm here, I can make sure." He picked up a strawberry and put it to her mouth. "Eat."

He wasn't about to take no for an answer, so she slowly opened her mouth and bit into the strawberry.

Satisfied, he continued, "Or, come to New York with me. There's nothing keeping you here."

Olivia looked around the small apartment. Truer words had never been spoken.

Overcome by a fresh wave of sadness, she dropped the plate on the coffee table. "What am I going to do?" She buried her face in her hands, releasing the tears she'd been holding in since they lowered her mother's body in the ground.

Stephon pulled her tight, caressing her back while she cried for a long stretch of minutes. After she pulled herself together, Stephon led her to the bedroom and made her lie down. Olivia didn't remember much after that, except his sticking his head in later, saying he had to go run errands and would be back in a bit.

Olivia raised herself up on the bed and glanced at the clock. She'd been asleep for four hours. She stretched and momentarily relished the quiet. But before long she found herself contemplating what she would do with herself next. Stephon's offer was enticing, but she couldn't go anywhere. At least not yet. She had some investigating to do. Her mother's last words were haunting her. *Her father wasn't dead?*

Olivia remembered, clear as day, when she was seven years old, her mother sat her down and explained how her father—a loving, hardworking man—had been killed in a tragic drunk-driving accident. That's why Olivia didn't drink when all her friends were indulging. She refused to allow herself to lose control and possibly cause someone else the pain of living without their loved one as she'd had to. Now, to learn that whole story had been an elaborate lie was shattering.

Olivia needed some answers and she knew just where to get them.

An hour and a half later, Olivia stood on the doorstep of her

Aunt Betty's apartment at the assisted-living center she'd called home for the past six years.

"Olivia," Betty said, surprised. "What in the world are you doing here? I'm sorry I left without waking you, but you were sleeping so soundly and my arthritis was kicking in—"

Olivia held up her hand to cut her aunt off before she got to rambling about her many ailments. "Aunt Betty, I need to talk to you."

Her aunt stepped to the side. "Well, come on in. Did Stephon bring you over here?"

Olivia entered the efficiency apartment. She had so much on her mind, she hadn't given a thought to Stephon. She'd braved the winter weather, hopped the bus, and made her way across town.

"No, I caught the bus." Olivia's tone caught Betty off guard, and the elderly woman stopped and stared at her.

"Aunt Betty, I need to know the truth," Olivia said, cutting straight to the reason she was here.

"What truth?"

"About my father. Right before Mama died, she told me my father wasn't dead, and that I had a half brother. She was apparently trying to get some money from him when she had her heart attack. Why in the world would she have lied to me about this for all these years? I need to know the truth."

The old woman looked extremely grave. "The truth doesn't always set you free."

Olivia ignored the warning in her aunt's voice. "I need to know what you know."

Betty shook her head like she had no idea what Olivia was talking about. "Baby, your mama was very secretive."

Olivia was not going to let her aunt off that easily. "Aunt Betty, my mother didn't carry a secret like this for that long without sharing with *someone.* And she was close to you. I know you know something."

Betty shifted uneasily. But she realized Olivia wasn't leaving until she got some answers. Finally, she motioned toward the sofa. "Sit."

"Is it true?" Olivia asked, not moving one inch.

"Well, if you're not gonna sit, I will." Betty plopped down on the end of the sofa and began massaging her calf as if it were in severe pain.

Olivia consented to sit on the other end. "Aunt Betty, please? Whatever secret my mother was carrying killed her."

"No." Betty stopped massaging and pursed her lips. "It was your mama's bad heart that killed her."

"Yes, but she was out that day trying to reach my father—a father I didn't even know was still alive. And the stress of that is what killed her. So I deserve some answers."

Betty nervously wrung her hands. "Sweetie, I'm sorry, but I swore to your mama—"

Olivia pounded the coffee table. "Mama's not here! She's gone and I need some answers." Olivia took a sharp breath, trying to calm herself down. "Besides, obviously she wanted me to know. She tried to tell me before she died. But I need to know: Was she delirious or was she telling me the truth? Is my father alive, and if so, who is he? Where is he?"

Betty looked to be weighing her words. "Okay," she said with a heavy sigh. "Your mama was not delusional. Bernard Wells is your father, and he's very much alive . . . and well-off."

Olivia's mouth opened in shock. Her father really wasn't dead. "Who is Bernard Wells?" she said after a moment. "Why do I know that name?"

"*The* Bernard Wells." Betty blew an exasperated breath. "The one who owns all of those department stores. I don't know much, but I can tell you that your mother used to work for the Wells family."

"Work for them?"

"Yes, she was their nanny for years in Los Angeles."

Olivia was stunned. She'd never known her mother lived any place other than Houston. She definitely didn't know she'd worked as a nanny "Well, what happened?"

"*You* happened," Betty said matter-of-factly. She leaned back on the sofa. "Your mother was madly in love with Bernard Wells, and he was in love with her."

Her mother, madly in love? "I'm confused. What was wrong with that? If they were in love, why wouldn't they be together?"

Betty narrowed her eyes. "You're no fool, Olivia. Your mother was the Wellses' nanny. Bernard *and his wife*."

Olivia's mouth dropped open as it dawned on her what her aunt was saying. "So, Mama was having an affair with a married man? She lived under this woman's roof and slept with her husband?"

Betty nodded and solemnly said, "Your mama ain't always been saved."

That scenario was hard for Olivia to fathom. Her mother had been deeply religious her whole life. She rose and ended each day with prayer. She read her Bible religiously and she practically lived in the church. It was hard to imagine her carrying on with a married man.

Olivia shook off her daze. "That's unbelievable."

"That's the truth."

"So, what happened?"

"Adele, Bernard's wife, found out and kicked you and your mother out."

"What do you mean, kicked us out?"

"Just what I said. She made your mother leave and she banned Bernard from having any contact with either you or your mother."

"So I was already born?"

"Not only were you born, you were three years old."

Olivia gasped. "Mama had an affair with this man, then lived there with me in the same house for three years?"

"She was so very ashamed of what she did," Betty said sadly. "And I can tell you, she called me many nights. She felt so bad, and she wanted to end the relationship, but Bernard wouldn't let her. Every time she tried, he came to her professing his undying love. Then she found out she was pregnant with you, and for some reason, she decided to stay. She might have been scared of losing her job—she was making a lot of money—I think it was because she loved him so much."

This was all crazy. How could her mother have been up in church every week, reading her Bible, and she was carrying a secret like this?

"I don't understand. So, they just kicked her out on the street? Why didn't she file child support or something?"

Betty released a mocking laugh. "Why didn't she file child support?" Betty shook her head, but Olivia didn't see what was funny. "Back in my day, we weren't as strong-minded as you young girls today. We just didn't file child support like that. Plus, they paid her off. I don't know how much, but they gave her money to never contact them again."

That stung Olivia's heart. "So, my mom sold me out for a lump sum of money?"

"No. The Wellses are a powerful family, and apparently, Adele is a woman you don't want to cross. She told your mom that if she ever contacted them again, she would have Lorraine deemed unfit and have you taken away and placed in a foster home." Betty wagged her finger. "And that woman had enough money to do it. So your mama saw she had two choices: take the money and run, or risk losing you."

"So she took the money?" Olivia said with tears in her eyes.

"Can you blame her?"

Olivia was stunned at everything her aunt had just revealed. So that's what her mother meant about Juilliard. Bernard Wells had enough money to pay for Juilliard, yet she couldn't afford to buy one book from the school. Her mother had been left to suffer and struggle while her father lived it up? Olivia found herself questioning everything about her past.

Betty leaned over and squeezed Olivia's hand. "I'm sorry, baby. I told you, some secrets are best left buried. But the question now is, now that you know everything, what are you going to do?"

To that question, Olivia had no response. But she knew one thing, she wouldn't rest until she got some answers. And the man who knew those answers was her father.

# Chapter 6

"This is utterly ridiculous," Adele barked as she waved the printed report in front of her husband's face. "The Murray Agency is going with another company! Do you see the fallout from this act of ineptitude? But I tell you this: we won't have this problem again. I told you before, if you can't handle your job, I will!"

She stomped out of his office and down the stairs into the textile area. Employees stood in front of mounds of clothing heaped on huge rectangular tables. They worked in unison, putting finishing touches on the items. Against the wall, several machines spun out the finest silk, which was transferred to another unit for processing. By the time Bernard caught up to his wife, she was standing in front of the assembly line.

"Walter!" The entire floor froze as they looked her way.

They feared Adele almost as much as Bernard did, and her mere presence sparked terror in everyone.

Adele motioned toward the security guard who stood off to the side. "Clarence, please escort Walter Maddox off the premises."

"What?" Walter's eyes widened in shock.

"You're fired," Adele said, folding her arms across her chest to let him know it wasn't open for discussion.

"Fired?" He looked stunned, but then immediately continued, "Look, Mrs. Wells, I am so sorry about that order." Panic filled his face. "You can dock my pay after the holidays, whatever, just please don't fire me."

"You should of thought of that before you fell asleep on the job."

Bernard had been severely disappointed in Walter, who supervised the packing of merchandise. He'd fallen asleep on the job several times, and the latest time it had apparently resulted in Macy's, one of their biggest clients, not getting a clothing shipment in time for Black Friday. Macy's executives had been furious. So, Bernard understood Adele's anger. But Walter was a good, long-term employee, and Bernard was willing to give him another chance. Adele, however, was fed up.

"Don't worry about cleaning out your locker. We will have any of your personal property shipped to you," she continued.

"But, Mrs. Wells," Walter said, his voice reeking of desperation, "it's because I've been working double shifts because my oldest is going to college. Then my daughter just had twins, and—"

"And none of that would be my problem," Adele said, cutting him off.

Bernard knew it was time for him to speak up. "Adele—"

"The decision is final." She waved her husband away before he could start protesting.

Walter's eyes darted back and forth between the two of them. "Mr. Wells, please?"

"The decision is final," she repeated.

Bernard had never seen a grown man cry, and it tore his heart as the tears started flowing down Walter's cheeks.

The entire floor stood in stunned disbelief as security hesitatingly approached the older man. "Come on, Walter," one of the guards gently said. "Let me escort you out."

Walter glared at Adele through tear-filled eyes. "Twenty-three years I gave this place. *Twenty-three* years and you do this to me?"

"Then it may be high time for you to retire," Adele said as she glared down the assembly line. All the employees ducked their heads, shaking in fear that they would be the next ones to feel Adele's wrath. England Enterprises paid its employees well, so no one wanted to lose his or her job.

Adele's gaze zeroed in on the shift supervisor. "Where's Jerry Cooper?"

The supervisor didn't say anything, just pointed outside to the gazebo that doubled as their smoking area. Adele stomped off in that direction. Before she could reach the door, it swung open and Jerry walked in looking disheveled and worried. When he spotted Adele, Bernard, and most of the crew staring his way, Jerry stopped.

"Wh-what's going on?" he stammered.

Adele looked at her watch. "Is it break time?"

"N-n-no. I just had to step out and make a phone call. My daughter is—"

"Mr. Cooper, save your excuses. I have heard them all. And honestly, I'm quite tired of them. So let me cut to the chase. You're fired."

Bernard let out a long sigh. The man had been through so much. His wife had died last year and his only child was waging an ongoing battle with leukemia. She passed in and out of the hospital, and the poor man was withering away as he tried to balance work with caring for her. That's why Bernard had been lenient with him. But the look on Adele's face told him Jerry's luck had run out.

"Fired? What do you mean, fired?"

"We have to let you go," Bernard said, stepping in before Adele could anger Jerry even more. Bernard had seen Jerry lose it on more than one occasion and knew this situation had to be handled gingerly.

"Come on, Mr. Wells. I just had to call and check on my daughter. I'm sorry."

"The decision has been made. Please clean out your locker." Adele didn't say another word as she turned and headed back upstairs to the office.

Jerry grabbed Bernard's arm before he, too, could walk

off. The strength of his grip frightened Bernard. "I'm sorry, Jerry."

"Don't do this, Mr. Wells, please don't do this." Jerry dropped to his knees and clasped his hands together in prayer. "I'm begging you, please don't do this."

Bernard shook his head as he sighed heavily. The entire floor was staring at Jerry, yet he didn't care. "I'm sorry, Jerry. You left us no choice."

As Bernard turned away, Jerry began sobbing uncontrollably. Walter walked over and tried to help Jerry up. "Come on. We got to go," he sadly said, trying to pull his coworker up off the floor.

Bernard could not bear to see them leave, so he made his way back into the small office he used whenever he came down to the textile factory. He actually liked it better than his plush downtown office, with the exception of today. He recoiled at the sight of Adele sitting behind his desk, flipping through a file.

"I cannot believe you," Bernard said.

"Well, believe it. Unfortunately, I have to do your job since it's obvious you don't have the balls to do it."

He ignored her obvious goading. "Was it necessary to fire Walter so publicly like that?"

She huffed in disgust. "I swear, I don't know how you are successful in this business because you have absolutely no backbone."

He glared at her. The sad part was, she was right. He had none. At least not with her. "I try to show some compassion.

It's not necessary to be such an evil b—witch," he said, catching himself.

His comment didn't faze her. "Whatever, it's done. And if you don't like my decisions, you know where the door is."

She rose to her feet and marched angrily out the door. Watching her leave, he once again had a thought he'd had many times over the years. He hated his wife.

He tried to start working again. He picked up the file his wife had abandoned, but the words on the forms blurred before his eyes. At times like these he didn't know what to do next, where to turn. Well, actually, he thought, he knew where to turn.

With that in mind, he picked up the phone.

Bernard glanced nervously around the small bistro. He hated driving across town, but he needed to get away from the office, and he needed to see the woman standing in front of him.

"Hey, honey," Alyssa said, looking around herself, making sure it was okay for them to embrace.

Bernard took her in his arms and hugged her tightly. "Hey."

"You okay?" she asked, studying him.

He sighed heavily. He'd called and asked her to meet him for lunch. She'd suggested her place, but he knew where that would end up, and today he just wanted someone to talk to. "I'm okay," he said, pulling her seat out.

She sat down and made herself comfortable. She looked stunning as usual, in a pearl-white, two-piece suit. He remembered the day he'd bought it for her. She'd protested because of the price, but he loved the way it looked on her. Then and now.

"So, did Adele really fire Walter and Jerry? Everybody is talking about it at work."

Bernard nodded.

"But I thought you said Walter knew about us."

Bernard nodded again.

Fear spread across Alyssa's face. "You don't think . . ."

This time Bernard shrugged. He'd been wondering about that all morning. It was part of the reason he wanted to see Alyssa, to warn her. Walter was a deeply religious man who, as far as Bernard could tell, had an extremely good heart, so hopefully, he wouldn't try to get revenge by spilling their secret. Bernard had been worried sick that Walter would blackmail him because he knew all about Alyssa.

As big as Los Angeles was, the maid cleaning the room at a hotel where Bernard had spent a weekend with Alyssa was Walter's wife. He had never said anything, but Bernard had no doubt that Walter knew because his wife had goggled in shock when she recognized Bernard. In fact, he had waited with bated breath for the call demanding money in exchange for silence, and when it never came, he came right out and asked if Walter knew. Walter didn't confirm anything, but didn't deny it either. He simply said anything Bernard was doing was "between you and the Lord."

"I don't think so, because Walter isn't that type of guy, but you never know. Desperation can drive men to do things they never thought of doing before," Bernard admitted.

"Oh, no." Alyssa fidgeted nervously. The waitress came and set a cup of coffee in front of Bernard and hot tea in front of Alyssa.

"I took the liberty of ordering for you."

"That's fine," she said sweetly.

He looked at her and finally smiled. Everything was fine with her. Why couldn't his own marriage be that way?

Alyssa dipped the bag up and down in her water. "I can't believe this. I hope Walter doesn't cause trouble. I don't understand why Adele just doesn't let you run the company. You're very good at it."

"That's the question I've been asking myself for years," Bernard said wearily.

Alyssa reached across the table and covered his hands with hers. "I'm so sorry you're having to go through this."

Bernard nodded his appreciation. "I just feel so awful. Walter has a family. And Jerry"—Bernard shook his head—"he lost his wife already and now his daughter is sick."

"Isn't there something you could do? You can't talk to Adele?"

Bernard felt a headache coming on. "You know there's no talking to Adele. She especially isn't going to make herself look bad by reversing a decision she made."

Alyssa leaned back and sipped her tea. "Then make it right in your own way. I don't really know Jerry Cooper, but I know Walter. He's such a sweet guy. Can't you help them find another job? At least if Walter thinks you're trying to help, he might not be tempted to cause trouble."

"The problem with that is, Walter is old, and Jerry, I don't know, sometimes he seems a little unstable."

"Then what about some type of severance?"

He instantly dismissed that idea. "But we don't offer severance packages to manufacturing employees."

"You're the boss, you can offer whatever you like." She shrugged. "And you're creative. I'm sure you can find a way to do it without letting Adele know about it."

He weighed Alyssa's words, surprised that he hadn't thought about that solution himself. "You're right. That's what I'll do."

Bernard finally felt the tension he'd been feeling all day seep away. As usual, Alyssa had made him feel better. And this time it had nothing to do with sex. Maybe there was hope for them yet.

# Chapter 7

The sounds of the television filled the room. Olivia was only half watching because her mind had been racing like crazy. What was she going to do now?

*Her father wasn't dead?* Not only that, but he was filthy rich. And she had an older brother, something she had dreamed of all her life. Mona had an older brother, Charles, and he was like a guardian angel to her. As a little girl, Olivia used to crave that and had even asked Charles could she be his sister. He'd said yes, but it wasn't the same. To know she'd had the two things she wanted most—a father and a brother—all along, had her mind jumbled up for the past few days.

Olivia finally focused on the TV when Oprah said something about living your best life. The show had to be on ABC because Olivia could only get three channels since the cable had been cut off. Her mother had had a small policy, just enough to bury her. Now, three weeks after her death, Olivia still had no idea what she was going to do.

She had been in a daze these past few weeks. Stephon had gone back to school for his final exams, but he'd said he wouldn't rest until he convinced her to move to New York with him. He was planning to come back next week to spend Christmas with her, but she'd told him that she had no intention whatsoever of celebrating Christmas. Both Stephon and Mona had been driving her crazy, sending people to check on her since she still didn't have a phone. Aunt Betty had even sent Mrs. Worthy over because they thought Olivia might be suicidal. She wasn't suicidal, but she definitely wasn't herself. In fact, Olivia had no idea who she was at all.

The only thing that had gotten Olivia out of bed these past few weeks was her overwhelming need to consume every piece of information about Bernard Wells that she possibly could. Thankfully, she still had Internet service, so she was able to google him and find all of the basic information about him. She'd even paid the $4.95 to get personal information, including his address and phone number.

But now that she was armed with all of this info, she had to figure out what to do with it. A commercial on television reminded her that she also needed to figure out what she was going to do about her job. The store where she worked, Eden's, was busy during the Christmas season, so she knew they needed her back at work.

A knock on the door jolted Olivia from her thoughts. She

pulled herself up off the sofa, where she'd been for the last three days. She knew that she couldn't keep ignoring everyone.

"Hi, Mrs. Worthy," Olivia said, after opening the door to her landlord.

"Hi, baby. How are you?"

"I'm making it," Olivia somberly replied.

"Well, I, ah, I . . . don't know how to say this." Worry lines creased Mrs. Worthy's face as she struggled to continue. "I'm so sorry and I've prayed about coming up here and tried to hold out as long as I can, but the mister said business is business, and, well, we gotta get something on the rent."

*"Rent?"* Olivia stared at Mrs. Worthy in a daze. After all that Olivia had been through, the last thing on her mind was rent. She'd had to use what little savings they had to make up for the insurance shortfall to bury her mother. "I don't have any money."

Mrs. Worthy was fighting back tears. "I understand that. It's just that . . . well, we got a lot of people that are interested in the apartment . . . and, well, they can pay."

Olivia was speechless. After everything she'd been through, she was now about to be kicked out of her apartment? Could God really be this cruel?

"I can give you to the end of the week," Mrs. Worthy said sadly. "But if I don't have something by then, I'll have to ask you to leave."

She flashed one last sympathetic look before easing away from the door.

After Mrs. Worthy left, Olivia broke down crying all over again. Yet as the tears dried up, she found a new resolve hardening inside her. She decided it was time she pulled herself up out of her slump, got herself together, and handled her business. Priority number one would be figuring out how to pay the rent. Maybe she could get an advance from work. At this point, that was her only hope.

This had to be a cruel joke.

Olivia stared at the life-size poster. She'd braved the winter weather to walk to the pay phone and call her supervisor, Emily, who'd been happy to tell Olivia that she still had a job. But Olivia had no idea she would be coming back to *this*.

"Wh-what is that?" she asked her friend Kelly, who was sitting in the break room reading the *National Enquirer*.

"Girl, I don't know. They just hung that up. A lot has happened since you've been gone. You know they were talking about us being bought out. Well, that's the new owner." Kelly smacked her gum as she flipped the page in the magazine. "He's supposed to be starting the New Year on some crazy 'Attitude Is Everything' campaign." Kelly rolled her eyes. "Tell you what. If he gives me a raise, that'll help boost my attitude."

Olivia continued staring at the picture of the man. She couldn't believe God would torture her like this. Or was it a sign?

Aunt Betty's words lingered in her head: *Bernard Wells is your father*. The same Bernard Wells that was now taking up half the wall in the break room.

Olivia searched for any resemblance in his eyes. His bone structure. Anything. But there was nothing. She didn't know if she *wanted* there to be anything. But the longer she stared at the smiling poster, the more her blood began to boil. If this man was indeed her father, he'd gotten her mother pregnant, then kicked her out on the street without so much as a phone call all these years. He'd let them wallow in poverty while he lived a life of luxury, taking over companies for sport. He was dressed in a designer suit, with Bruno Magli shoes, while she hadn't been able to afford new shoes in years—even with her associate's discount. And worst of all, her mother had died trying to get him to give her some of his money.

Olivia couldn't help it as she let out a piercing scream and charged the poster. *"Arrrghhhhh!"*

Kelly blanched in shock as Olivia snatched the poster off the wall, screaming as she ripped it to shreds. "Olivia, what's wrong with you?" Kelly asked, wide-eyed.

At that moment their supervisor, Emily, raced into the room. "What's going on in here?"

Olivia had torn the poster to shreds. She stood, her chest heaving, crumbled-up pieces of the poster surrounding her feet.

"Are you okay?" Emily asked as she eyed the shredded mess.

Olivia had destroyed the poster. Nothing else was left on the wall but a corner of the shoes. "No, no. I'll never be okay again." Olivia sobbed as she buried her face in her hands and slid to the floor.

"Oh, my God, what is wrong?" Emily asked as Olivia's crying intensified.

Olivia sobbed for a few more minutes, then tried to pull herself together. She glanced up at the now-filled break room. Her coworkers were looking at her like she'd completely lost her mind.

"Ummm, you know what?" Emily finally said. "Maybe it was too soon for you to come back to work."

"I . . . I need the money," Olivia managed to say.

Emily looked around, then leaned in and whispered, "I'll make sure you get paid today, just go home."

Olivia sniffed. One day's pay would do nothing for her. But she was in no condition to work—she didn't know if she could ever work here again now that she knew Bernard Wells was her new boss.

"Okay." She allowed Emily to help her up off the floor. She ignored the stares of Kelly and everyone else as she walked toward the door. That's because Olivia knew she would never return.

She also knew that now, more than ever, the only place she was going to get the answers she needed was straight from the horse's mouth. The torture of not knowing the whys was driving her insane. The bitterness that was building up inside was driving her mad.

As she made her way back out to the bus stop, Olivia knew what she had to do next. If Bernard Wells was her father, he was about to see her wrath, up close and personal.

# Chapter 8

Bernard took a deep breath, clicked the remote to lock his car, then buried his hands in his pockets in an effort to contain his anxiety. Maybe this hadn't been such a good idea. As soon as he pulled up, the guys standing out front had begun eyeing the luxury automobile. Bernard considered turning around, but Walter's son was among those standing outside, and he'd already spotted Bernard.

"Hi, Mr. Wells," the young man said uneasily. "What you doin' over here?"

"Is your dad here?" Bernard nervously asked.

"Yes, sir. He's inside."

Walter's son had always been pleasant, and under any other circumstance Bernard would've stood around and made conversation, but he was anxious to get inside. Bernard tapped the tattered screen door a couple of times before a young girl opened the door. She looked about six or seven years old.

"Is Walter here?" Bernard asked

The girl held the door open for Bernard to come in, then took off running toward the back. Bernard assumed he was supposed to follow her in and walked down the short hall and into the living room.

"Mr. Wells," Walter said, shocked to see his former boss. He jumped up from his seat. "What are you doing here?"

Bernard couldn't help but notice the long, orange extension cord that ran out the side window.

"Sorry," Walter said, when he noticed Bernard studying the cord, "things are a little tight and we're having to borrow some electricity."

That twisted Bernard's heart. He had never imagined that Walter and his family would have to do something like that.

Walter's wife appeared at the door, a baby on her hip. Unlike her son, she didn't bother to be pleasant. Her disdain was written all over her face.

"Honey, you remember Mr. Wells?" Walter asked.

"Hmph," she said before spinning around and walking back into the kitchen.

"I'm sorry. You'll have to excuse her," Walter said. "She's a little hurt behind the way everything went down."

"No, I understand. That's actually why I am here. How are you doing?"

"Well, you know jobs ain't easy to come by, specially for someone my age, so I'm having a hard time finding work and my unemployment check barely covers the rent on this place. My wife broke down and tried to go get public assistance, but there's a waiting list for housing, and, well, since she refused to lie about being married, they won't give her food stamps. But we making it work," Walter added with a smile. "Sorry for the breakdown on my last day. The firing came as a shock. I know Jerry is taking it just as hard, if not harder."

Bernard could not bear the man's unflagging cheerfulness. "Walter, I'm so sorry about what happened."

Walter nodded knowingly. "I know it wasn't you. And I know God doesn't give us more than we can handle, so I'll be all right."

Just then a little boy ran into the room. "Hey, Paw-Paw, come on, we're about to sing 'Happy Birthday' to Ernie," he said, tugging on Walter's arm.

"Sorry, Dad," a woman said, scurrying into the room and scooping the little boy up.

"Come on. It's my grandson's birthday," Walter told Bernard. "Come out back with us so we can sing 'Happy Birthday.' It won't take but a minute, then we can come back and finish our conversation."

Truthfully, Bernard would rather have waited right where he was. He felt so out of place, but he followed Walter into the back.

Bernard was shocked at the warm and loving greetings he got when he walked out the back door. The apartment had no backyard, but they'd set up a table and three balloons in the small courtyard. Several people—adults and kids—were bundled up, crowded around a little boy seated in front of a homemade cake. It was unusually cold, but no one seemed to notice.

Bernard couldn't help but smile as they happily sang to the grinning little boy sitting at the head of the table. Bernard couldn't believe how happy they were, given how little they had.

"We don't have a lot we can give him, but we got love," Walter said after they'd finished singing, responding to the expression on Bernard's face. "Too bad you can't wrap up love. Five-year-olds don't quite get that."

Bernard immediately noticed that there were no gifts, yet the boy looked so happy and everyone seemed to be having a great time.

"Come on," Walter said, motioning for Bernard to follow him back inside.

"So, can I ask you something?" Bernard said once they were back in the living room.

"Ask away."

"So he, I mean, um, your grandson is gonna be okay without getting any gifts?" Bernard couldn't imagine Kendall ever being excited at a party with no gifts. He would've pouted the whole time if he didn't have the latest whatever—but that was probably because they always gave him the best of everything.

The silence that followed made Bernard wonder if he'd offended Walter. He was just about to reframe his question when Walter said, "Mr. Wells, you know I respect and admire you, and losing my job hurt me to my core. Still, you have to understand. We may not be rich in material possessions, but we're rich in spirit and love, and in the end, that's all that matters. I ain't never seen a hearse with a U-Haul on the back, if you know what I mean. As much as I want to be able to provide for my family, my wife in there, she's the best thing God ever created. She's the love of my life and I would die for her. Now, I was downright mad at your wife for firing me, but my wife convinced me that God does everything for a reason. And while we can't see it now, He had His reasons and I don't need to wallow in anger. So, I've let it go, thanks to her."

"What are you saying? You're okay with getting fired?"

"Of course I'm not okay with getting fired. But I can't let a job steal my joy. It's hard because I pride myself on taking care of my family, but I also know what's most important. Does that money keep you warm at night? Does it give you unconditional love? While that money may buy you the best facilities, ain't nothing like someone to love you when you're in pain, to be by your side and nurse you back to health when you're sick. I'm not talking about someone who will leave if the checks stop coming, but someone who genuinely cares about you. I hope you don't think I'm out of order for saying this, and honestly, I probably am, but I guess it doesn't really matter anymore anyway. As much as I'd love to have a tiny portion of your money, I wouldn't trade places with you for nothing in the world." Walter shook his head to emphasize his point. "You're a good man, but unhappiness lives right there." He pointed to Bernard's heart. "You and your son are two of the most unhappiest people I've ever met in my life. You need to find some happiness in your world. And you're not gonna find it in the arms of some pretty young thang. Find your joy. Or one day you'll look up and you'll find your money has made you miserable."

They sat in awkward silence as Bernard tried to process what his former employee was saying. How could money ever make him miserable?

Walter broke the spell. "But I know you didn't come here to hear a lecture from me, or to wish my grandson happy birthday, so what's going on?"

"Well, I-I," Bernard stuttered. Walter was right. He hadn't expected to get a life lesson when he came over here, especially about a subject that he'd been thinking about a lot lately. "I came because I wanted to bring you your severance package."

Walter looked surprised. "Huh?"

"You know, I, umm, I just, ah, wanted to personally bring it to you because I felt really bad." Bernard reached in his pocket, pulled out a check, and handed it to Walter. He had thought long and hard about what he was about to do and ultimately decided it was the only way he'd be able to make peace with the way they'd fired Walter. Plus, hopefully, the money would be enough to keep that blackmail call from ever coming.

Walter narrowed his eyes. "Are you trying to bribe me, Mr. Wells?"

"No," Bernard said hurriedly. "Of course not. I mean . . . Adele shouldn't have . . . well, you know how Adele is."

Walter took it, still looking unsure. His mouth dropped

open when he saw the number on the check. "Mr. Wells, what is this?"

"It's, like I said, your severance package."

"Mr. Wells," Walter said suspiciously, "I work down in manufacturing and I ain't never heard of nobody in manufacturing ever getting a severance package."

"It's a new policy," Bernard said, shifting uncomfortably. Adele would kill him if she knew what he was doing. But he didn't care. Walter had worked for them a long time, and Bernard needed to do something. Bernard had tried to do the same for Jerry, who had also been with them a long time—although Jerry's money was considerably less. But Jerry no longer lived at the address they had listed for him.

Walter shook his head and handed the check back. "You don't need to pay me off. I'm a godly man and I have my own cross to bear. I don't worry about others. You don't have to worry about me saying anything."

Bernard breathed a sigh of relief. Deep down, he knew that about Walter, but he wanted to be sure. Yet that wasn't the main reason he'd written the check. He wanted Walter to have the money. "Please, just take it and take care of your family. I know it's not a lot but, well, I hope it helps."

Walter eyed the check. "It definitely would help."

"Then, please, take it. You gave us twenty-three years. It's the least I can do for you."

Walter released a heavy sigh. "Thank you so much." He clutched the check to his chest. "You don't know how much of a blessing you have been to me." He actually started to cry. "Me and the missus prayed this morning, and she said if we stayed faithful, God would deliver." Walter raised his arms to the sky. "Thank you, Jesus."

The religious praise made Bernard uncomfortable. He'd given up on any type of religion a long time ago. The only time he and Adele set foot in a church was when they had to make an appearance.

"Walter, what's going on?" his wife asked, reappearing in the doorway.

"Honey, look what Mr. Wells gave us," he said, racing over to show his wife the check.

Mrs. Maddox looked at Bernard skeptically, then down at the check her husband had thrust in front of her. Her eyes widened. "Wh-what's that?"

"What does it look like?" Walter exclaimed.

"It looks like a check for a hundred thousand dollars."

"That's what it is, baby! That's what it is."

She returned her attention to Bernard. "We don't need to be bought off."

"It's not for that," Bernard said too quickly. "Your husband was a good employee. He deserves it."

Even though her expression looked like she wanted to protest, she teared up as she turned to face her husband.

He read her mind. "It's real, honey. And it's ours."

Her hands started shaking as she threw her arms around her husband's neck. Watching how overjoyed they were, Bernard actually felt bad. He spent $100,000 on suits in a year. It was a drop in the bucket, and they were acting like they'd won the lotto.

Walter was right: Bernard's priorities were all wrong.

Mrs. Maddox broke free and came over to hug Bernard tightly. "Thank you so much! I'm so sorry I was nasty earlier, but Lord, Jesus, Lord Jesus!"

"It's okay," Bernard said, trying to ease loose from her suffocating hug. "I hope it helps."

"Oh, it helps, all right. It most definitely helps!"

Bernard finally cracked a smile as he backed up toward the door. They'd resumed their rejoicing and dancing around as if he'd given them the greatest gift ever. "Well, I'm gonna get going. You all take care, okay?"

"God bless you," Mrs. Maddox said, her eyes filled with tears.

"Thank you, Mr. Wells," Walter added. As Bernard stepped out the door, Walter called, "And remember what I said, find you some happiness. You deserve it!"

# Chapter 9

"So, what are you going to do?"

Mona ran her fingers through her wild, curly mane as she lounged on the sofa and watched Olivia pace back and forth across the living room. They'd been talking for the past hour, trying to decide what Olivia should do.

She had been all set to head to Los Angeles and confront Bernard Wells, but her aunt Betty had warned against it, and so had Stephon, and now she was doubting her original impulse. Mona was the only one gung ho for her to "hit the road and give that fool a piece of your mind."

"I just don't know," Olivia sighed.

"I told you what you need to do," Mona said, wagging her finger as if she were scolding a child. "If that man really is your father, it makes no sense that you're sitting up here struggling while he's living in the lap of luxury. He needs to pay for back child support or something."

Mona had been singing that same song since Olivia had first told her about Bernard. Mona had been stunned, to say the least, but after they'd done some more searching on the Internet, Mona became convinced that Olivia looked just like Bernard and "needed to go claim what is rightfully yours."

Olivia massaged her temple. She'd had a steady throbbing headache lately—and she knew the pounding was all stress-related.

"I mean, I was all ready to go, but Stephon is right. What am I supposed to do, walk up to the man and say, 'Hi, I'm your long-lost daughter'?" Olivia finally said.

"Yes, that's exactly what you're supposed to say," Mona said without hesitation. "Followed by, 'Can you please write me a check?'"

Normally, Mona's sarcastic quips brought a smile to Olivia's face, but today she was too flustered to make light of the situation. She'd played this scenario over in her head several times. Aunt Betty had reiterated how powerful the Wells family was. But really, what could they do to her? Destroy her livelihood? She had none now. Take her money? She couldn't pay her rent. Sully her name? Please. They couldn't do a thing to her because she had nothing to lose.

"I don't know what to do," Olivia said. "I just can't believe my mom had an affair with a married man."

"You need to let that go. No one is perfect. So your mom was doing some scandalous things back in the day. Big deal."

"It is a big deal, Mona."

Mona tsked and pulled out a cigarette, a nasty habit she'd picked up when she was fifteen.

"I hope you're not about to light up in here." The last thing Olivia needed was some secondhand smoke aggravating her headache.

Mona rolled her eyes and dropped the cigarette back in her purse. "Anyway, you know I loved me some Miss Lorraine, but I'm sure thirty years from now, when I look back on my youth, I'll remember a lot that I'm not proud of." Mona flashed a wicked smile. "You're the only prude that will be able to honestly tell your kids that you have a clean slate."

Olivia bit her nails nervously. "I don't know. Maybe Stephon is right. Maybe I just need to go to New York with him."

Mona groaned in displeasure. She liked Stephon okay, but she found him too controlling sometimes, which he could be whenever he didn't get his way. "Now, you said yourself, living in New York and not being able to go to Juilliard would be torture. And what are you going to do, go to New York and move into his dorm room?"

"He has an apartment. Besides, he's the one that offered."

Mona shrugged as she stood up. "You do what you feel is best, but if I were you, I'd be California-bound."

"Can I use your phone? Because I have to make a decision soon. Mrs. Worthy gave me until the end of the week to leave."

"I can't believe that old bat is actually going to evict you after all you've been through." Mona reached into her purse for her cell phone. "I wish you could come crash with me, but I'm already sleeping on the sofa now that Donna moved back home with all them doggone kids. But you know, if necessary, both of us can squeeze onto that sofa."

"Thank you, Mona, but no."

Mona half-smiled as she handed Olivia the cell phone. "It's cool. Here. Call your stupid boyfriend. Or ex-boyfriend. I'm going to use the printer in your room. Is it working?"

Olivia nodded. "It is, and don't go smoking in my room."

Mona waved an airy hand as she bounced off. Olivia didn't miss that Mona had her cigarette and a lighter ready.

Olivia pushed the issue of Mona's smoking aside and stared at the phone. Going with Stephon, she tried to convince herself, was her only choice. Finally, she took a deep breath, then dialed Stephon's cell phone number.

"Hello?" a woman on the other end said.

Olivia frowned, then removed the phone from her ear and checked the phone number. Stephon's name was displayed on the screen. She put the phone back to her ear. "Ummm, may I speak to Stephon?"

"May I ask who's calling?"

"This is, ah, this is . . . Olivia."

The woman informed her firmly, "Stephon is not available. This is his girlfriend. Is there something I can help you with?"

Olivia felt sick to her stomach. *"Girlfriend?"* she managed to say.

"Yes," the woman replied, her voice filled with attitude. "Do you want to leave a message? I can let him know you called when he gets back home. He had to run to the store and get me some pistachio ice cream. Our baby is kickin' like crazy because she seems to crave it twenty-four-seven."

Olivia nearly dropped the phone. She had wondered before if Stephon was dating—they *had* been broken up. But why would he invite her to come stay with him when he was living with his pregnant girlfriend?

"Don't worry about it. You don't have to tell him I called," Olivia muttered.

"Are you sure?" the woman asked, suddenly trying to sound pleasant.

"I'm sure." Olivia ended the call before she burst into tears.

"You know, if I were you, I wouldn't mind getting out of this dump," Mona said as she walked back into the living room a few minutes later. "I don't know why Mrs. Worthy thinks—" She stopped when she noticed the stunned expression on Olivia's face. "Oh, my God, sweetie. What's wrong?"

"I-I just called Stephon . . . and a girl answered."

Mona's hand went to her hip and she cocked her head. "Excuse me?"

"She said . . . she said, she was his girlfriend. His *pregnant* girlfriend."

That was all the news Mona needed. She launched into a tirade. "Unh-unh, see, I told you, all men are dogs. Even the ones that want to front like Stephon, acting like the only thing he wants to concentrate on is his schoolwork. How he gonna ask you to come stay with him and he has his knocked-up girlfriend there?"

"That's what I wondered." Olivia shook her head in disbelief. She added another thought she'd had. "Maybe I should give him a chance to—"

"Maybe you should nothing," Mona said before Olivia could start making excuses. "Maybe Stephon is a lying dog like all the rest of them."

Olivia started full-fledged crying. *Stephon had someone pregnant?* This could not be happening to her. How much pain was one person expected to endure?

Mona sat down on the sofa and took Olivia's hand. "Girl, you'd better stop crying over that man." That had no effect, so Mona reluctantly added, "Okay, maybe Stephon isn't as bad because it's not like y'all were officially together."

Olivia continued trying to process everything that had happened. She'd known Stephon since the eighth grade, and he had his issues, but she'd never known him to be a liar and a cheat. "Maybe I should give him a chance to explain."

Mona's thoughts were trending in another direction. "Maybe you need to take this as a sign. What you need to do is get your butt on a Greyhound, go to California, and get paid." Mona dropped a piece of paper that had been rolled up in her hand onto the coffee table. "Look at this."

"What is it?" Olivia said, wiping her eyes.

"Read it."

Olivia picked up the paper. "'*Forbes*' richest companies

list,'" she read. "'Apple. AT&T.'" She stopped and looked up at Mona. "And?"

"Keep going." Mona jabbed at the bottom of the paper. "Look at number twenty-three."

Olivia's eyes moved down the list. "England Enterprises." She was still confused. "Okay? And?"

"Yeah, guess who is the president of England Enterprises?"

"Who? I mean, the name sounds familiar."

"Your daddy dearest! Bernard Wells." Mona nodded triumphantly, and Olivia remembered seeing the name in all the information she had pulled on Bernard. "That's right. Your daddy owns one of the richest companies in America." Mona motioned wildly around the apartment. "And you, his daughter, you're living *here,* in this dump, waiting to get evicted. I don't think so."

Not for the first time, Olivia noticed how squalid the apartment was. The once-white walls were now a deep beige. Water stains covered the ceiling, which looked like it could collapse in the next windstorm. Olivia and her mother had kept the apartment clean, but no amount of cleaning could get rid of the rust around the appliances, the creaky floorboards, or the paper-thin walls.

"Handle your business, girl," Mona continued. "If Bernard Wells really is your daddy, it's high time he paid for abandoning you. And if he won't, I'm sure the *National Enquirer* or one of those TV shows would be willing to pay big money for your story."

Olivia had never even considered the possibility. "You're talking about blackmailing him?"

"I'm talking about doing whatever you need to do to get paid. Shoot, maybe you won't have to blackmail him. Maybe he will feel guilty and write you a hefty check on the spot. Either way, you won't know until you go. Now, I just checked and a bus to Los Angeles leaves at eleven in the morning. I got paid today, so I'll cover our tickets."

"Our?"

Mona's hands went to her hips. "You don't think I was sending you to Hollywood by yourself, do you?"

"What about your job?"

"What about it? I'll call in sick. They cut my hours anyway."

"So you would go with me?" Olivia said, relieved. She didn't know how she could make that trip without her best friend. Mona was so many things she was not—aggressive, innovative, outspoken. Olivia would need all those assets if she was going to settle in a place like Los Angeles.

"Girl, yes. I told you, everything happens for a reason. Mrs. Worthy put you out. They told me they were cutting my hours yesterday. All of that stuff is happening because God wants us to go to the City of Angels."

Olivia smiled for the first time all day. "That's what God wants, huh?"

"It sure is."

Olivia released a heavy sigh. "I've never been outside of Houston."

"Yeah, you have. You apparently lived in Los Angeles until you were three years old." Mona stuck her hand out for Olivia to take it. "It's time to go home. Let's go pack. Everything, because I have a feeling we won't be coming back."

Olivia slowly took her friend's hand. Together they walked into the bedroom to pack for California. At last Olivia would start what she hoped would be the beginning of a brand-new life.

# Chapter 10

The excited voice of a football announcer filled the condominium as the soft patter of rain fell outside. It was perfect football-watching weather. Everything about this afternoon was perfect.

"Hey, babe. Would you like another beer?" Alyssa stood in front of Bernard, wearing nothing but a Dallas Cowboys football jersey, which stopped right below her bikini line. Her long curls hung loosely down her back.

Bernard licked the last of the hot-wing sauce from his fingers, then picked up his Heineken and downed the final suds.

"Yes, please," he replied with a smile. He leaned back and put his feet up on his coffee table. He couldn't help but smile as he thought of the reaction Adele would have if she ever walked in and caught him with his feet up on any of her prized possessions. In fact, this whole scene would turn Adele's stomach. Hot wings and beer. T-shirts and warm-up pants, lounging in front of the TV, watching football. Yeah, she would definitely have a lot to say about this. Which was exactly why Bernard was here.

"Yes!" he said as the Atlanta Falcons made another touchdown. "Can you believe Julio Jones caught that ball?"

"You can get excited all you want, but the Cowboys are still gonna come out on top."

"In your dreams." Bernard laughed as the announcer pitched a commercial. He pulled Alyssa down on his lap and planted a long, deep, passionate kiss on her. She responded, her body instinctively reacting as if it craved him. So many things about this scene felt so right, and yet not right enough to fully commit to Alyssa. She never verbalized her desires for a happy-ever-after, but Bernard knew that's what she really wanted.

Sometimes he felt guilty about Alyssa. That's why he showered her with gifts. Not once had she ever asked him for a thing, and on more than one occasion she had turned his gifts down, which only made him want to give to her more. He knew a lot of his colleagues had gold diggers on the side, but Alyssa was far from that. He never quite understood why she stuck around. She didn't pressure him for his time, for his money, even for a commitment. She was just happy whenever he showed up. He didn't know if she saw anyone else. He never asked because he didn't know if he could handle the answer. All he knew was that moments such as this were priceless.

"Don't start anything," she teased, pulling away from him. "Not if you want to finish watching the Falcons get this beating."

"Forget the Falcons." He pulled her back toward him. She didn't fight him, instead quickly removing her Cowboys jersey with a graceful ease. Bernard showered her face and neck with kisses until their bodies once again came in concert with one another, creating a symphony of pleasure.

Thirty minutes later, Bernard lay across her sofa, spent. Only one other woman had loved him so. And he'd loved her. Could it be? Could he possibly be falling in love with Alyssa?

Bernard shook away that thought. He knew better.

"Let me get your beer and wrap your blackberry cobbler up," she said, slipping her jersey back on. He smiled. Yes, she'd made him a blackberry cobbler—his favorite—from scratch. Another small favor his wife would never dream of doing.

Bernard slipped his clothes back on, then turned his attention back to the television. But his mind was no longer on the game. The memory of loving Lorraine had a hold on him now. He was blissfully traveling back to the first time he fell in love with blackberry cobbler—and became enamored with the woman who made it.

Bernard had just graduated from Harvard Business School and had stopped in a diner right after moving to Los Angeles to start his new job at England Enterprises. Lorraine Dawson had come to LA from Texas looking for work. Her dream was to open a catering business for the stars. The very moment she took his order, he was smitten.

"So, would you like anything else?" Lorraine asked after she'd cleared the last of the cobbler he'd taken four hours to eat, just so he could sit there and watch her serve the other customers.

Bernard tried not to appear desperate, as he was sure she was onto him now and he didn't want to come across as a stalker. But he couldn't help himself. The pie was delicious, yes, but she was divine. She had an innocence in her smile that he found captivating.

"No, I guess I'm good."

"You sure?" she said with a smile. "Because I might be able to go in the back and whip you up another pie that you can nibble on for the next three hours."

He held up his hands in surrender. "Okay, I'm caught." He extended his hand to shake hers. "I'm Bernard Wells. Umm, so you made the cobbler?"

She shook it. "Hi, Bernard Wells. Yep, I do double duty as the cook and the waitress." He knew his gaze was making her uncomfortable because she shifted, then added, "Is there anything else I can get you?"

Her smile continued to light up the dim diner. She wasn't the most beautiful woman he'd ever met, but she possessed the most natural beauty. With just a dab of lip gloss, her smooth skin, deep-set eyes, and beautiful mane, she could go toe-to-toe with any of the model types he had dated in the past.

"Your phone number," he said before he realized it.

She didn't lose her smile. "Unfortunately, I don't give out my phone number."

"How can I change your mind?"

"You can't."

He wasn't ready for her to walk away, so he blurted out, "Are you from around here?"

"No, I'm from Texas."

He seized upon the opportunity to continue the conversation. "You're a long way from home."

"Yeah, I know." She tore a piece of paper off her notepad, and for a moment he got excited. "Here's your bill."

His heart sank when all he saw on the bill was his total.

"I'll take that whenever you're ready," she said, smiling as she removed his silverware from the table.

He tried not to hide his dejection. "Well, can I take you out for coffee, since you won't give me your number?"

She finally lost her smile. "Actually, I work. A lot. And when I'm not working, I'm looking for more work. But thank you anyway." She took his empty plate and walked away.

Bernard wasn't used to rejection. The women that flocked around him were attracted to his ambition, his drive, his education. That's not to mention his rugged good looks and charming personality. But none of that impressed Lorraine Dawson, and that only made him want her more.

"Look, I really would like to take you out," he said when she came back to get the check. He couldn't believe he was begging a woman for a date.

"And *you* look," she replied, showing the first sign of irritation since he'd come to the diner. "I already told you that wasn't going to be possible."

That's what she had said, again and again, day after day after day.

Finally, one evening she asked him. "Aren't you tired of these stale BLTs?"

"I'm going to keep coming in here, being a BLT-, blackberry-cobbler-eating fool until you say yes."

"Yes." She flashed her dimpled smile.

He wanted to do a happy dance, but maintained his composure. "In that case, I'll have the steak."

She laughed, and that was the beginning of a whirlwind romance. He loved her with every particle of his being. He started to look forward to where their relationship was heading. And then he made the biggest mistake of his life.

His boss, Hampton England, announced that he had a woman he wanted Bernard to meet. Bernard should immediately have said he wasn't interested, let Hampton know that he was already involved with someone. But you just didn't say no to Hampton England.

That next day, Hampton brought in his cherished daughter, Adele, to meet Bernard. From the start, Bernard thought Adele was pretty and educated, but she was too stuffy for his taste. Besides, he was in love with Lorraine. Still, he took Adele out, and before he knew it, Adele had fallen hard for him. Mr. England made it clear that if Bernard wanted to advance in the company, Adele was his ticket to do so. Bernard definitely wanted to advance. His dream since college had been to head a Fortune 500 company.

As the days progressed, Bernard's time with Lorraine grew shorter and shorter. He gave her lame excuses as to why they couldn't spend as much time together anymore as he pursued a relationship with Adele. He hated doing Lorraine wrong, but he was being sucked in by the spell of the fabulous England riches. After all the family dinners, European vacations, and private outings with his boss, Bernard found himself in too deep. Adele took control of their relationship—just as she took control of everything else—and before Bernard knew what had happened, he was planning a wedding. . . .

The sound of Alyssa's humming as she worked in the kitchen brought him back to the present. He watched her move effortlessly to the stove. She looked . . . blissful, and it made him sad. What was he doing? She deserved so much better. When did he turn into such a selfish person? No, he told himself, he wasn't selfish. He was just strong-willed. He had to be to claw his way from poverty to graduating at the top of his class at Harvard Business School. He never wanted to return to the crack-riddled environment he'd endured as a child. Bernard loved Lorraine, but he wanted the power that came with being a member of the England family more. Only he now regretted the decision because he'd chosen money over love, and the money had made him miserable.

Still, watching Alyssa, he couldn't bring himself to let everything go for her, which proved he wasn't in love with her. Maybe he didn't know how to love.

Suddenly, Bernard felt the urgent need to leave. His mind was getting jumbled and he needed to be by himself.

"Hey, Alyssa, I'd better get going," Bernard announced as she walked back into the living room.

He could tell by the way her shoulders sank that she was disappointed, but she didn't say a word as she handed his blackberry cobbler to him, then walked him to the door.

# Chapter 11

Olivia and Mona had arrived in Los Angeles only an hour ago after what seemed like a three-day bus ride. Exhausted, Olivia had wanted to go find a cheap hotel and get some rest, but Mona insisted that they go to Bernard's office first so that they didn't "have to spend a dime if we can help it."

On the long cross-country ride, Olivia had replayed her mother's last conversation. She'd analyzed and dissected the whys behind her mother's actions—and Olivia still didn't understand. She prayed that by coming to Los Angeles, she'd get some answers.

She had second thoughts as she stood in the crisp December sun. Everything inside Olivia was telling her to turn around. This wasn't a good idea. But Mona was right. Bernard Wells had gotten away with too much for too long, and it was now time for him to pay.

Finding his office building was easy, and just the sight of it made Olivia mad. Everything about it reeked of elegance. The brushed-brick outside was beautiful, and the inside left her speechless. The lobby was painted white from ceiling to floor. Headless mannequins sat and stood in various poses throughout the lobby, all draped in what Olivia assumed were the latest England Enterprises designs. Even the furniture was white, accented with gold trimmings. Olivia glanced over at Mona, who whispered a slow "Daaaaaammmmn."

"May I help you?" the prissy receptionist asked as Olivia approached the front desk. The woman looked like she should've been sauntering down a runway instead of manning a front desk. From her perfectly wrapped French roll to her all-white suit, she looked like an accessory to the lobby decor. Her eyes darted back and forth between Olivia and Mona, who had plopped down in one of the white leather lobby chairs.

"Yes, I'm here to see Bernard Wells," Olivia said.

"Is he expecting you?"

"No, but . . ."

The lady narrowed her brow and set down her pen. "I'm sorry. If you don't have an appointment with Mr. Wells, I'm afraid you won't be able to see him."

"Oh, he'll want to see us," Mona called out from her seat. Olivia shot her the evil eye. She'd made Mona promise not to say a word before agreeing to let her come inside.

"May I have your name?"

"Olivia Dawson."

The woman picked up the phone, then turned her back and mumbled something into the receiver.

After a few minutes, she spun back around. "I'm sorry, Mr. Wells is not in."

"Well, we'll just sit here and wait until he gets back," Mona announced.

Before Olivia could say anything, two security guards appeared by her side.

"Is there a problem?" one of them asked.

"No, there's not," Mona calmly said. "We're just going to sit over here and wait for Mr. Wells."

"Our offices are actually about to close, so you won't be able to do that," the guard said.

"What part of *we're not going anywhere* do you not get?" Mona snapped.

Normally, Olivia would've stepped in when Mona started getting aggressive, but something was telling her to let Mona handle this.

"Ma'am, we're going to have to ask you to leave the premises," the guard said.

Olivia contemplated leaving peacefully, but she had to see Bernard. "I'm sorry, but I need to speak with Mr. Wells and it's very important."

"I told them Mr. Wells wasn't in," the receptionist chimed in.

"Well, call him on his cell phone or something," Mona snapped. "You called security on us like we're some terrorists or something, so call your boss and tell him you got someone here who ain't leaving until she talks to him."

The receptionist looked about to respond, but her gaze was deflected to the front door. Olivia turned and looked as well. There stood the man that until a few weeks ago she had no idea existed. He looked like his photos on the Internet. Tall, clean-cut, and rich. He had smooth skin and his clothes draped his body perfectly. If not for his salt-and-pepper hair, she would've pegged him for forty. And no matter how hard she tried, Olivia couldn't see her mother ever having loved a man like this.

"Is there a problem?" he asked.

The receptionist jumped to her feet. "I'm sorry, Mr. Wells, but this woman is determined to talk to you. She and her friend are being rather belligerent."

"We got your belligerent," Mona said, shooting the receptionist the middle finger.

Bernard, who had walked in with two other people, stared at Olivia. For a moment, a flash of recognition passed over his face. But then it faded.

"Is there something I can help you with?" Bernard asked, confused. He continued to study Olivia, and his laser focus was making her uncomfortable.

"I need to speak with you," Olivia said, trying to keep the shakiness out of her voice. She had never been so nervous about anything.

"About what?"

Olivia's eyes darted over Bernard's shoulder to the young man who'd walked in right behind Bernard. He was the spitting image of his father, except he looked a lot—Olivia couldn't quite put her finger on it—looser. But the instant connection she felt told her that he was her brother.

"Yo, Dad, what's up?" he asked Bernard.

Bernard ignored his son. He continued to study Olivia, seemingly fascinated. Then recognition set in because his eyes widened and he mumbled, "Lorraine."

*So he knew who she was!*

Olivia didn't say a word. She didn't need to. Bernard took her elbow and pointed toward the elevator. "Please, come with me to my office."

Everyone watched as the two of them walked away.

Mona smacked her lips. "Now we get started."

# Chapter 12

Bernard felt as if he were seeing a ghost. He'd immediately recognized Olivia, but then he'd told himself that it couldn't possibly be . . . yet the more he looked at her, the more he knew beyond a shadow of a doubt. She had her mother's eyes. Her mother's deep dimples, her deep-set eyes. She even had that narrow line in the crevice of her forehead that popped up whenever Lorraine was stressed. Bernard might as well have been looking at Lorraine the very first time they'd met.

By the time Bernard reached his office, he'd managed to compose himself. Over the years, he'd often wondered what Olivia would grow up to look like. Several times he'd come close to hiring a private investigator to find her, but he knew if Adele ever found out, their marriage would be over. The same day that she put Lorraine out, Adele made him sign a document forbidding any contact with Lorraine or Olivia. He only signed it because Adele threatened to divorce him and he would have lost everything he'd worked so hard for. But he mostly lost his nerve to contact them because too much time had passed. What could he possibly say? How could he possibly get Lorraine or Olivia to forgive him for abandoning them?

Even so, he wasn't about to have this reunion play out in his company's lobby. England Enterprises would be hurt by a scandal like that.

"Can I get you anything?" he asked after he'd invited Olivia to take a seat on the leather sofa in his office. The bravado she'd worn earlier was now gone, replaced by nervous energy as she fiddled with her purse strap.

She was watching him intently, and Bernard assumed it was because of the way he was staring at her. But he couldn't help himself. Seeing her—seeing *his daughter*—made his heart turn flips.

"I-I don't know where to begin," he finally said, taking a seat in the chair across from her. He stared at her in awe, extending his hand toward her like he wanted to touch her to see if she was real.

"How about my beginning?" Olivia said, her voice filled with anger. "Is it true?" She paused when he didn't respond. "I mean, I did some research, and my mom did work for you for a while, but . . ."

Bernard swallowed. He wanted to shout, "Yes!" and take her into his arms, but he held back. "What did your mother tell you?"

"That's just it. She didn't tell me anything until very recently."

Olivia took a deep breath. "But she told me you were my father—right before she died."

Bernard felt like someone had taken a sledgehammer and hit him in the chest. He hadn't talked to Lorraine in almost two decades, but news of her passing tore at his soul.

"Died? Wh-what happened?" Olivia looked at him like how dare he have the nerve to act hurt by the news. But she just didn't know. He'd never stopped loving Lorraine, and hearing this was devastating.

"The doctors say it was her heart. I think it was the stress over the years of struggling to raise a child by herself, of trying desperately to make ends meet." Olivia paused, as if she had so many questions she didn't know where to begin. Finally, she asked again, "So, is it true?"

"Olivia . . ."

"Is it true?" she repeated, her voice getting louder.

What was he supposed to say? As much as he'd missed both her and Lorraine over the years, he'd almost convinced himself that it had never happened. Almost.

Bernard was just about to tell her what she wanted to hear when his son poked his head in the door.

"Hey, Dad, is everything all right?" Kendall looked back and forth between his father and Olivia. He entered the room and stood at her side like he was waiting for an introduction.

"Kendall, I've asked you not to come in my office when I am in the middle of business."

Kendall continued staring at Olivia. "Just wondering what

kind of business you had going on with . . ." He waited for Olivia to give her name. She didn't.

"Son, this doesn't concern you. If you would please, go on home and I'll talk to you later."

Kendall raised his eyes skeptically. "But I thought we were going to—"

"Kendall, I said later!" Bernard snapped.

Kendall looked shocked, probably because his father rarely raised his voice to him. But the news of Lorraine's death, plus seeing Olivia after all this time, was overwhelming.

"A'ight," Kendall said, sliding back out the door, but his eyes met Olivia's with intense curiosity as he exited.

"So, that's my brother, huh?" Olivia's voice was low and strained.

Bernard took a deep breath. "Olivia—"

Before he could finish, Kendall stuck his head back in the door. Bernard was about to blow a gasket, but the frantic look in his son's eyes stopped him.

"Ummm, sorry, Dad, but, ummm, just wanted you to know Mom is coming this way."

A flash of panic passed over Bernard. Adele would definitely recognize Olivia, for she looked too much like Lorraine. And even if she didn't, she would raise hell if she found him with a young woman in his office, especially when he didn't know what Olivia would say. But more than anything, he couldn't risk Adele's running off his daughter again. Not before they had a chance to talk.

Bernard inhaled deeply. "Where are you staying?" he said in a hushed tone.

Olivia looked unsure.

"I just wanted to know so that we can talk—away from here."

"I actually haven't gotten a place to stay," she admitted.

Bernard had an instant solution for that problem. "Kendall, can you take Olivia over to the Four Seasons and get her set up? Just use your American Express."

Kendall raised an eyebrow. "But I thought you had it cut off."

"It was just restricted. I'll call and have the restriction lifted. Just please."

"But I rode here with you. My car is at home."

Bernard hurriedly reached in his pocket and fished out the key to his Rolls-Royce. "Take my car."

Olivia looked uneasily between them.

"I'll come by this evening and tell you everything." Bernard looked over at his son, then back at her. "Just don't say anything before we have a chance to talk."

Bernard heard his wife's voice getting closer and bolted toward the door. "Please?"

Kendall stepped forward. "I got it, Dad."

"What about my friend?" Olivia said, remembering Mona.

"I'll have a car bring her to the Four Seasons. Just go out the back, please?" He prayed that she wouldn't give him a hard time. "Please?"

"Fine."

Bernard went to ward off his wife and give Kendall and Olivia time to slip out. He flashed one last look at Olivia. "I promise, I'll tell you everything tonight." He breathed a sigh of relief when she nodded and followed Kendall out the side door.

# Chapter 13

Olivia reclined in the plush leather seats of the luxury car. She'd never been in a car this nice. The ride was so smooth, she felt as if they were floating on air. She hadn't said two words since Kendall had whisked her down the stairway. She'd been tempted not to go, to stand her ground. After all, she had planned to give this man a piece of her mind.

But if he was her father, she needed to hear what Bernard had to say. She drummed the seat with her fingertips. She hated that nothing was going as planned. All the way to California, she'd imagined doing something scandalous to get revenge. She even imagined the ways she would stomp into Bernard's office, curse him out, demand to know why he'd abandoned her and her mother. What was to happen after that, she hadn't given much thought. She'd fully intended to go ahead with her plan to go off until she saw the look in his eyes. The way he looked at her, especially when she told him that her mother had died. He'd looked stricken. It was almost as if a piece of him died, too. But that couldn't be possible. No way could this man have truly loved her mother, not if he'd let her live in such utter poverty.

"Are you okay?" Kendall asked. Those were the first words he'd uttered to her since they'd gotten in the car fifteen minutes ago.

Olivia just nodded, then pulled her jacket closer as a chill crept up her body.

Kendall took the hint and didn't say anything for the next few minutes. Finally he said, "Where are you from?"

"Houston."

"Yeah, well . . . uh, if you don't mind me asking, how do you know my dad?"

He's *our* dad, she wanted to say. But she knew she couldn't go there. Not yet. That reply would surely be followed by a slew of other questions that she was in no position to answer.

"How far until we get to the hotel?" Olivia asked instead.

"Oooo-kay," he said with a grin. "Shut up, Kendall, and mind your business. I get it."

His smile was infectious and she relaxed a little. "Sorry. It's been a long day."

"It's cool." He paused, and she could feel the heat of his gaze. "I know my dad doesn't tell me everything, but it seems that he would've mentioned you. I mean, with the way he acted after seeing you, you got some kind of hold on him."

She chuckled. "You're reading way too much into it."

"Then what is it?"

"You should talk to him about that," Olivia said, willing Kendall to just let up.

He let out a small snicker. "Yeah, my family, we don't talk much. We don't do much of anything, at least not together."

Suddenly, Olivia wanted to bombard him with questions, find out more about Kendall's relationship with his father. Find out what it was like growing up with a father who cared about you. As a little girl at her neighborhood dance recitals, she used to watch the other girls get flowers from their fathers, and she desperately craved that. She wanted someone to shower her with kisses and love after a job well done.

The irony wasn't missed, though. She and her mother had nothing, yet they were extremely close. Kendall and his father had everything, and here he was talking about how distant they were.

"I don't know what you have to complain about," Olivia found herself saying. "I imagine you're on top of the world. You know, living it up like this." She motioned around the car.

He laughed loudly. "Please. This material stuff don't mean sh—I mean crap. If people only knew . . ." He shook his head. "Yeah, the esteemed Wells family got everybody fooled. If you look up *secrets* and *lies* in the dictionary, it'll have our family photo." He caught himself like he'd said too much.

Olivia wondered if he had some idea about his father's affair with her mother, if that's what he was talking about. "Well, trust me, the alternative ain't pretty." She gazed out the window at the shockingly bright scenery. It was hard to believe she was actually in Los Angeles, a place she'd only seen on TV. She took in the palm trees as they sped down the freeway.

"What's the alternative? Yeah, you might not have had money, but I bet your mother used to make you homemade muffins and knit your outfits. Your daddy used to take you on trips to the park."

She turned her nose up. "Not hardly." While she adored her mother, Olivia didn't know any of that stuff. For as long as she could remember, her mother worked two jobs, and that meant Olivia had a lot of lonely days and nights. That's how she and Mona had become close. Since Lorraine was never home, and Mona's house was overflowing with people, she started spending a lot of time at Olivia's so that she wouldn't be alone. "All I'm saying is you wouldn't want to walk in my shoes. Trust me."

Once again she took in the slick interior design of the Rolls-Royce, so immaculate it looked like it had come right off the showroom floor. Then her gaze scanned Kendall's designer watch, his expensive clothes, even his $300 Jordans (she knew how much they were because they were the hottest shoes in the country). Who wouldn't want his life?

Olivia initially wanted to label Kendall ungrateful, but she had a feeling there was much more to Kendall Wells than met the eye. She'd just have to find out what that was.

# Chapter 14

Bernard tapped his fingers nervously on the corner table in the small deli. He'd made arrangements to meet Jerry Cooper here and was truly hoping that Jerry wouldn't cause a scene. He'd thought about just mailing this severance check to Jerry, but he knew he needed to face Jerry like a man. Bernard looked toward the door as it opened and was shocked to see Walter walking in with Jerry.

"Hey, Jerry. Hey, Walter."

"Hey, Mr. Wells," Walter said, while Jerry stood behind him, shifting nervously.

"What are you doing here?" Bernard knew the two of them had been friends at work, but he didn't know the extent of their relationship.

Walter looked nervously over his shoulder at Jerry. "Just thought it best if I came along for moral support."

"You okay, Jerry?" Bernard asked as they slid into the seats across from him.

"I'm not doing too well, Mr. Wells," Jerry said, fidgeting. "Walter here, he's been helping me out a lot."

Bernard wondered how Walter had been helping. Surely, as badly as he needed money, he wouldn't have given Jerry any. Besides, this check Bernard had in his pocket should help Jerry some.

Walter gave a reassuring nod. "I don't mean to intrude, but Jerry is in a bad way. And I'm hoping you can help him out."

"I fully intend to." Bernard reached in his pocket to remove the envelope.

Jerry jumped in, "You don't understand, Mr. Wells. It's not just the money that I needed. It was the benefits, the health insurance."

Bernard nodded. "I know your little girl had leukemia and—"

"Has!" Jerry said, getting worked up. "She *has* leukemia. And without insurance, I don't know how we can fight it."

"What about COBRA or Medicaid?"

Walter shook his head as Jerry went on, "COBRA costs an arm and a leg, and Medicaid takes forever to get."

"I'm sorry—"

"Mr. Wells, this is killing me. She's all I got left. I need my job, Mr. Wells. Or you need to call someone and help me get another job."

"I—Jerry, you know I tried to work with you," Bernard stammered. He'd considered calling a colleague about hiring

Jerry (none of them would touch Walter), but with Jerry's erratic track record, Bernard couldn't put his name on the line like that.

"Try harder," Jerry snapped. Fury seemed to be building in his eyes. "Grow some balls."

Bernard's mouth dropped open in shock, then he quickly composed himself. "I understand you're distraught, but you will not disrespect me."

Walter put his hand on Jerry's arm to calm him down. "Mr. Wells, I don't think Jerry meant any disrespect. He's just hurting right now."

Jerry continued his death glare. The eerie silence was interrupted as the waitress approached their table.

"May I help you?" she asked with a jovial grin.

"No, you may not!" Jerry screamed at her, and she immediately retreated.

"Jerry, you need to calm down," Walter said soothingly.

Jerry snatched his arm away. "Don't tell me to calm down. Until you lose your wife, until you have a daughter lying in the hospital fighting for her life, who was about to have an operation but now she can't because she doesn't have insurance, until you've experienced that, you don't know what I'm feeling. The only saving grace is that I was able to provide for her. And now you've taken that away from me. And for what? A couple of measly screwups? As long as I've been with that company?"

"I understand that, but you cost us a lot of money," Bernard said, trying to get through to him.

"And for you, that's the bottom line on everything, isn't it?" Jerry said.

Bernard was starting to regret he'd come. "Here, just take the check. Maybe it can help."

"Maybe, maybe not," Jerry said, although he took the check. "I hope you're happy with how easily you can destroy people's lives. I hope when you look in the mirror, you can live with what you see." Jerry stood up, knocking over the chair before storming out the deli.

Walter and Bernard sat in silence for long seconds. Then Bernard remarked, "Wow, that didn't go as planned."

"He's just so angry." Walter took a deep breath. "Mr. Wells, I don't know if you've been rich all your life, but there's nothing that can strip a man's dignity faster than not being able to provide for his family. Trust me, I know."

"But I went behind Adele's back to give him some money."

"And I'm sure when he comes to his senses, he'll appreciate that."

Bernard bore enough guilt. He'd gone above and beyond to help Jerry. "He'll be fine."

"Until that money runs out. And that's what concerns me. Once it's gone, I don't think he has a clue what to do from there."

"Just so you know, I haven't always been rich," Bernard felt compelled to say. "Adele came from money. I didn't. I had to work hard for everything I had. I have worked long hours for years."

"I'm sure you do, and I don't think anyone is trying to take that away from you." Walter stood up himself. "I just think you don't realize that there are some things more precious than money. And to Jerry, that is his daughter." Walter looked in pity at Bernard before saying, "Good-bye, Mr. Wells."

Bernard remained seated long after they left. Walter didn't know how much Bernard could relate to that because he'd finally found something that was just as important to him as money—his daughter. But he wasn't a complete fool. If he played his cards right, he could keep his money and power, and his daughter. He just had to figure out a plan.

# Chapter 15

Mona was acting like she'd died and gone to heaven. From the moment the car service had dropped her off, she'd been acting like she was meant for this life. They were booked in the Presidential Suite, which, Olivia had read on the back of the door, was over three thousand square feet. That was bigger than both of their apartments put together. The spacious suite was adorned with contemporary artwork and modern furniture. The balcony had a panoramic view.

Yes, this was unlike anything else they'd ever experienced. So Olivia couldn't blame her friend. They'd both come from nothing, and while Mona had dated a few guys with money, none of them had ever come close to giving her this type of lifestyle.

"Okay, that's him," Olivia called out through the bathroom

door. "I know you've been in there for over an hour, but just stay there until he leaves."

"Girl, this bathroom doubles as a steam room. My hair is gonna be jacked, but this is so freakin' unbelievable!" Mona shouted over the Mary J. Blige tune blaring in the bathroom.

"Well, just stay in there and let me handle this. Don't come out until I tell you."

"I won't bother a soul," Mona sang.

"And turn that music down!"

Olivia took a deep breath. She'd been here almost three hours, and her stomach had been in a twisted knot the entire time. Bernard had called and told her what time he'd come by. She'd tried to ask him questions, but he asked her to be patient. Now her patience had run thin. She needed to know the truth.

She opened the door to the suite to find Bernard standing nervously in the entrance.

"Hi. May I come in?"

She didn't say anything as she stepped to the side.

"Did you get settled?"

"I did." She'd been floored when the concierge had taken her to the penthouse suite. She had been about to tell him that she didn't need all that space when Mona had showed up. "It's a bit excessive. . . ."

"Oh, don't worry about that. I want to make sure you get whatever you want."

She glared at him. *Now* he wanted to give her what she wanted. She had *wanted* a father. She had *wanted* money for college. And the more that she thought about it, she wanted this life that rich folks such as he and Kendall took for granted. Instead, she was saddled with a broken heart and broken dreams, all of which could've been prevented had he decided to include her in his life.

"Look, let's cut the small talk. I need some answers."

He nodded. "Do you mind if I fix a drink first?"

She shrugged in irritation, then waited while he went to the full bar and poured himself a glass of brandy. He took a swallow like it was some type of liquid courage, then walked back over to her.

"Okay, ask away. Anything you want. But first, can you answer a question for me?" She gave a slight shrug. "What happened to Lorraine?"

"Why?" she asked, not bothering to hide the coldness in her voice.

He glanced down solemnly and then back up at her. "Believe it or not, I loved that woman with all my heart."

"You have a hell of a way of showing it!" Olivia exclaimed. "How do you turn your back on someone you love?"

"It's complicated."

"This isn't some Facebook status."

"Huh?" he said, confused.

"Nothing." She inhaled sharply. She had promised herself she wouldn't get worked up. "Are you my father?"

He nodded and she felt her heart drop into her stomach.

"I'm just trying to understand all of this, okay? Up until a few weeks ago, I had no idea that my father was even alive, let alone *the* Bernard Wells. I mean, did you ever think about us?"

"Every single day."

She rolled her eyes in disbelief. "I don't have children, but I can't imagine that when I do, I'd completely turn my back on them."

"The day I let you and your mother walk out of my life was the worst day of my life," he said quietly. "I don't expect you to understand. All I ask is that you forgive me."

He must be on some kind of drugs, she thought. She had come here for answers, and, yes, maybe even money. Forgiveness wasn't an option.

"What can I do to make it right? How can I make this up to you?"

She heard Mona's voice in the back of her head. *Get his money, girl.* But she couldn't bring herself to utter the words demanding money.

"I don't want anything from you. All I want is the truth," she found herself saying. She shook her head, fighting back tears. "Now that I think about it, I made it this long without you, I'll continue making it. I shouldn't have come."

"I'm glad you did." An uneasy silence filled the air between them until he added, "So what are you gonna do now? I know your mother didn't have much family. Did she ever marry?"

*Ha,* Olivia wanted to say. Not only did her mother not ever marry, the only other man she'd ever given her heart to had also broken it. Flashes of Ray Joseph filled Olivia's mind. She didn't have any horror stories like Mona, who'd been molested by her stepfather. But Ray had definitely made Olivia's life miserable. He'd treated her like someone he had to endure to be with her mother. He didn't have a nurturing bone in his body.

Then, one day when she was twelve, Ray vanished. Her mother cried for days, saying Ray had taken what little money they had left.

"We were so poor. We struggled every day. I couldn't even go to college." The tears Olivia had been holding back were threatening to burst free.

"I'm so sorry. Your mother had money when she left. We-we gave her two hundred and fifty thousand dollars."

Hearing about the lump-sum payment made Olivia even more outraged. "Is that what I was worth to you? I was a two-hundred-and-fifty-thousand-dollar mistake?"

"No," he protested. "I loved you. I loved you both."

Olivia threw her hands up in frustration. "You know what? I can't do this. I'm going home. I made a mistake coming here."

He gently grabbed her arm to stop her from walking off. "Tell me, what do you have to go home to?"

He was so right about that. Mrs. Worthy had probably rented the apartment by now and set what little Olivia had left behind out on the curb. Still, she snatched her arm out of his grasp.

"Stay in Los Angeles. Let me make up for lost time."

She looked at him like he had lost his mind. "Let you make up for lost time?" she repeated incredulously.

"Yes. I want to take care of you, do right by you."

She felt utter disgust at this bald-faced offer. So once again, he wanted to toss some money at his "inconvenient trouble" and that would make everything all right?

"I don't want your handouts," she spat. "I work for everything I get. I always have and I always will."

He looked shocked, then a small smile spread across his face. She couldn't believe he was looking proud.

"A child with my work ethic," he muttered.

"I don't have anything of yours but supposedly your DNA. Any kind of work ethic, values, morals that I have, I got from my mama."

He held up his hands in surrender. "Okay, I don't want to take anything away from her. Your mother has done an excellent job. But she's gone. And I want to help you."

"She'll stay."

Olivia spun around and glared at Mona, who was standing behind her, her arms folded, her eyebrows raised.

"Didn't I tell you to stay in the bathroom?"

"Unh-unh, girl, you did." Mona sauntered into the living room, the plush white hotel robe wrapped tightly around her body. "But somebody got to be the voice of reason because you and all this self-righteous crap is ridiculous."

"This is my best friend, Mona," Olivia said, formally introducing Mona to Bernard.

He shook her hand.

"How are you doing, Mr. Wells?" Mona said, grinning like

a Cheshire cat. "Since me and Olivia are like sisters, can I call you Uncle B?"

Olivia couldn't believe Mona's nerve. But the exchange actually broke the tension.

Bernard smiled. "You can call me whatever you'd like."

"Mona, can you go back in the bathroom?"

"So here's the deal." Mona jutted a finger in Olivia's direction but kept her eyes on Bernard. "My girl ain't got nowhere to go. She was kicked out of her apartment. Her ex had asked her to come live with him, but then she found out not only was he cheating, but he was about to be a daddy. So she ain't got nothing in her life right now but a lot of heartache and drama. That means she needs you, whether she wants to admit it or not."

"Mona!"

"I'm just keeping it real." She side-eyed Olivia. "Even if you won't."

Her announcement over, Mona headed for the bedroom. Yet a thought struck her and she stopped short. "Uncle B, do you mind if I order some room service?"

"Yes, help yourself," Bernard said eagerly. "Order food, spa services, car service, whatever you like."

"Whatever?"

"Whatever."

"Oh, yeah, I ain't never had no lobster and Don Periyon," Mona sang as she bounced into the bedroom.

"Sorry about that," Olivia said. If she didn't know Mona's

heart, she'd swear her friend was only along to see what she could get out of the deal.

Bernard didn't see any issue with what she'd said. He looked relieved that someone asked him for a favor. "No problem. I'm glad you have a friend to help you through everything."

"Look, I don't know why I came here. I just needed some answers. I needed to hear from your mouth if it was true you're my father. But this"—she shook her head—"this was a mistake."

"No, your friend is right. There's no reason for you to go back. Let me help." She continued shaking her head, but he knew of more ways than one to break through. "If you won't take money, at least let me give you a job."

*A job?* That thought had never occurred to her. Plus, Mona was right. What options did she have? Technically, Bernard owed her all that and then some. But that wasn't her nature. Her mother had taught her to work hard for everything in life, and she couldn't change just to be spiteful. At least if she was working for him, she wouldn't feel like a total leech.

"Work for you doing what?"

He shrugged like he didn't have a clue. "What do you want to do?"

All of the model photos she had researched flashed in her mind. "I have an eye for fashion. I guess that's because my true passion is dance."

"Is that so?" He was very pleased by this news. "My mother was a dancer," he said, smiling. "I actually opened a dance studio in Beverly Hills in her name." He paused, screwing up his lips. "It's a nonprofit, so you wouldn't make any money over there, but if you ever want to go train or help out, or anything, just let me know."

Olivia was flabbergasted by this coincidence. Here she'd been struggling with dance for so long, and her father owned a dance studio, named after his mother.

It suddenly dawned on Olivia that she didn't know if his mother—her grandmother—was dead or alive. She didn't know anything about that side of her family. Yes, she'd met Kendall, but did she have any cousins? Where did her family live? A whole part of her family tree was barren. There was so much that she didn't know. She would never get answers if she left.

"Or, you could come work at England Enterprises and maybe just go to the dance studio in your free time," Bernard added.

She'd thought before, while she was tracking down everything about him, what it would have been like if she'd been able to work at a place like that. "Well, I could use the job," she finally said.

He looked ecstatic. "Well, there you have it! We can discuss your salary, what you'll be doing. You said you like fashion. I'm the fashion king. We can find something for you to do."

"Okay," she finally said. But she refused to smile. She refused to give him the satisfaction.

Bernard reached into his pocket and pulled out a business card. "Here's my private number. You call me if you need anything. Anytime. I know it's been a long day, so I'm going to let you get some rest."

He took a step toward her as if he wanted to hug her. She took a step back to let him know that wasn't an option.

"Okay," he conceded when he noticed her apprehension. "I'm gonna go." He looked so happy. "I promise you're not going to regret this," he added before walking out the door.

As soon as he was gone, Mona reappeared. She walked over and rubbed Olivia's arm. Mona wasn't a touchy-feely person, so the move caught Olivia by surprise.

"What are you doing?"

Mona was looking at the fingers she'd used to touch her friend. "I'm trying to get some of that luck to rub off on me because, baby, you just hit the lotto."

# Chapter 16

Bernard had been trying to devise a plausible story all day long. He could easily slide Olivia in. After all, he didn't discuss all of his hires with Adele. But since the Walter and Jerry fiascoes, Adele had made her presence more known at the office, and the last thing Bernard wanted was her digging for answers about Olivia. He also had to figure out a way to explain to Olivia that she would need to use a different last name—because the instant Adele heard the name Dawson, her antennae would go up.

As for his own plans with Olivia, Bernard hadn't yet figured that out. He had to take full advantage of this opportunity, and he couldn't let Adele, or anyone else, jeopardize his shot at redemption. He knew that he would eventually have to come clean with Adele, and it would not be pretty. But not yet. Not before he had a chance to get to know his daughter, and if he was lucky, bond with her, and even get her to forgive him.

The maid, Vianessa, stuck her head in his study. "So will you be dining with Mrs. Wells, or will you take your dinner in your study again?"

This was the perfect opportunity to start setting the stage. "No, Vianessa, I'll dine with my loving wife. Just give me a few minutes to change for dinner."

Bernard continued to spin out possible scenarios as he made his way up the spiral stairs to his room. He changed, then headed back out, but not before stopping at the top of the staircase and taking in the beauty that was his home. The house, one of the Spanish colonials built in the 1800s, was well maintained, its rich history preserved. From the intricately carved ceilings and paneled walls to French doors and balconies, arched ceilings and floor-to-ceiling windows, which overlooked a cascading waterfall to the pool, the home was everything Bernard had ever dreamed of. He'd been ecstatic when they moved in. It felt like he'd finally arrived. Granted, his father-in-law had purchased the house outright as a gift, but it was still Bernard's home. Now, looking at the spectacular layout that looked as if it came from *Architectural Digest,* he couldn't help but wonder why they needed all of this house. There was more staff here than family. Bernard had hoped to one day hear the pitter-patter of grandchildren through the house, but something told him that if Kendall did ever settle down and get married, the chances of his returning to visit would be slim to none.

Bernard made his way into the dining room. Adele sat perched at the end of the table, looking like royalty in a burgundy designer dress and immaculately styled hair. Just once, he thought, he'd like to show up for dinner in some sweatpants and a T-shirt. That's how he ate when he was with Alyssa. But Adele would die if he didn't "dress for dinner."

"Hello," he said, taking his seat at the other end of the long table, which could easily seat twenty people.

"Hello to you, too," she replied curtly.

They waited as Vianessa served their food, then quietly began eating.

The tension in the air was palpable, so Bernard decided to try to ease it. "How was your day today?" he asked as he cut a piece off the peach-glazed salmon.

Adele sipped her sparkling water, taking her time before replying, "It was fine. The Junior League is trying to get me to head up the fund-raiser. I told them last year was my last time and I plan to stand my ground."

Bernard tried to act interested. Truthfully, he could not care less about her Junior League, Senior League, or any of those other charities she did for show more than anything else.

"Vivian and her friends are going to Rome in a few months. I was thinking perhaps we could accompany them," she said, changing to her other favorite topic—keeping up with her high-society friends.

*Oh, joy,* he thought. *Just what I want, to go on vacation with you.* "Sounds like fun."

"Fun." She gave a terse chuckle. "I don't think we know

what that is anymore. Still, it would be relaxing and it would give you a chance to network with Charles."

"That would be nice." Bernard tried his best not to lose his smile. Charles was a pompous wannabe who, like Bernard, had married into money, but Charles looked down on everyone who wasn't in his tax bracket. The last thing Bernard would ever want to do would be to hang out with him. "Well, the new campaign kicks off tomorrow," he said, trying to steer the conversation in another direction.

"Yeah, the 'Attitude Is Everything' campaign," she said with a sneer. "I swear, you and these ridiculous campaigns. We need to be focusing on the bottom line and not worry about emotions."

"But if your employees are happy, you have a more productive workforce."

She waved him off with her fork. "All I want to know is, was the purchase of Eden's successful? You know I don't agree with your decision to buy up all of these mom-and-pop stores."

"I know you don't, dear, but it's all part of a strategic plan."

She rolled her eyes like she wasn't impressed. "You and your strategic plans."

Bernard realized the time was ripe. Drop it in like another strategic plan. "Oh, by the way, I'm bringing in some graduates from USC for the professional management program."

"For what?"

"Some program they contacted us about. They're trying to get Fortune 500 companies to participate, so they're sending us over three students. I'll have one working in the marketing area, another in the textile department, and one in the business division." Bernard made a mental note to call USC first thing in the morning and get some interns.

"Oh," Adele said, a small smile spreading across her face. "Could it be my husband is finally finding a way to incorporate charitable work into the business?"

She had been asking Bernard for a while to get involved in more philanthropic activities, but he was never interested. He wanted to leave that to her so he could run the business. "I wouldn't call this charity. Just trying to help the university out."

"Well, whatever, I'm happy to see you doing it." She paused, studying him as if she'd seen something odd.

"What?" he finally said.

"I don't know. Maybe you like being charitable more than you realize because something seems different about you."

Bernard tensed up. "Different how?"

She shrugged, then picked up her tea and sipped it. "Just different. But in a good way. You seem, I don't know, happier than you have in a while." She studied him some more.

Bernard forced a laugh. "Trust me, sweetheart, you're reading way too much into my demeanor. I'm the same executive I've always been."

Adele looked like she wanted to say something more, but decided against it. She leaned back as Vianessa came and removed her plate.

"Would you care for dessert?" Vianessa asked.

"No, thank you, but I will have a glass of sherry."

It was Bernard's turn to glare at his wife. He'd had numerous conversations with her about her drinking. He'd even told Vianessa not to offer wine with dinner. Over the years, Adele's one glass of wine had turned to two, then two to four, then from wine to bourbon. Although she would never admit it, she was a functioning alcoholic. He'd long ago stopped trying to get her to seek help. She wouldn't admit it, so how could she get help? Besides, she kept up her appearances and only got out of control in the privacy of their home, so both he and the staff had learned to stay out of her way when she got belligerent.

"Would you like some sherry as well?" Vianessa asked, turning to Bernard. He could tell she was nervous about getting the wine, but she also knew that she would incur Adele's wrath if she didn't. Bernard knew it, too.

Since he was trying to play nice, he nodded. "Sure, I'll take some as well." He waited as Vianessa filled both of their glasses, studying her. Her plump cheeks were rosy and her eyes glistened as she spoke, but she still looked weary. He really liked Vianessa, and although she'd been with them for more than eleven years, she should've retired twelve years ago. Bernard and Adele had never spoken about it, but Bernard had long ago noted how, after Lorraine, any staff that Adele hired were either old, severely overweight, or extremely unattractive.

As soon as Vianessa left the dining room, Adele said to him in a businesslike tone, "Well, would you like to have sex tonight?"

Bernard wanted to laugh. That offer was pathetic. "That's

okay," he said mildly. "I'm sure you're tired after your day with the Junior League."

"I am, but I missed our appointment last month and I know how you get. So despite my exhaustion, I am willing to fulfill my marital duties." She smiled, Bernard guessed, to let him know that she was joking. But he didn't see anything funny.

"No, I'm good, actually."

She looked stung. "And would that be because you're having your needs met elsewhere?" While her voice was filled with sarcasm, a hint of vulnerability escaped. It was a side of her he rarely saw and it caught him off guard.

Still, he refused to respond in kind, although he didn't know what in the world she expected. Did she really think he would accept a life of sex-when-she-felt-like-it? Did she think he had any desire to pound on his wife as she lay there and waited for him to finish? Did she expect him to ignore his needs because she couldn't be bothered?

Ultimately, Bernard decided he wasn't in the mood to argue with his wife—again. He thought about calling Alyssa, but then held back. All of his attention needed to be focused on Olivia. And after their last conversation, he had a feeling that Alyssa was finally reaching a point of wanting more in their relationship.

Bernard simply said, "I assure you, darling, my needs are not being met." But he couldn't help but add, "By you or anyone else." Then he rose to his feet formally and retreated to his room.

# Chapter 17

"Girl, I could so get used to this."

Mona bounced into the living area of the hotel suite. She was wrapped in the plush Four Seasons bathrobe. She had a chocolate-covered strawberry in one hand and a mimosa in the other. The funny part was that she looked like she belonged in an expensive suite with her wild, curly hair and sun-kissed skin as she sashayed over to window, opened the blinds, and took in the magnificent view.

"Why do you have on that robe?" Olivia asked.

Mona swirled around, then gently ran her hand down the material. "That's what it's here for. To wear. So what's up? What are we doing today?"

"We? I thought you were going home today." Mona's job had called and given her two days to get back to work or else they would replace her.

"No," Mona corrected her, "I said they called and told me I needed to come back today. I didn't say I was going."

"So, you're really not going to go back?"

Mona held her hands up like two sides of a scale. "Ummm, let's see, should I go home to that cramped apartment with seven people? Or, should I chill here at the Four Seasons with my bestie? Yeah, I'll take door number two, Alex."

They both laughed. "You are silly," Olivia said.

"Besides"—Mona motioned up and down her body—"all this isn't meant to sit behind a desk pushing paper." She flashed a wicked grin. "And I have a feeling we're on the verge of a whole new life."

"There you go with that *we* stuff again."

Mona waved away her friend's words and picked up a brochure off the table. She tapped a fingernail on one item in particular. "You know, I was thinking we could schedule a spa day. This place actually has a masseuse that will come to the room. Heaven," she said with an orgasmic groan. "I hope he's sexy."

"We are not having a masseuse come here," Olivia said, snatching the brochure out of Mona's hand. "And would you act like you have some class?"

"I don't." Mona snatched the brochure back. "But I know just what can help me get it: chillin' here at the Four Seasons. You can't get much classier than that."

"Mona . . ."

Mona let out an exasperated sigh, as if tired of her friend's objections. "Olivia, you said yourself, this man's wife is crazy.

Obviously, if she banned your dad from talking to you all these years, you know she's capable of anything. But he owes you, and you need to get what you can before she finds out and shuts down the pipeline."

Olivia hadn't thought about Adele's reaction. She didn't know how the woman was going to respond to Olivia's being back in their lives. She wondered how Bernard even planned to tell her. And what if Mona was right? What if Adele made him cut off contact with Olivia? Bernard had obeyed Adele before. Who was to say he wouldn't do it again? And the question remained, what did Olivia want from him? Yes, she could use the money. But what did she want now? Answers? She'd gotten those. Bernard and her mother had a torrid affair and she was the product. She had always longed to have her father in her life. Now that could be a reality. Olivia also wanted to get close to Kendall. She'd always wanted a sibling growing up, and Kendall seemed like a lot of fun. What if they really connected?

"Look, girl, all I'm saying is, if this man wants to let you live in the lap of luxury, you do that. If he wants to spend his money on you to make himself feel better, you let him do that. Because really, what other choice do you have? Save you some money and figure out what to do from there. Hell, save up enough money for Juilliard."

Olivia considered her friend's words. That was definitely a valid point. Could she save up enough money for school? Her heart raced. That was her greatest dream. Maybe she could take him up on his offer of work at the dance school. That way she could hone her skills while working up the nerve to ask him to pay for Juilliard.

The silence was interrupted by Mona's ringing cell phone.

"Hello." Mona immediately turned up her lips as she walked over to the window. "What? She doesn't want to talk to you." That got Olivia's attention. "Look, Stephon, don't call my phone anymore. We know all about your little pregnant girlfriend."

Olivia shouldn't have been surprised, but she couldn't believe Mona was calling him on the carpet like that. Olivia sighed. Mona had a right to be mad, but Olivia owed it to Stephon to hear him out, so she jumped up and stepped in front of her friend.

*Let me speak to him,* Olivia mouthed.

Mona shook her head and abruptly turned her back to Olivia. "Whatever, Stephon. You must think she's Boo Boo the fool. She don't want to hear nothing your triflin' behind got to say."

"Give me the phone," Olivia demanded, then snatched it away. Otherwise, Mona would have continued on.

"I guess she *is* Boo Boo the fool," Mona mumbled, shaking her head.

Olivia took a deep breath, then said, "What, Stephon?"

"Hey, how are you doing?" He had the nerve to sound as if nothing were wrong.

"What's it to you?"

"Come on. Don't be like that," he said smoothly. "You know I care about you. I've been worried sick."

"You care about me?" Olivia released a pained laugh. "How does your pregnant girlfriend feel about that?"

He hesitated like he wasn't sure exactly what Olivia knew. Part of her waited in anticipation, wanting him to tell her that it was all a big misunderstanding. That someone was playing a cruel prank. Instead he said, "I'm sorry. I didn't know how to tell you."

She swallowed the lump in her throat. So it was true, he'd gotten someone else pregnant?

"I didn't mean for it to happen. I was just as surprised as you are."

Olivia gasped as she fought back tears. "So what was all this 'come live with me' stuff?"

"I meant it."

Olivia couldn't believe he thought so little of her. "What, me, you, and your baby mama?"

She could feel him cringing through the phone. He hated that term. "She doesn't live with me. And, yes, she'll be the mother of my child, but she's not my girlfriend."

That didn't make Olivia feel any better.

"All I'm saying is, I meant every word. I never wanted to break up in the first place. You broke up with *me*."

"Now I'm glad I did because this hurts enough. Imagine how I would feel if we were actually together."

"Don't be like that. We've been through too much together."

"And I've been through even more this last month. I can't deal with any added drama."

"I don't have any drama," he said defensively. "Can we not

fight? I just wanted to see how you were doing. Your aunt said you went to see your dad. I thought you were going to leave that alone."

Olivia rubbed her eye in annoyance. She wasn't going to let Stephon brush this under the rug and act like everything was okay. "Stephon, don't worry about me. Worry about your pregnant girlfriend," she said angrily.

"She'll just have to understand," he protested. "I love you. Not her. I want to be with you. Not her."

"That's not what it sounded like when she answered your phone."

"She had no business answering my phone. And just because she's having my child doesn't mean we can't make things work between us."

Olivia couldn't believe she was having this conversation. Stephon had been her first and only love. She'd only let him go because she'd been scared of his cheating on her, but she'd always believed in her heart that they would end up back together. Now that could never happen. The last thing she needed was some baby-mama drama.

Olivia took a deep breath. "Stephon, I have enough going on in my life right now. I'm not mad at you," she lied. "You were right. I was the one that broke up with you, so enjoy your new family. Just leave me alone, okay?" She hung up the phone before he could reply.

"That's what I'm talking about!" Mona exclaimed from the far end of the room, where she must've been listening the entire time.

Olivia didn't reply. She hardly felt like celebrating whatever victory Mona thought she'd won. Inside, she was torn apart.

Mona eased over to her friend's side, draping an arm around her. "All I'm saying is, you did the right thing, although I do think you let him off too easily. You're heading places. Stephon is your past. You have to look toward your future now."

Olivia had never been so unsure in her life. "Where am I headed, Mona? Like really, what are we doing here?"

Mona shrugged, turning serious. "I don't know. All I do know is that we just need to lay back, kick it, and enjoy the ride."

Olivia gave her a half smile.

"Yes, I said *we*. I'm here to stay, baby." Mona tightened the belt on her robe, snatched up the brochure again, and pointed it at her. "Now, let me go call the spa. I'm hoping they send me a tall, sexy Swedish guy," she said, bouncing out of the room.

A spa? A masseuse? Then again, that's what Bernard wanted them to have. He'd offered her a job, an office job at a company. She could ace that job. She could make something of herself at last.

For the first time since arriving in Los Angeles, Olivia started to feel hopeful.

# Chapter 18

Bernard groaned as he walked down the stairs. He could hear Adele and Kendall going at it again. He was on his way to Alyssa's, and he had been wrestling back and forth about whether he should break things off with her. All he wanted was to get out the door. The last thing he felt like doing was refereeing a shouting match between his wife and son.

"This makes no sense. Either you get a job or you get out!" Adele yelled.

"Fine. I have no problem with getting out," Kendall shot back.

Bernard knew he couldn't pretend he didn't know what was going on. He needed to go in and break up this recurring fight.

He took a deep breath and walked in the kitchen. "Son, don't raise your voice at your mother. Show her some respect."

"How about she respect me sometimes?" He looked at his mother in disgust. "I'm in here minding my own business and she comes in givin' me orders. Maybe if she laid off the sauce she wouldn't be trippin' all the time."

"You're worthless just like . . ." Adele didn't look drunk, but Bernard saw the half-empty wineglass on the counter.

"I'm worthless like who? Dad?"

Bernard knew what she wanted to say. But he had to give it to Adele. That was one area that she left alone.

Adele sighed and tried to calm herself. "For the record, I'm not drunk. I had one half glass of wine."

Kendall rolled his eyes. "Yeah, okay."

"My point is," she continued calmly, "I will not continue to support this ridiculous rap career. You either go back to school or you get a job. End of discussion." She stormed out the room without even speaking to Bernard.

"Ugggh," Kendall huffed as he paced back and forth across the kitchen. "I thought mothers were supposed to be loving."

"Just because your mother is being hard on you doesn't mean she doesn't love you."

Kendall looked at his father as if he were crazy. "Hard? Is that what you call it? Half the time she acts like she can't stand me. The other, she acts like she can't stand you. Why is she so freakin' bitter?"

Bernard had to muster up a defense. He knew where some of her bitterness came from—well, a great portion of it. That didn't mean, though, that she had to take it out on their son.

"Look, your mother and I just want what's best for you.

You have so much potential and we hate to see you not living up to it."

Exasperation filled Kendall's face. "I mean, she can't even respect me enough to talk about what makes me happy. I want to produce music, not just rap, but all she hears is the word *rap* and she shuts down about anything else." Kendall looked like he was about to cry, which was definitely out of the norm.

Bernard said gently, "Son, you know how your mother is."

"She just frustrates me so much," Kendall growled, his fists balled up like he wanted to punch someone. "All my friends, they love their moms."

"And you love yours."

Kendall stopped pacing. "But sometimes I wonder if she loves me. A lot of times, in fact."

"She does." Bernard sighed. "You're both mad right now." This version of his usual song had worn thin, even to him. He tried going another way. "Look, let's make a deal. I know we tried you working at the company, but that was a few years ago, so let's try it again just to appease your mother."

Kendall cocked an eyebrow.

"And you can do your music thing on the side," Bernard quickly added. "If you hang in there for six months, I'll front your start-up studio."

Now he had his son's undivided attention. "Oh, my God. Are you serious?"

Bernard hadn't thought through his offer. But his son had been searching for something he wanted to do with his life for so long, and no matter what he tried, his heart always came back to his music. "I am. You just try the job out, give it your all," Bernard said sternly, "and at the six-month mark, I will pay for everything. That will appease your mother and at the same time show me that you can remain committed to something, even when things get rough."

Kendall was flashing all of his pearly whites. "Seriously, Dad?"

"Seriously, dude."

"Dad, please, don't ever say *dude* again." Kendall hugged Bernard.

Bernard embraced his son with all his might. He loved that boy to death. But he did understand Adele's frustration with him. Kendall was smart and had been right from the cradle. In the eleventh grade he designed a patent that had won the science fair, and he'd received all kinds of awards. So it was disheartening that he wanted nothing more than to be a musician. Bernard hoped that it was a phase Kendall was going through. A friend had told Bernard it could be rebellion. At this point, though, Bernard just wanted everyone to be happy.

"So what now?" Kendall asked.

"So, you report to work Monday morning at nine a.m."

"Nine a.m.? Man, you don't have any late shifts?"

Bernard narrowed his eyes.

"Okay, okay." Kendall threw up his arms in surrender. "I'll be there at nine." He considered something else, causing him to lose his smile. "Can you let Mom know because I don't even feel like talking to her?"

"I will." Part of Bernard should've encouraged Kendall to go talk to his mother himself, tell her about his commitment to the job. But the other part understood—because he had no desire to be around Adele either.

"Hey, what's wrong with you?" Alyssa said as she opened the door and stepped aside so Bernard could walk in.

He immediately began loosening his tie.

"You had a fight with Adele?"

"No, it's not that. Just had a long day."

Alyssa started helping him with his tie. "Well," she said slyly, "I have just the thing to help you relax."

He took her hands and stopped her. "No, Alyssa." He paused, trying to figure out how to say what he'd been thinking about all the way over. "You know how much I adore you."

She stopped, wondering what was up. "And I adore you, too."

"And I appreciate how you've handled . . . everything. I know this situation hasn't been easy."

She nodded knowingly.

"But—"

Alyssa cut him off. "But if you think that means I don't want you, I do. I love you, Bernard. I understand your situation is complicated. And I'm okay with that."

"And that's not fair to you," he said, swinging into his prepared lines. "You need to find someone who loves you for you."

Her eyes began watering. "What are you saying?"

"A lot of things are changing in my life, and I'm trying to do right."

"But you said things were complicated with you and Adele."

"They are and they probably always will be." He lowered his head. "But I've caused her a lot of pain in our lifetime."

"But that's been true all along."

"That's just it. And I've justified it for so long. I'm just trying to live right."

"Bernard, what is going on?" Alyssa shook her head in disbelief. "What are you trying to say?"

"We can't see each other anymore." He added hastily, "I mean, I'm going to make sure you're taken care of financially."

She stepped back out of reach, insulted. "I don't want your money. I made it clear I was never with you for your money."

"I know that. That's why I want to do for you."

She realized he really meant to break up. "Bernard, don't do this," she pleaded. "Please, don't do this." Her voice shook.

"Honey, I know it's hard."

"So, I've held on for nothing? I've wasted two years of my life?"

"Alyssa . . ."

She began pacing back and forth across the room. "Of course I knew what the score was, but I thought you would one day wake up and come to your senses and leave her and we could be together."

Now at least he felt on firmer ground. "I know, but I kept telling you that wasn't going to happen."

She stopped, spun around, and glared at him. "I know what you told me, but what you *showed* me was something entirely different."

He reached out to hug her. "Alyssa."

She slapped his hands away. "No. Get out."

"Here, at least take this." He handed her a check he'd already filled out.

She stared at the check in disgust. "That's the answer to all your problems. Throw some money at it and make it go away." She was reeling, almost losing her balance. "You can't keep playing with people's feelings like this, Bernard. Or one day you'll regret it."

"But, Alyssa—"

"Just get out, go."

"Can we—"

"Just get the hell out!" she screamed.

Bernard didn't want any trouble. He took the check and set it on the table. She might not want it now, but when she came to her senses, she'd take it. Everybody always ended up taking his money.

# Chapter 19

Olivia took a moment to pull herself together before she walked through the front doors. This time she regarded the mannequins with a new eye. She admired the silk peasant blouse on one of the mannequins, yet noted how the shirt would look so much better with some loud green capris. That would make the outfit much more trendy and give it some pop. She smiled at how she'd already gone to work.

Then she caught a glimpse of herself in the large floor-to-ceiling lobby mirror. She was wearing beige, wide-leg pants and a new cashmere mock turtleneck that Mona had picked up. She looked cute, but the right accessories would've definitely set the outfit out. She made a mental note that she'd have to step up her fashion game because cute would no longer cut it.

The receptionist that she had seen last week looked over the rims of her glasses. Her face twisted in a frown when she recognized Olivia. "May I help you?" she asked, not bothering to hide her disdain.

"Yes, I'm here to see Elijah Brown," Olivia said, glancing at the name Bernard had written down.

"Is he expecting you?"

"He is. It's my first day," Olivia answered nervously. "I'm supposed to start working today."

The woman eyed her skeptically, then dialed a number on her phone. She turned her back so Olivia couldn't hear what she was saying and mumbled into the receiver. Getting the okay, she turned back around and pushed a sign-in book across the counter.

"Please sign in and I'll buzz you in. You're going to the third floor."

"Thank you," Olivia replied, ignoring the woman's attitude. She was too nervous to worry about anything other than this job. She'd tossed and turned last night, both with excitement and anxiety. She also didn't know how she would be able to work for Bernard when she had so many unanswered questions.

Olivia had allowed the masseuse—who was Latin, not Swedish, which was even better for Mona—to give her a massage. That had put her into a deep sleep. After they lunched, Bernard had told her to go shopping for some work clothes. When she asked how she was supposed to pay for them he had given her the names of some boutiques and told her to put everything on his bill. Olivia didn't even know they did that in real life. She thought that was stuff you only saw on TV. Mona was in heaven, though, especially because Bernard told her to get a few things, too. While Olivia tried to be frugal in her shopping, Mona had tried on every outfit in the store. That is, until Olivia had to nip her shopping spree in the bud.

"Hi, Ms. Howard," a portly man said as he walked up to Olivia and shook her hand.

"Howard? Oh, no, my name is Olivia Dawson."

He looked confused as he glanced down at his paperwork. "Oh. It says here your name is Howard."

Olivia hadn't filled out any paperwork, so obviously someone had made a mistake. Then a sinking feeling filled her gut. Maybe Bernard didn't even remember her last name.

"No, it's Dawson."

The man aimed to please. Clearly, he had received orders from the top. "Well, how about I call you Olivia?" He motioned for her to follow him. "Come on, I'll show you around."

Olivia followed him back through a set of double glass doors. He was quite chatty, but she spoke as little as possible. She had to be careful of what she said. Bernard had asked that she not tell anyone who she was just yet. She didn't know how she felt about that, but a part of her understood how he wouldn't want to spring a surprise daughter on everyone.

*If* she was even his daughter.

He'd never questioned if she was really his daughter and had balked yesterday when she'd suggested that they take a DNA test.

"Trust me," he had said, "you're my daughter. I knew it the moment I first saw you."

Olivia had a dream last night that this was all a big misunderstanding and that Bernard had just been charitable in giving her this job. But for every ounce of doubt she had, he responded with extreme certainty.

Elijah walked her into his office, gave her a key card, and explained some basic procedures. "You're going to be training with another new hire today," he said with a smile.

"Okay." She followed him to a small conference room. He opened the door and she saw Kendall sitting at a rectangular table, playing on his iPhone. The expression on his face said he'd rather be anywhere else. "Hey."

He looked up in surprise. "Hey, yourself. What are you doing here?"

"Starting my first day at work. I didn't know you worked here." She was thrilled to see him. He'd called the hotel to check on her a few times, and she had appreciated his concern.

"I didn't until about"—he looked at his watch—"twenty minutes ago."

She was taken aback. *How can he just now be starting at his father's company?*

"Long story," he said when he noticed the confusion on her face. "The folks say I gotta get a job. Might as well get one where I can't get fired."

"Well, I'm glad you two have already met," Elijah said. He pulled a TV on a standing trolley to the front of the room. "We're gonna start with this." He turned the television on and pressed the play button on the DVD player. "All employees have to watch this orientation video."

As Kendall was about to protest, Elijah added, "Even those who have already seen it."

Kendall groaned and slumped back in his chair. As soon as Elijah left the room, Kendall pulled his iPhone back out and started playing Angry Birds.

Olivia couldn't believe how lax he was about the whole situation. This was an awesome opportunity, and he was acting like he couldn't care less. How could he not realize how lucky he was?

As the video began, she pushed away thoughts of Kendall and focused on the screen. The presentation wasn't as boring as she thought it would be. It had the basic spiel about respecting co-workers, but when they toured the textile area, she found herself engrossed in all the processes needed to bring fashion to life.

After a few minutes, Olivia noticed Kendall staring at her. "What?"

"Are you really watching this mess?" he said, pointing to the TV.

"Yeah. I'm trying to, anyway."

She could tell he had asked about the video only as a way to start a conversation because he immediately followed up with "So, is that why you were here to see my dad, so he could get you a job?"

She hesitated. "You sure ask a lot of questions."

"You sure don't answer any questions," he said with a sly grin.

The last thing Olivia wanted was his getting suspicious, so she said, "Umm, yeah. That's why I'm here. I wanted a job."

"Why didn't you just say that, then?"

"Because I don't normally like strangers in my business," she said with a smile. "But"—she pointed at the television—"don't you think we should be paying attention?"

"This training video is stupid. I don't understand why we can't just get to work."

"Because it's company policy," Elijah said, walking back in the room. "And you wouldn't want us to begin making exceptions for you just because you're the CEO's son. You might have people like Olivia here complaining about preferential treatment for family."

She feigned a smile as Kendall rolled his eyes.

Elijah checked the video. "But you only have about twenty-five more minutes." He grinned. "You can do it," he said, looking directly at Kendall.

Elijah exited the room again and Kendall immediately shifted back into I'd-rather-be-anyplace-else mode. Olivia soon found herself tuning the video out as well. It had moved from the fashion part and was now talking about company policies. However, she was able to watch it without interruption because Kendall had dozed off.

After the video finally ended, Elijah had them fill out more paperwork. Like Kendall, Olivia was ready to get to work.

By noon, Elijah finally seemed ready to turn them loose. "You guys can go grab lunch. There's a small cafeteria down the hall," he told Olivia. "Kendall can show you where it is. When you get back, the two of you will get started in merchandising, although you will spend some time in all departments."

"We're working together?" she asked. Throughout the morning she'd seen glimpses of Kendall's personality, and she was starting to like him more and more. But spending time with him also made her nervous. What if he started asking more questions?

"Yep," Elijah said. "Since you two are coming in together, we thought it would just be easier to have you go through our Management Training Program together."

Kendall clapped his hands in excitement. "All right, maybe this won't be too bad after all."

Elijah shot him a warning look.

"What?"

"Remember the training video" was all Elijah replied. Olivia had no idea what he was talking about, but he was gone before she could ask what she had missed.

"So, what you eatin'? Lunch is on me," Kendall said.

"I . . . I can buy my own lunch."

"I didn't say you couldn't. I was just being a gentleman. Geesh."

She relaxed. "Sorry, I'm just a little tense. I'm real nervous about this job."

He smiled warmly. "No problem. But chill, it's really not that bad. This is a cool place to work, if you're into that work thing."

She laughed as she followed him into the cafeteria. Over lunch, Olivia was pleasantly surprised at how well she and Kendall clicked. She had never laughed so hard in her life with some of the jokes he was telling her. She also learned that he was hoping to get into the music business, and he spouted a couple of rap lyrics for her. She was no fan of rap, but she had to admit that he was pretty good.

Throughout the day, Olivia imagined what growing up with him would have been like. Would he have protected her from people like Terrance Shackleford, who tortured her relentlessly in the fifth grade? Would he have beat up the guy she lost her virginity to, then didn't speak to her the next day at school? A couple of times she caught herself gazing at him as she imagined the what-ifs.

One time he caught her staring and looked at her strangely in return, before flashing that charming smile. She was actually searching his face for features that resembled her own. At lunch, when he'd pushed all his food apart because he didn't like it touching, she'd almost told him the truth—because mixing food was her biggest pet peeve as well. But she had to tread lightly. She had yet to see Bernard today, and she wanted to make sure that things went smoothly.

"So, was your first day everything that you thought it would be?" Kendall asked as he walked her downstairs after they got off.

"It was good. Honestly, I didn't know what to expect."

"Well, it was boring—just like I expected," he joked as they went through the double glass doors into the brilliant LA sunshine. "How are you getting home?"

She was unsure how to answer, but since he was walking out

with her, she couldn't lie. "Umm, I have a ride coming." She didn't want to tell him that Bernard was sending a car service for her because then Kendall would be questioning why.

"I'm meeting my friend out here," Olivia added, looking up and down the sidewalk for Mona. "She went out today to try and find an agent. And she's supposed to meet me back here."

"Oh, she's an aspiring actress. Why does that not surprise me? Every female in LA wants to be an actress."

"Not everyone."

Kendall smiled at her. "So, where are you staying?"

Her eyes narrowed in confusion. "At the Four Seasons, remember? You dropped me off."

"No, I mean permanently. You can't live there forever."

Yet another practical detail she hadn't thought about. Bernard had told her to stay in the suite for as long as she wanted, but she knew that didn't mean indefinitely. "I guess when my money gets right, I'll find a place."

"Well, let me know if you need any help," he offered just as Mona walked up.

"Hello, hello, hello," Mona sang. Four shopping bags hung from her arms. She had on a pair of oversize sunglasses and wore a long, fitted, plum maxi dress, which had to be new because Olivia had never seen it before.

"Oh, my goodness," Mona said, recognizing Kendall. She flashed a sly grin at Olivia. "Well, we're moving on mighty quickly, aren't we?"

"Oh, it's not like that at all," Olivia interjected, embarrassed. "He works here with me," she said, pointing at Kendall.

"Remember, he came in with B—Mr. Wells on that first day? That's his dad."

"Oh, yeah?" Mona leaned in to get a good look at Kendall from head to toe. Even though he had on a pair of khaki slacks and a button-down dress shirt, Olivia knew Mona was impressed with what she saw.

"Kendall, this is my best friend, Mona."

Mona took his hand and stepped in closer. "Umph, how you doin'?"

He chuckled at her flirtation. "What's up?"

"Gas prices, the cost to do my hair, my rent," she joked.

Olivia grimaced. Why did her friend have to come across so strong?

Luckily, Kendall didn't seem fazed. "I feel you," he said, running his hand through his short, wavy hair, "my perms now cost me twice as much." Olivia did a double take before he quickly added, "I'm kidding."

All of them laughed.

Olivia said, "I don't know, maybe you were on some Al Sharpton kick."

"Yeah, I wish someone would come near my hair with some chemicals," he replied. "So, what you ladies getting into tonight?"

"You tell us," Mona said sweetly.

"We're getting into our car, going back to our hotel, and resting," Olivia responded.

Mona groaned and rolled her eyes. "My girl here is such a prude. She's the only person that could come to LA and want to sit inside."

"Well, we're gonna have to change that," Kendall announced. "I'll let you ladies rest tonight, after Olivia's big first day, but tomorrow I'm taking you to this new spot called the Vine. I'm picking you up and I'll show you how we party, West Coast style."

"I'm from Missouri, so show me, baby," Mona said, laughing.

Olivia let out a groan, but Kendall grinned and continued to take Mona's flirting in stride.

"Cool. Olivia, you still have my number, so you holla at me if you need anything."

Olivia nodded as a Town Car pulled up. The driver jumped out, raced around, and opened the door for them.

"See you ladies later," Kendall said as they got in the car.

"Bye," both of them said in unison.

"Oh, my God. I just met my future husband," Mona said breathlessly as the car pulled off. "He did not look that fine the other day."

"Girl, please."

Mona turned around and looked out the rearview window. "Lord, have mercy. He's getting into a fire-red Porsche. Yes, ma'am, that man is as good as mine."

"Umm, that would be no. He is so off-limits," Olivia warned.

Mona settled back into her seat. "My, is someone protective of their brother?"

*Brother?* She really had a brother. That was going to take some getting used to, but the thought sure brought a smile to her face. "Naw, it's not even like that. I just . . . I don't know."

"Well, I'm just glad you're getting it together. But I know you don't mind me snagging him, right? I mean, we are besties. We share everything?"

Olivia pointed at the bags. "Obviously, since you're spending up my so-called father's money."

Bernard had told them to go on Rodeo Drive and buy some clothes. He'd said all they had to do was give the clerk his name and bill it to his account. Olivia had never heard of such a thing and was sure they were going to get embarrassed, but not only had it worked, when the stores found out they were on Bernard Wells's account, they got first-class treatment.

"Well, someone needs to spend some money because you only bought a few pants and some shirts. They weren't even designer."

"Because I'm not trying to take advantage of anyone."

"Please. What I spent is a drop in the bucket to that man." Mona patted Olivia's leg with excited little taps. "But if I play my cards right, I might not need Uncle B's money because his son might be taking care of me just fine."

Olivia shook her head. She knew her friend was joking. At least she hoped she was. "Anyway, did you find an agent? Or did you spend all day shopping?"

Mona sighed and fell back against the leather seat. "No. Everybody wants a referral."

"So, what are you going to do?"

"I found out about some open auditions. I'm gonna do those, then do some cold calls until I can find an agent and, hopefully, work."

"Why don't you try to find some other kind of job if you're gonna stay?"

Mona removed her sunglasses and looked at Olivia like she'd lost her mind. "Now, why would I do something like that?"

"Because I'm going to have to get an apartment. And if you stay with me, you're going to have to help me with the bills."

"News flash!" Mona tossed her hair over her shoulder. "Your days of worrying about bills are long over. Daddy Warbucks is ready to make up for seventeen lost years, and I say you let him!" Mona clicked her teeth as if she had made her point. "But seriously, you know I'm not gonna just mooch off you—for long. I told you all of this is divine intervention, my chance to get into acting and modeling, and I have a feeling my big break is right around the corner."

Olivia side-eyed her friend. Mona had always fantasized about being a famous actress, but Olivia had never taken her seriously because she'd never taken one acting class or done anything other than hope she got discovered somehow while walking down the street.

"What's that look for? You don't think I'm serious?"

Olivia would've told her no, but she knew her best friend. Once she set her mind to something, she could make anything happen. "I didn't say a word."

"Good, because I don't want to have to tell everyone in my Academy Award speech about how you didn't believe in me."

*Academy Award speech,* Olivia thought, groaning. "So, you're going to try and find some acting classes?"

"Nah, I'm going straight for the auditions. Some people

naturally have it, and I naturally have it." Mona slid her sunglasses back on and leaned back in the seat.

Olivia couldn't help but laugh at her friend. She wished she had Mona's confidence. Still, things were looking up for both of them. Mona was prepared to grab her moment. Now Olivia needed to reach out, in a more practical way, and take hold of hers.

# Chapter 20

Bernard was happier than he'd been in a very long time. That's because in the last four weeks his relationship with Olivia was going better than he could've ever imagined. He didn't disturb her at work, but he stopped by her hotel every day. Sometimes they had dinner. Sometimes they went out for coffee, and sometimes they just sat and talked. She'd taken him up on his offer to go to the dance studio, and she'd stepped in and given some one-on-one tips to the young dancers. He had gone to watch her twice and was amazed at how graceful she was, especially since she said she hadn't danced in two years. At work, he'd beamed with pride as Ms. Barrows raved about her performance. Ms. Barrows had told him that they definitely needed to hire Olivia full-time because she was a natural at the job, adding that it was so refreshing to see someone so talented with such a wonderful work ethic. Thrilled to hear this report, Bernard wanted to brag and announce that she was his daughter, but he'd just listened attentively.

One day soon, Bernard hoped, he could tell the world. Olivia hadn't completely opened up and let him in, but she had shared some stories about Lorraine and growing up in Houston. She didn't ask him about Bernard's relationship with her mother, almost as if she was scared of the answers. But when she did bring it up, he would tell her everything—well, almost everything.

In the meantime, he would take what she offered. Bernard already relished that as the days wore on, Olivia's answers weren't as abrupt. Her voice wasn't laced with as much anger. The hurt and pain of years of neglect still showed, but he knew that in time he would break down that barrier. He wanted nothing more than to get his daughter to forgive him and spend the future together with him as her father.

"So, what do you think, Mr. Wells?" the Realtor asked, indicating the last room in the condo.

"It's beautiful. I love it, and if she wants it, I want her to move in by the weekend."

"You want it to be in her name, right?"

"Yes, I do. But I want this to be her decision. Just let her know everything is taken care of already—after she tells you that she wants it." Bernard would've told her himself, but he'd learned that his daughter didn't like handouts and people feeling sorry for her. She was the complete opposite of Kendall.

Luckily, her friend Mona was the complete opposite of Olivia as well, and Mona was on his side. *Well, Mona is on my money's side,* he thought wryly. But whatever worked. That's why he had offered up his convertible Benz for Olivia last week in front of Mona. He knew Mona would make sure Olivia took the car. As he'd expected, Olivia had protested, but ultimately, Mona had convinced her that they needed transportation in LA, and Olivia had given in. So, Bernard knew this condo couldn't be his idea. Sure, the Realtor would have to tell her that he'd paid for it, but only after he'd sold her on it.

"I really hope she likes it," Bernard repeated.

Olivia was going to say the gated community, the high-vaulted ceiling, and the spacious living area were all too much, which was yet another quality he loved about her. Kendall would have complained that the place was too small. Bernard wanted Olivia to be safe, and he thought this pick wasn't too fancy or overboard. It was just right for her.

"I told her that you'd be coming to help her to find an apartment," Bernard told the Realtor, who was nearly salivating at the idea of a cash sale of this magnitude. Bernard didn't usually buy real estate in cash, but he didn't want Olivia to have any issues, and he didn't want Adele to find out. "There's a little something in it if you can convince her to take this one," Bernard added.

The Realtor did lick his lips this time, and Bernard knew it was a done deal. He wanted Olivia to live here for a number of reasons: the security was great, and it was a three-bedroom condo, so it was large enough for her friend to stay. But most important, it was only ten minutes from his home. He hoped to be spending a lot of time over here. He had to make up for so much lost time, but he had to tread carefully, because if Olivia was anything like her mother, she could be a quiet storm.

Bernard's heart ached when he recalled the last time he'd seen Lorraine's wrath—the day he'd broken the news that he was marrying Adele.

"That was a delicious meal," he said, leaning back in his chair and rubbing his stomach. Lorraine had cooked a mouth-watering meal of smothered chicken, rice, cabbage, and salmon croquettes. She was a flat-out fabulous cook.

Bernard had been trying to get up the nerve for weeks to tell Lorraine, but he could never bring himself to utter the words he knew would crush her heart. Now, with his wedding to Adele scheduled in just a couple of weeks, he knew he had to come clean. Lorraine already suspected something because he hadn't been visiting as much, and when he did, he was often distant.

"I'm just happy you're here. I'm hoping that you can tell me if I did something wrong," she meekly said.

He took her arm and pulled her down onto his lap. "You could never do anything wrong." He kissed her hungrily. That made her relax and she sank into his embrace.

After a few minutes, she pulled away, then stood up. "I made you a blackberry cobbler. Let me go get you some."

He took a deep breath and stopped her just as she reached the entrance to the kitchen. "I have something to tell you."

Lorraine stopped, then slowly turned around. She took measured steps back to the table, then eased into the chair across from him as if she anticipated the news that was about to come.

"I don't know how to say this. . . ."

"Just say it." Her eyes danced with panic.

"Ummm, I don't . . . I'm . . . I'm getting married," he blurted out.

She sat stunned, like that was the last thing she ever expected to hear. "W-what?"

He saw a film of tears start to build in her eyes, and he almost lost his nerve, almost told her this was just a horrible joke, but he couldn't lie to her anymore. "I am so sorry to do this to you, but it's true. I'm getting married." The words hurt leaving his mouth. The pain he saw on her face hurt more.

"To who?" she whispered in disbelief.

"To my boss's daughter."

The expression on her face said she was trying to process what he'd just said. "Are you kidding me?"

"No. I wouldn't play like this."

"Oh, my God!" Her bottom lip started quivering. "Married?"

Bernard knew this would be a devastating blow. They'd been together for over a year, and he'd never stopped telling her how much he loved her. He never wanted to stop telling her. They'd talked about their plans, their future, their family.

He raced over to her end of the table and dropped to his knees in front of her. "Baby, I am so sorry. It just happened, my boss, his daughter is so controlling . . . things just got out of control. I don't know."

*"Married?"*

"Please forgive me." He reached out to touch her arm. She jerked out of his reach and stood up.

She took deep, labored breaths, trying to keep from hyperventilating. "Bernard, tell me something, anything to make this make sense. Where did this come from? Why did this happen?"

"Sweetheart, I am so sorry, but I don't have a choice. You have to understand. This is everything I've worked my whole life for. I went to school for this. I worked hard for this position. And it's a great opportunity." His words sounded crazy as they left his mouth. But they were true. He'd been on a mission since the day he set foot in Los Angeles. He'd been determined to be a success and prove all the naysayers, including his estranged father, wrong. Falling madly in love with Lorraine hadn't been a part of his master plan.

"The marriage is a *great opportunity*?"

"No, I . . ." He struggled to find the right words. He'd thought this decision through extensively, and he knew he was making the right choice. Bernard's mother had married for love, and their family had all been miserable ever since. He couldn't live like that again. He'd vowed at the age of ten that he would never be poor again, and marrying Adele would ensure that.

"So, let me get this straight," Lorraine said slowly. "You've been cheating on me and now you're about to marry the woman you were cheating with?"

"It's not like that at all," he protested. "I have to do this. It's like a package deal. If I want to run this company, I have to marry her."

"So you're leaving me so you can get a promotion?"

"Don't make it sound like that." He stood up and began pacing in front of her.

"What other way is it supposed to sound, Bernard?" she asked, dumbfounded.

"Please. I don't really love her, but—"

"If you don't love her, don't marry her," Lorraine cried.

"I don't have a choice."

"Oh, my God, I do not believe this."

The rest of the night had been more of the same. He'd tried to comfort her, but she'd gone ballistic, and before the night was over, the remaining smothered chicken was splattered all over the wall and her tiny apartment was in shambles. She'd called him everything but a child of God as she cursed and cried, and he endured it all. Each word told him the pain she felt. He was devastated over what he'd done to her . . . and later, even more so over what he'd done to himself.

Lorraine had packed her bags and left that day, so even if he had been thinking about changing his mind—which he had considered over the next few days—it was a moot point. She was gone. With a regret that would only grow more agonizing with the passing years, Bernard pulled himself together, put on a happy face, and married his future.

"Mr. Wells! Hello!"

Bernard jumped at the sight of the security guard tapping on his car window.

"Sorry, didn't mean to startle you. I was just worried about you. You've been sitting out here a minute."

"Just getting my thoughts together," Bernard said, flustered.

"Guess that's what you businessmen do." The guard chuckled.

"Guess so." Feeling troubled, Bernard got out of the car and tried to push away the memories. There was no longer any sense in wallowing in the past. All his attention needed to be on his future. That's why he'd had to let Alyssa go. He just hoped that Olivia would see that he really was a good man.

# Chapter 21

Bernard's smile couldn't get any bigger. Olivia couldn't help but be touched by the way his eyes lit up whenever they were together. He treaded so lightly most of the time, as if terribly afraid of doing the wrong thing, but he couldn't hide how he felt about her.

As she took a seat across from him at the Starbucks near England Enterprises, Bernard looked on top of the world. She'd stopped in the coffee shop this morning to get her mocha and saw him reading the *Wall Street Journal*. She was surprised to see him sitting out in public at a place so close to the office.

"I just love the peaceful atmosphere here," he'd explained before asking if she'd join him.

"Well, I just wanted to tell you that I found a place," she said, setting down her steaming café mocha.

"That's wonderful. Is it one of the places the Realtor showed you?"

She nodded, smiling. "It's the one that's closest." She gave him a sincere look of thanks. "I don't have much to go in the place, but I'm trying to fill it up."

Mona had had her brother Charles pack up both her and Olivia's meager belongings. Before Olivia had left, she had packed all her mother's things and the things she wanted to keep from that apartment, which wasn't much, and put them in storage at Charles's house. Once Olivia and Mona had decided that LA would be their new permanent home, Charles had everything shipped to them.

"Well, you know if you need anything else—"

She held up her hand to stop him. "I know. Thank you. But I'm good. I mean, you've done more than enough by paying for the condo."

When the Realtor had shown her and Mona the condo, Olivia had loved it immediately. However, she knew she couldn't possibly afford it. But then the Realtor had explained that it had been bought and paid for in full—if she wanted it. While her initial reaction had been to say no, she wasn't a complete fool. So, much to Mona's elation, she'd gladly signed on the dotted line.

"It's the least I could do." The way Bernard was staring at her sent a funny feeling through her. Not for the first time, she wondered how strongly she reminded him of her mother.

"Well, I need to pay you back," she said, breaking their gaze.

He nodded, even though the look on his face said he'd never

accept a dime from her. "Just the fact that you offered to pay me back means the world to me. I'll be honest. I don't see character and integrity like that often in my line of work."

Olivia took a sip of her coffee. What a 180-degree turn her life had taken. "I've never lived in a place that we didn't rent," she said wistfully.

"Well, it's high time you did." He paused like he was carefully considering his words. "I know I wasn't there for you while you were growing up and I can never make up for that, but I want to make your life from here on out as stress-free as possible."

"Well, I . . . I don't want to take advantage of your generosity," she softly said.

He looked offended. "You could never do that. I see your heart." His expression turned solemn before he added, "You know, you're just like your mother. I mean, any other person would've walked in my office trying to see what they could get out of me. But not you. Not your mother. She was never impressed with wealth."

That was her opening to ask him about her mother, but Olivia couldn't bring herself to do it. She'd yet to ask him detailed questions about their relationship. She was still grieving for her mother, and she wasn't ready to have her image shattered as Bernard shared the filthy details of their illicit affair.

Bernard shook away his nostalgia. "Is your friend Mona going to stay on in Los Angeles?"

"Probably."

"Good," he said, beaming. "I just want you to be happy,

because no matter what you think, I do love you." She shifted uncomfortably again, so he quickly changed the subject. "Ummm, so everything else is going okay with you?"

She nodded, grateful that he was sensitive enough not to push himself on her. "But, have you told Kendall yet?"

He paused as worry lines creased his face. "Not yet. The timing isn't right," he finally said.

She had been trying not to get frustrated with Bernard, but she was slowly reaching that point. She'd never been a liar. Her mother had instilled that in her for as long as she could remember. Olivia considered briefly the hypocrisy of her mother's words about always being honest, but then turned her attention back to Bernard.

"It's been over a month. When will the timing be right? I like Kendall and I don't want to keep lying to him. I don't want to live a lie, period."

Bernard stared blankly at her, and for a moment she wondered if he was trying to have her all to himself. She quickly shook off that thought. No, Bernard was just trying to take the easy way out. The road that was filled with denial and "if we don't talk about it, it will go away." But that wasn't her world and she didn't know how much longer she could wait for him to come clean.

The problem was, she didn't know how she would do it if Bernard didn't.

# Chapter 22

At times like these Bernard wished that he had a personal assistant. He'd had back-to-back stressful meetings all day, and his head was throbbing. He had just left work, and instead of getting on the 405 to go home, he'd stopped at a local grocery store to purchase some aspirin. Two of the mergers he'd been working on had fallen through, and the board members were not happy. Then a knitting machine had broken and a supervisor quit. It had been the day from hell.

Bernard couldn't remember the last time he'd stepped inside a grocery store, but he desperately needed some Tylenol and a six-pack of Heineken for later. A quick tour of the aisles and Bernard found what he needed.

"Will that be paper or plastic?" the clerk at the checkout counter asked.

"Plastic, ple . . ." His words trailed off when he saw Walter at the end of the counter, bagging his groceries. He wore an apron with the grocery store's name across the front.

"Walter? How are you?" Bernard asked as he handed the clerk a $20 bill.

"I'm on this side of the soil, so I guess I'm still doing all right." Walter's smile was genuine.

Bernard got his change, then Walter handed him the bag.

"How long have you been working here?"

"Just a couple of weeks. Do you need some help with this out to your car?"

Bernard could tell the question was routine, but he felt compelled to say yes. Walter grabbed the small bag and followed him outside.

"Why are you working here?" Bernard asked once they reached his car.

Walter looked at him like that was the craziest thing he'd ever heard. "I need a job."

"But, I mean, you know, you got the severance money."

"And I appreciate that, but I told you, I have two children in college. That money is a big blessing, but it's not going to be enough to feed my family from here on."

Bernard understood that, but he couldn't believe Walter couldn't find anything else. "But bagging groceries?"

Walter shrugged. "A man's gotta do what a man's gotta do."

"I'm so sorry."

Walter waved him off. "Don't feel bad for me. No, I don't want to be here and I don't understand what part of my master plan this is, but I learned long ago that when you don't understand something, that's God working it out. I just have to stay faithful and know even though I don't understand it, I know he's working something out."

Bernard couldn't help but look on in admiration. Even in the face of adversity, at his lowest point, when he had every right to be bitter, Walter stayed faithful. It's a trait Bernard didn't ever see himself possessing.

"I actually got Jerry Cooper a job up here as well," Walter said, "but they wanted to switch him to the night shift, and you know that wouldn't work with his daughter. Besides, he really needed something with benefits anyway."

"So you don't have benefits here?"

Walter flashed a you-know-the-answer-to-that smile.

"How is Jerry?" Bernard asked, trying to shift the subject. "After that day at the deli, I was a little worried."

"Truth be told, I'm worried about him, too. He's not the same man he used to be, you know, back before he lost his wife and his daughter got sick."

Bernard nodded. "And you, how are you holding up?"

"Like I told you, I'm blessed. Regardless of my circumstances." Walter shuffled a foot. "But I best be getting on back inside before I lose this job." He smiled. "Have a good life, Mr. Wells. I'm still praying for your happiness. And I pray that one day, you'll learn to pray for yourself. Maybe then, you just might get it."

# Chapter 23

"I don't believe this."

Olivia waited with bated breath as Angela studied the lobby mannequins. Olivia didn't know if that was a good "I don't believe this" or a bad one.

Angela walked around the mannequins, studying them from the back and the front. "So, you just took it upon yourself to change the design of our lobby mannequins?"

Olivia had known she was taking a gamble doing this without asking. It had taken nearly an act of Congress to get the receptionist to agree to allowing the changes long enough for Olivia to show off her magic. "Yes, ma'am. I-I just thought I could show you my vision better than I could tell you."

Angela fingered the emerald-green capri pants. "Wow, those are really loud."

"I know they are, but I think we should be trendsetters. The pants give the outfit flair."

"And you had the seamstress make this from discarded material?"

Olivia nodded. "Yes, I simply had her change the way they were cutting the shirts from the men's Elsik line, and the left-over material could be used for the pants. That way we maximize our material without incurring any additional costs. And by putting the splash of color in the lobby, it maintains our classy feel but shows we're also a company that keeps up with the changing trends."

Angela finally delivered her assessment: "Girl, you are brilliant."

Olivia released a breath as a huge smile spread across her face. "Oh, my God. I was so nervous that you were going to hate it."

"Hate it? I love it! This is exactly the concept we were looking for. Mr. Wells had been trying to verbalize what he wanted, but none of the designers were able to capture it because I don't think they were clear on what he wanted. This captures the style exactly." Angela was giddy with excitement. "I can't wait for him to see what you did with both of these!" she said, pointing to the other mannequin, which Olivia had outfitted with an electric-blue, off-the-shoulder maxi dress.

If anyone had ever told Olivia that she would enjoy something else as much as dance, she would've said that was crazy. But after four weeks in the Management Training Program at England Enterprises, Olivia was loving her job.

She'd mastered the marketing division, impressing her supervisor, Angela, so much that she'd moved Olivia to the design department. Olivia had been responsible for the costumes in her dance school back in Houston, so she had an eye for color and fashion in general. Her fashion expertise and keen eye helped her see what people wanted, and she had already impressed two wholesale clients.

But all the work had left Olivia with little time to finish setting up her condo. Thank God for Mona—at least she got all the stuff moved in and settled while Olivia worked.

Kendall, on the other hand, had no interest in his job. He never got to work on time, and when he did arrive, he was never focused. But still, Olivia loved being around him. They had a natural connection and had grown extremely close over the last month. Now, even though they were in different divisions, she looked forward to lunch, which they ate together every day. He'd called in sick this morning, but he'd secretly told her that he was really going to an industry luncheon to hobnob with record execs.

Olivia took her tray with her chicken Caesar salad and eased down at a table where two young women were sitting.

One of them, Shawn, she recognized from the mailroom. The other she'd seen a few times in the PR department but had never officially met.

"Umph, she's dining alone today. Guess her man didn't make it," Shawn giggled to her friend.

Olivia should have ignored them, but she frowned and asked, "Excuse me, are you talking to me?"

The girl rolled her eyes like she couldn't appreciate Olivia's interfering in her conversation, even though she was obviously talking about Olivia. "Well, I wasn't talking *to* you." The girl looked at her friend and laughed. "But I was talking *about* you."

Olivia leaned in, pushing aside the little voice urging her to ignore Shawn. The last thing she needed was anybody speculating about her, because once the truth came out, that could get real ugly. "I'm not sure what man you could possibly be referring to," Olivia said anyway.

Shawn raised an eyebrow. "Your man. The boss's son."

Olivia sighed in frustration. She decided to try to play nice just to keep the drama at a minimum. "Oh, no. Kendall and I . . . it's not like that at all."

"Whatever," Shawn said, turning up her lip.

The other woman flashed a smile. "You'll have to excuse my friend." The woman stuck her hand out. "I'm Alyssa. I work in public relations."

Olivia shook her hand. "Hi, Alyssa."

"No need to apologize for me," Shawn interjected. "Everyone sees you guys together all the time. You ain't gotta front with us. And truth be told, I ain't mad at you. Baby Moneybags got it going on," she cackled.

"Well, it's not like that at all. Seriously," Olivia protested.

Shawn seemed intrigued by the denial. "Okay then, hook me up."

"Excuse me?"

"Hook me up. If there's nothing going on between you two,

put in a good word for me. He's a little younger than I like them, but his wallet makes up for any deficiencies."

As Shawn laughed, Olivia was dumbfounded. Was Shawn serious? As if Kendall would even want someone like her. Her hemline was too high and her neckline was too low. She looked as if she were going to the club instead of to work. Olivia didn't know a whole lot about her brother—yet—but she definitely didn't think he'd be attracted to someone like Shawn. With a tight smile Olivia said, "I'll see what I can do."

"That's what I'm talking about." Shawn stood up and grabbed her tray. "Let me get back downstairs. I'm already late and I don't need ol' lady Cusack trippin'." Shawn said good-bye to Alyssa, then grabbed a piece of paper and scribbled her number down. "I'm serious, tell Kendall to call me." She licked her lips. "He won't regret it. I'll rock baby boy's world."

Olivia grudgingly took the number. "Okay, I'll pass it on." As she folded the piece of paper, she found herself wondering what type of women her brother actually did like. He had only mentioned one ex, named Tina. Other than that, he said he'd stayed clear of serious relationships. Kendall had told Olivia and Mona that he was selective in whom he dated because he was never sure if they liked him or his money. At first Olivia had thought he was being a little cocky, but after seeing all the women at the club constantly throwing themselves at Kendall, she could believe him.

Still, if that was the only downside to being rich, Olivia would take it over her life any day.

"Give it here," Alyssa said, holding her hand out after Shawn was gone.

"What?" Olivia said, confused.

"Give me that number so I can throw it away for you." Alyssa laughed. "I know you were just being nice. Shawn doesn't have a shot at being with Kendall Wells."

Olivia smiled as she handed Alyssa the number. Alyssa balled it up and tossed it on her empty tray. "That settles that problem."

They made some small talk, and at first everything was cool. But then, Olivia started feeling like she was on some kind of job interview.

"So, what made you come here for work?"

"I don't know." Olivia shrugged. "Just seemed like a good place to use my talents."

"Did Kendall refer you?"

Olivia hesitated and debated lying, but she didn't want to keep track of a trail of lies. "No, actually, his father helped me get the job."

Alyssa's whole body tensed up. "So, how do you know Ber—Mr. Wells?"

The sharp tone of her voice told Olivia this conversation needed to wrap up. "You know what? I need to be getting back to my desk myself." Olivia stood and started gathering up her tray.

"Do you have to go?" Alyssa sounded panicked, but then she relaxed. "I mean, I was enjoying our conversation."

*You mean your inquisition,* Olivia wanted to say. "Sorry. Some other time. I've got so much work on my desk."

"Well, I guess I'll see you around."

"Yeah, enjoy your day." Olivia hastily exited. She didn't know what was up with Alyssa, but something about her didn't feel right.

Olivia shook away the thought. It was probably her own paranoia about saying the wrong thing. She silently cursed. Enough was enough. Bernard was going to have to step up to the plate and be honest because she couldn't walk around paranoid about everything and everybody.

# Chapter 24

Olivia was loving the previews she was perusing for New York Fashion Week. Angela had shocked her when she gave Olivia a coveted invitation to go with her to the event. So Olivia was soaking up all the research she could so that she could be fully prepared.

"Psssst, Olivia!"

Olivia looked up from her desk to see who was calling her name. She frowned when she saw Kendall poking his head around the corner. He had a huge grin across his face.

"Boy, what are you doing?"

"Meet me in Dad's office," he whispered.

"For what?"

"I don't want anyone to see me. You know I called in sick."

"What is it that has you doing some double-oh-seven stuff?" she asked, getting up from her desk.

"Just wait a minute, then meet me there."

Olivia gave him a few minutes, then made her way back to Bernard's office. She wondered how they would get past Bernard's secretary, but as usual, the elderly assistant wasn't at her desk.

"What's going on, Spy Kid?" she asked, once she was standing in front of Kendall in his father's office.

"Oh, my God." Kendall could barely contain his excitement. "You're not going to believe this."

"Believe what?"

He held his hands out in a ta-da motion. "Your boy is on his way."

"On his way where?" Then she remembered why he called in sick. "Oh, wow, the luncheon. Did you make some connects?"

"Did I? I gave my demo tape to this record producer with Sony and he loved it."

She was happy to see him so excited. "Of course he loved it," Olivia said proudly.

"I know this could mean nothing. It could go nowhere, but you don't know how major this is for me."

"Yes, I do."

"I've been working for so long for this, waiting on an opportunity like this."

His excitement was infectious and she was thrilled. "I am so happy for you."

"Thank you for believing in me." He sounded so sincere. "I just hope that I don't blow it."

"You won't. You got this, boy. You are so talented, and they'd be crazy not to sign you."

"This is a dream that I have that nobody has believed in."

"Well, I've been a believer from the beginning."

"I will always be grateful to you for your encouragement." Kendall reached out and took her into a big bear hug.

She hugged him back, then froze when she felt him nuzzle her neck. "Whoa, what are you doing?" she asked, jumping back.

Kendall pulled her back and leaned in to try to kiss her. "Come on, Olivia. You can't deny that there's electricity between us."

Olivia didn't know what came over her, but she punched Kendall in the chest so hard that he stumbled backward. "Ewww! Get away from me!"

Yes, they'd grown closer by the day, but it had never dawned on her that he would think their connection was sexual.

Kendall was about to respond when they heard Bernard's voice. "What is going on here?" He stood in the doorway, stunned. Olivia hadn't heard the door open, so she wasn't sure how much he'd seen.

Kendall rubbed his chest, looking confused. Olivia knew that she had hit him hard, but he was about to cross the line and she'd just reacted.

Olivia glared at Bernard. This was all his fault. If he had been honest with Kendall, this would never have happened.

"Dad, I was just—"

"I saw what you were trying to do!"

Bernard stomped into his office. Olivia didn't know what to say. This entire incident had caught her completely off guard.

"Are you okay?" Bernard asked her.

Shaken up, Olivia could barely reply.

"Dang, I'm sorry," Kendall said, mystified by her reaction. "I wasn't trying . . ."

Bernard's venomous glare stopped him midsentence.

Olivia didn't say a word as she headed toward the door. This was getting too far out of control.

"Olivia, are you sure you're okay?" Bernard asked.

"Yes." She nodded, but kept moving toward the door, keeping her eye on Bernard. "But you better handle this," Olivia said sternly. "Because if you don't, I will. Believe that." She marched out of the office.

# Chapter 25

Bernard had to take deep, slow breaths to keep from completely losing his temper. He was more sickened than angry. Thankfully, Kendall didn't actually kiss Olivia, but Bernard could tell Olivia was livid.

He closed the door after Olivia left and spun around to face his son. "I can't believe you did that!"

Kendall stared blankly at his father.

"You don't have anything to say?"

"What do you want me to say?" Kendall shrugged like he couldn't understand the big deal. "I'm attracted to her. I thought she was attracted to me. Maybe we have something. . . ."

Bernard needed to tell him why that could not happen, but he still couldn't bring himself to utter the words. "You can't do that."

"Why?"

Bernard took another deep breath. *Just tell him.* "Because it's not right."

"I don't understand what's so not right about it. I'm single, she's single. So what's the problem?"

A part of Bernard wanted to come clean. But the other part knew Kendall would never understand Bernard's betrayal of Adele, and he wasn't ready to shatter his son's image of him. Nor was he ready for the pain such news would inflict on Kendall.

"Obviously, she's not interested in you."

"You don't know that," Kendall protested. "Maybe she just needs time to warm up to me."

Another deep breath. "Son, trust me when I tell you. Leave it alone. This is not the time or the place," he said firmly.

"Are you worried about sexual harassment or something? If so, Olivia's not like that."

Bernard slammed his hand on his desk. "Dammit, Kendall, what did I say?"

Bernard's stern tone caught Kendall off guard and he shot his father a suspicious look. Probably because he could count on one hand the number of times he'd seen Bernard get upset.

Bernard inhaled, then lowered his voice. "Son, we can't handle another sexual-harassment case. We can't even handle the appearance of any improprieties. I need you to keep this professional. Please, stay away from her."

Kendall crossed his arms and studied his father. "Would that be," he said slowly, "because *you* want her?"

"Excuse me?"

"Yeah." A smile formed on Kendall's lips. "This is all starting to make sense. She shows up here ready to make a scene. You whisper something to calm her down, you set her up in a suite at the Four Seasons, giving her carte blanche to buy what she wants. You give her one of your cars to drive. And I'm sure you had something to do with that nice condo she's set up in." He studied his father some more. "So, is that your mistress?"

"What?" Bernard exclaimed. The conversation was making him uneasy for reasons that had nothing to do with Olivia.

"If that's what it is, that's all you have to say. I mean, I don't condone cheating on Mama"—Kendall shrugged nonchalantly—"but I can't say that I blame you either."

"Kendall!" Bernard didn't know whether to be more upset that Kendall thought he was having an affair with Olivia or that he didn't care. "I'm not having an affair with her," he said with conviction.

"You don't have to . . ." Kendall's words trailed off as Adele walked into the office.

"What are the two of you looking all intense for?" She stood in the doorway, dressed in her signature black St. John suit. Her hair was neatly done, like she'd just stepped out of a beautician's chair.

Bernard's heart quickened. What had she heard? He didn't need any questions about Olivia.

But she walked in, dropped her Hermès bag on his desk, and turned to Kendall. "How is work going? Or have you quit yet?"

"Hello to you, too, Mother." He frowned at Bernard. "I'm

out." He headed out the office, not bothering to hide his disdain.

"Can you teach your son that it's bad enough that he uses that slang, but the workplace is not the place for it?"

"Hello, Adele." Bernard sighed. "You know, maybe just once you should try saying, 'Hi, Son, how was your day?' You could try to act like a caring mother."

"Obviously, I care. I raised him."

*Technically, you didn't, the nannies did,* Bernard wanted to say. Instead, he released a long breath. "Okay, Adele. What can I help you with?"

Her usual forbidding visage opened up into a big grin. "I brought you something."

He stood speechless, trying to remember if it was his birthday or anniversary.

"Oh, don't look like that." She set a tall paper bag on his desk. Then she reached in and pulled out a bottle of wine. "I know I'm the wine drinker and you're the wine collector, so I thought you'd appreciate this."

Bernard shook himself out of his stunned trance and took the bottle. Adele had bought him a gift? Just because? "Oh, my God," he said, reading the bottle. "Is this what I think it is?"

She smiled. "If you think it is the Terrantez 1715, it is."

"B-but this is the oldest known bottle of wine in the world."

"And I had to move heaven and earth to get it," she said proudly. "But I thought you would enjoy it."

"Adele, I-I don't know what to say."

She smiled as if his excitement was enough. Bernard couldn't believe this. He'd commented on the famous Madeira a year ago but had long ago given up any hope of tracking it down. "Thank you," he said, taking a step toward her to hug her, something he hadn't done in a long time.

The hug felt momentarily awkward, then he felt his wife sink into his embrace.

"Bernard, I saw . . ."

Bernard dropped his arms and jumped back as both of them turned toward the door. Olivia had stopped at the entrance, her eyes darting between the two of them. It was the first time Adele and Olivia had seen each other in seventeen years.

Bernard swallowed a lump in his throat, praying that Adele didn't recognize Olivia.

Yet Adele rose to her full height, crossed her arms, and said, *"Bernard?"*

"I mean, Mr. Wells," Olivia quickly corrected herself.

Adele cocked her head at her husband and he immediately stepped in. "This is the new hire I told you about. For the Management Training Program," Bernard said, jumping to Olivia's defense.

"And you allow her to call you by your first name?" she asked with a raised eyebrow.

Olivia lowered her gaze, almost as if she was ashamed—or didn't want to be recognized. Bernard wondered what she was thinking, and he prayed that she didn't say anything.

"Sorry," she muttered.

Adele took a step toward Olivia. "Well, young lady, around

this office I am addressed as *Mrs. Wells* and my husband as *Mr. Wells*. Is that clear?"

Olivia muttered a low "Yes."

"I swear, Bernard. Sometimes I wonder how you've been so successful, because your judgment is so skewed in the people you hire." So much for their sensitive moment. She snatched up her purse in disgust and stormed out the room.

Olivia and Bernard stood in silence for a moment before she said, "I'm sorry. I should've knocked."

"No, I'm the one that's sorry." He couldn't help but breathe a sigh of relief. That could have been absolutely disastrous.

"Obviously, she doesn't know about me?"

Bernard shook his head. "Not yet."

"Would that be why you gave HR a different last name?"

He could see the hurt in Olivia's eyes. He had meant to talk to her about that, but it had slipped his mind. He made sure her info was correct on the W-2, but he'd given Elijah a different last name because he was one of the employees that was loyal to Adele.

"It is. I just need time to work all of this out," he felt compelled to add. "As you can see, my wife can be a bear. And I want to break this to her the right way." He wasn't really concerned with Adele's feelings anymore, but he knew the havoc she was capable of causing, so he had to tread lightly. "I need you to be patient with me, okay?" He felt a flutter in his heart. This was déjà vu.

"You have a lot of things you need to work out." He could

tell Olivia's patience was running thin. "Your wife, okay, that's your call. But I'm not going to keep lying to Kendall much longer."

She turned and walked out, without telling him why she'd come back in the office in the first place.

Olivia was right. He had to tell both his son and his wife. Both of them would be furious when they found out, but he had to tell them nonetheless. He couldn't risk everything blowing up and losing all of the progress he had made with his daughter.

# Chapter 26

Kendall grunted as he navigated the TV through the front door. He and Olivia had been a bit uncomfortable with each other this past week, after the incident in Bernard's office, but he'd shown up at her place this morning, sticking to their plans to go shopping for a television. She had asked him to go with her so that she didn't get gypped, but after what had happened, she didn't think he would still show up. But he merely muttered an apology about being "caught up in the moment," then acted like it never happened. Since he played it cool, she eventually relaxed as well. What bothered her most was that Bernard still hadn't said a word. After all this time, how was she supposed to tell Kendall now?

"Man, I'm tired," Kendall said, setting the huge television box down on the floor.

They'd been out shopping all day and had finally found a television in her price range a couple of hours ago.

"I don't believe I'm doing manual labor," Kendall huffed. "I must really like you because this makes no sense. We should've just had it delivered."

"And I told you at the store, what made no sense was paying a hundred dollars extra to have them deliver something we could carry ourselves."

*"We?"*

She smiled and held up a piece of paper. "I carried the receipt!"

That made him chuckle. "Whatever! Fix me something to eat, woman." He stretched out on the plush zebra rug that Mona had purchased.

"First of all, I'm not your woman." She playfully kicked his foot. "Secondly, I have no food."

That a woman might not cook must never have occurred to him. "What are you and Mona eating?"

"Takeout. Neither of us are ever even here."

"Not here? Well, I know you're working all the time. What is Mona doing?"

"She's going out on auditions and stuff. She even shot a commercial yesterday. But you know Mona is a social butterfly."

He sat up. "So she's dating already?"

Olivia squinted at him. "I'm sorry, why are you all up in her business again?"

He waved away Olivia's comment. "Please. It's not like that at all. I was just wondering."

She was relieved to hear that. As much as Mona joked about getting with Kendall, Olivia didn't want that at all. She was having too much fun getting to know her brother.

"Besides, Mona isn't my type."

"What is your type?"

He smiled mischievously. "Hmmm, why do you ask? You having second thoughts? You want to dump that old man you're seeing?"

She immediately lost her smile. "Umm, no. Not at all. And what in the world are you talking about, 'old man'?"

He gave her a long, studying look. "Nothing. You just strike me as the type to date older men."

"I told you I'm not seeing anyone—young or old."

His face twisted into a contorted mask. "Then can I ask you what it was that so disgusted you, you know, the other day in my dad's office?"

"It's not like that," she stressed. She got up and headed toward the kitchen, just to have something to do. This conversation was so out of order.

"What? You don't find me attractive?" he asked, following her.

The thought made her gag. She took a deep breath as she tried to figure out how best to nip this in the bud. "You're cute and charming, in a brotherly kind of way."

He turned up his nose, offended. "Brotherly? Well, that's the ultimate shutdown." He threw his arms up, like he ruled wherever he went. "Do you know how many women want me?"

"Yeah, I saw the first night at the club." Olivia had never seen so many women blatantly throw themselves at a man. While Kendall had flirted, he hadn't paid any real attention to any of them.

"So then you know. But you wanna give me the brotherly brush-off?"

*If only you knew,* she thought.

"Seriously, though, I didn't mean to make you uncomfortable. I just erroneously read something when there was obviously nothing there."

"It kind of caught me off guard," she said, not sure what else to say.

"Well, you made it clear that you're not feeling me that way," he said with a playful pout.

"No, I'm not," she said, not leaving any room for doubt.

He put his hand to his heart like he was hurt. "Dang, can you be any more hard on me?"

Luckily, Kendall didn't harp on it. As she was quickly discovering, he didn't take a lot to heart.

"But, seriously, about your girl, she's fine as all get out. But she's a little over the top for my taste. Definitely fun to hang out with, but not anyone I can see myself in a relationship with."

"She really likes you," Olivia teased, grateful that he'd reverted to his jovial, carefree self.

"She likes my pockets!"

Olivia winced, shocked that he read Mona so well.

"What?" he said when he noticed her reaction. "Don't act surprised. Your girl might as well have a sign on her forehead that says 'Looking for a Sugar Daddy.' But it's all good. She's cool people and I don't mind spending money on people I like hanging out with."

"Oh, you're definitely Mona's kind of man, then."

He laughed as Olivia began unpacking the television. "A little help, please?" She motioned toward the box.

"If you had a man, what would he do?"

"He'd help me get this TV out of the box."

"But since you don't have a man"—Kendall plopped down on the couch and folded his arms behind his head—"don't strain your back."

She picked a throw pillow up off the sofa and tossed it at him. He giggled as he ducked, but he did get up and help her get the TV set up.

"So, are you going to stay at England Enterprises?" Olivia asked once the TV was screwed together and positioned firmly on the entertainment console.

"That ain't my cup of tea. I'm just putting in my time to get the money for my start-up."

"So you're really gonna try to be a rapper-slash-musician?"

He lost his smile and turned serious. "Why, you don't think I can do it either?"

She frowned. "Whoa! Slow down. I never said that. As a matter of fact, I know you can."

That made the smile return.

"I've heard you, and you were just playing around. I can only imagine what you sound like in a studio. I don't even like rap and I love your sound."

He paused, as if stunned by her words. "That means the world to me, you just don't know. No one believes in me or supports my dream."

She found that hard to believe. "Well, no one did—until now."

Their bonding moment was interrupted when Mona came bouncing in. "Hey, hey, hey," she sang. "The superstar is in the building."

"Do you ever subtly walk in a room? You know, without the grand entrance?" Kendall asked, shaking his head.

"That's boring, and as you know"—she paused for dramatic effect, striking a pose—"there is nothing boring about me."

"You can say that again," he mumbled, his eyes roaming down her backside. He caught Olivia giving him the side eye and quickly said, "So what's on tap for tonight?"

Olivia brushed off his ogling of Mona. Most hot-blooded men couldn't keep their eyes off her perfect Playmate figure.

"Look at this place," Olivia said, pointing around the room. "You see all this stuff that needs to be put up? That's what's on tap for tonight. That and work."

"And all this stuff will be here tomorrow," Mona said drily. "Where are you taking us?" she asked Kendall.

"How about you take *me* out?"

"Oh, don't say it like it's not possible." She did a slow twirl toward Olivia. "Because yours truly just booked her first pilot."

"Get out!" Olivia reached out to hug her friend. "Already?"

"Already. Honey, these folks weren't ready for me."

Kendall flashed a genuine smile. "Dang, congrats, girl. I guess I am going to have to take you out."

Mona grinned. "Yes, you are. But only if Brad, Denzel, or Idris isn't available tonight."

Olivia had no intention of going anywhere. She'd have to celebrate this weekend. Right now she had too much on her plate trying to get ready for Fashion Week. "You guys are going to have to party without me tonight."

"I can't believe you're not coming with us," Mona said, her lips pouty.

"Seriously, I'm taking over the dance class for Adrienne tonight. She has a family emergency, so she needed my help. Then I need to finish up here and get ready for Fashion Week. The last thing I have time for is partying."

"Uggh, you and those bratty kids." Mona turned to Kendall. "She is serious about her dance, so we can hang up getting her to come." Mona leaned in closer, like she was telling a secret. "My dear friend acts like she's fifty years old. I keep telling her she really needs to learn to live, love, and enjoy life."

Kendall shook his head in mock pity. "I haven't known her anywhere near as long as you, but I can tell she's too uptight."

"Hello? Can you two not talk about me like I'm not here?" Olivia protested. "And you might as well give it up because you're not going to guilt me into going."

Both of them turned to her and smiled. "Well, it was worth a try," Mona said.

"Have fun." Olivia turned her attention to the television. She had noticed something was wrong before, and now she realized the TV wasn't exactly centered on the console.

Mona draped her arm through Kendall's. "Oh, well, I guess it's just you and me, handsome."

Olivia didn't miss the way he tensed up at her touch. "Don't forget, you have a meeting in the morning, Kendall," Olivia reminded him.

He relaxed and released a small laugh. "Yeah, okay. I'll be there bright and early, and I'll bring the doughnuts."

Olivia watched the two of them walk out. They did make a cute couple.

Olivia relaxed and told herself that Mona was doing what she always did, taking advantage of an opportunity to have a good time at someone else's expense.

Olivia fixed herself something to drink, then stared at the mound of work in front of her. She had to decide which to tackle first—the folders strewn across the kitchen table or the boxes and bags that needed to be put away. She decided on the folders, and as she slid into the chair, she couldn't help but think that she could learn a lesson or two from her friend about living, loving, and enjoying life.

# Chapter 27

Bernard couldn't do it. He'd promised Olivia that he would come clean. But every time he came close, he lost his nerve. Or something happened. Like this morning. Bernard had psyched himself up all night and had finally been prepared to tell Adele. But the moment she entered the kitchen, he lost his nerve.

"Knock, knock."

Bernard looked up from his office desk and almost passed out at the sight of Alyssa standing there. He looked around nervously to see if his secretary saw her.

"Don't worry, I waited until Nicole went to lunch." Alyssa sashayed into the office.

"What are you doing?" Bernard whispered. "Why are you here?"

Alyssa did a slow stroll around the room and landed in one of the large wingback chairs. "I saw you the other day."

"Saw me where?"

"At Starbucks. With your new woman. The woman you dumped me for." Alyssa was smiling like she'd busted him cheating.

"Alyssa, what are you talking about?"

"That new hire. The intern. Honestly, Bernard, I can't believe you would stoop to having an affair with an intern. What is she, twenty?"

Bernard was dumbfounded. "An affair? With what intern?"

"The cute one," Alyssa said, trying to hide her disdain. "What's her name? Olivia."

Bernard couldn't help it, he laughed out loud. First Kendall, now Alyssa. Why did both of them automatically assume the worst?

"I'm glad you find this amusing," she said, losing her smile.

Bernard came over and sat down next to her. "Alyssa, I assure you, I am not having an affair with Olivia—or anyone else, for that matter."

She looked like she was trying to decide if she believed him. "I saw the way you were looking at her."

That made him uneasy. Like Kendall, he didn't need her getting any ideas, especially now that he had broken off with her. He didn't see her spilling his news, but he didn't want to take any chances.

He was about to reassure her some more when his secretary's voice came over the intercom. "Mr. Wells, your two o'clock is here."

He sat up straight, at a proper distance from Alyssa, as if Nicole could see him. "Give me a minute." He dropped his voice, wanting to get the personal matter over with. "Alyssa, I'm being honest. I'm not having an affair with her." He sighed. "But you know, we talked about this. You can't come to my office. People might start talking."

She lowered her head like a chastised child. "I'm sorry. I just miss you so much and I don't understand."

He took her arm and helped her stand. "I know, but now's not the time. Pull yourself together and we'll talk later, okay?"

She dabbed her eyes and nodded as he walked her to the door. He gave her a once-over before opening his office door. Nicole looked up, and Bernard didn't miss the look of worry that flashed over her face when she saw Alyssa.

"Mr. Bertran is here for his presentation." Nicole nodded in the direction of the gray-clad textile supervisor. He was trying to convince Bernard to invest in a different type of cloth-sorting machine.

"Give me a few minutes, then send him in." Bernard didn't bother looking at Mr. Bertran as he turned to go back in his office. He needed to pull himself together.

Exactly how had he been looking at Olivia? If his behavior was enough to raise the eyebrows of those closest to him, it was just a matter of time before Adele caught on. That reaffirmed that he needed to tell her and tell her now. Then he remembered the charity event they had to attend in San Diego this weekend. That would be the perfect time. No, on the way back. The last thing he wanted was to have to ride an hour and a half both ways with her wrath at its fullest, so he would tell her when they were almost home.

Bernard used to be scared of losing all that he had, and a part of him still was. But that was not as important now. With Olivia back in his life, he was most afraid of losing her.

Olivia had a lot of fire inside, just like her mother. Bernard used to call Lorraine the quiet storm. She seldom got upset, but when she did, she was a force to be reckoned with. Now, as he sat behind his desk, his heart once again ached when he recalled the last time he'd seen Lorraine's wrath—the day she found out she was pregnant with his child.

"Lorraine, stop crying," Bernard said, handing her yet another Kleenex. Three years had passed since he'd found her working back at the same diner as before. Apparently, Texas hadn't been good to her and she'd returned to LA. He never expected to run into her again, but would often visit the diner just for old times' sake. Once he discovered she'd returned, he'd started going back regularly. At first Lorraine wouldn't even talk to him. Finally, she said she forgave him and even understood why he made the choice that he did.

When the diner closed its doors for good and Lorraine found herself without work, Bernard convinced her to come be a nanny for his newborn son. Initially, she balked at the idea, spewed curse words he didn't even know she knew. But after a few weeks of persuasion, she decided to take him up on his offer, with the promise that their relationship be strictly professional.

Bernard knew her being in the same house was a bad idea. But he was so unhappy, and he missed Lorraine so much. He could have very well just given her money, but he hoped that having Lorraine near him would help fill the void he felt inside. And they managed the new setup well, staying away from one another and keeping their relationship professional.

For three years, just being able to see her every morning, seeing her lively personality engaging with his son, was enough for Bernard. Until it got to the point that he couldn't take the torture anymore.

"Stop crying? My life is over," Lorraine sobbed, breaking him from his thoughts.

"No, it's not," he said, his hand going to her stomach. "I mean, it's not the best of situations."

"I'm pregnant and you're married. How much worse can it get? What am I gonna do?"

Lorraine had lost both of her parents when she was a teen. She couldn't go back to Houston. She'd stayed with her aunt Betty the last time she was there, but Betty and her husband were barely scraping by in a rented efficiency.

"I guess I could always go back home and find a job, find me some place to live."

Bernard's heart filled with panic at the idea of her leaving. "Have you . . ."

She looked at him in horror as she anticipated what he was about to say. "I'm not aborting our baby," she said with conviction.

"What? No, I wasn't going to say that. But we can make this work."

"Are you prepared to leave her?"

Bernard was silent. Everything inside him wanted to scream, *Yes. Let's run away and live happily ever after.* But he knew that if he left Adele, there would be no happily ever after. If he left, they would both be miserable.

"Exactly. You're not trying to leave," Lorraine said when he didn't answer.

"I love you."

"But you love your fancy life more. If you didn't, we wouldn't be having this discussion."

"Fine, then you want me to just march in there and tell Adele it's over? That I'm leaving her to be with you? How do you think that would go over?"

Lorraine didn't respond. She knew Adele would go to her grave making them both pay.

"How would we take care of this baby if I do that?" Bernard knew he was being selfish, but he needed some time. He needed to come up with a plan. "Just stay on. I'll work something out." He seized her hands urgently. "I'll go crazy if you leave again. I just need time to get a plan together, set aside enough money so that we can be together."

"So you're planning to steal from her?"

"Of course not. I'm not going to steal anything. I work hard, Lorraine, running that company. I just need some time, time to build up a nice nest egg."

"I don't want you stealing her money," she said sternly.

"I'm not a thief, Lorraine. You know that."

"I don't know what you'll do for money."

"You know that I'm not a thief," he insisted. "Every dime that I set aside will be something that I earned so that we can have our life together."

Lorraine got up and took a new seat at the other end of the park bench. They'd driven to the other side of town to have this private conversation. "I don't feel right about this."

"What other choice do you have? Do you know how much it costs to raise a baby? Do you want her living in poverty?" Lorraine flinched, and he knew she was thinking along the same lines he was. "Please, stay here, and our child will have the best of everything, and you can have the best for her future. Think about it, you make good money here. Where else can you go and make that kind of money? You're going to go be a waitress in Houston for minimum wage? Who's going to keep the baby while you work long hours?"

Fear gripped her as she weighed his words, and Bernard knew he was breaking her down.

"All I'm saying is, stay here. Let's work it all out. I promise, we'll go back to the old relationship, totally hands off."

"What am I supposed to tell Adele?" She pointed to her stomach. "It'll be a while before I'm showing, but eventually I will show."

Bernard ran his hand over his hair. He didn't want to create any unnecessary lies to Adele, but what other choice did he have? No way could Lorraine walk around with child and Adele not ask questions.

"We'll tell her the father is someone from your church."

"More lies," Lorraine said, shaking her head.

"I'm so sorry." He moved over beside her and squeezed her tightly. "About everything." He pulled back and stared in her eyes. "Everything." She wept as he continued, "I wish I could turn back the hands of time. I would do things so differently."

"I don't want to lie to her."

"It's just a little white lie. You just tell her it's someone from church and that he's gone in the army."

"See, this is what I'm talking about. We're just making a bed of lies." Lorraine inhaled deeply. "And how long am I supposed to do this?"

"Long enough for us to figure out our next move." He massaged her stomach. "I don't want you to leave. I don't want you to take my baby from me. You know that I love you. You know about my relationship with Adele, how it's in name only."

"Then why stay?" she pleaded.

"Lorraine, we've been through this so many times. You know how I grew up. I don't want you—I don't want us—to have to suffer. So just be patient. Please."

He took her in his arms. He'd promised her right before she moved in as Kendall's nanny that they would one day be together. She had been beyond patient as one year turned into two, and two into three. Bernard really was trying to come up with a plan to leave, but then, three days before Olivia's first birthday, Hampton England, Adele's father, died.

His will bequeathed everything to his only daughter and made it very clear that if Bernard ever left her, he would leave penniless. A board of directors kept a tight rein over the finances, so funneling money away had become almost impossible. He'd managed to set aside a little money, but nothing that could afford them the lifestyle that she deserved.

Bernard shook his head. He hated that memory of Lorraine because it reminded him that that was the start of the pain he caused her over the years. Bernard didn't know why he continued to hurt the people he loved. He liked to think he was kindhearted, but he had a way of hurting people he loved that he simply didn't understand.

"Mr. Wells, sending in Mr. Bertran now."

Bernard took a deep breath, then brushed aside all thoughts of anything except work. At least at work he could be in command.

# Chapter 28

Olivia gave Kendall a measuring gaze as he headed in her direction. She was trying to gauge if Bernard had come clean. But when Kendall walked over with that charming smile on his face and said, "What's poppin'?" she knew that once again Bernard hadn't said a word.

"Same story, different day," she said, trying not to show her frustration with Bernard. He was putting her in the awkward position of having to tell Kendall herself, and she hated that.

Kendall sat on the edge of her desk.

She patted a stack of paperwork. "Work. One of us takes our job seriously."

He picked a piece of paper up off her desk, scanned it, then let it airily float back down on its pile. "Man, you're really into this stuff."

"This *stuff* is your job, too."

"This stuff is my *punishment,*" he corrected her. "So, I'm doing good to even be here."

"Oh, I forgot you're just trying to get your seed money for your recording studio," she said with a hint of sarcasm.

"And if it all works out, I'm as good as gone. If that record executive from Sony gives me a shot, I'll quit so fast."

"You would just walk away from the family business?"

He pantomimed a dagger to his chest. "In a heartbeat. Man, being here every day is torture."

"You call this torture?" She laughed.

"Yes, especially working for that old, stuffy Ms. Barrows." He stood and began stiffly walking around Olivia's small office. "'Young Mr. Wells, I understand you are the boss's son, but we expect you to remain committed and have respect for your job,'" he said, mocking their supervisor, Angela Barrows.

Olivia laughed because he imitated Ms. Barrows perfectly. "Come on, she's really nice. And besides, she's just doing her job."

He plopped back down and looked around the small room. "I'm still trying to understand how you got your own office. I'm the boss's son, and all I got was a friggin' cubicle."

"Maybe because they know you're not serious," she chastised him. "And you know I'm only stationed here temporarily. When Kim Haynes gets back from maternity leave, I'll be right back out there with you."

"When Kim gets back, hopefully I'll be gone."

"Whatever."

He scooped up a handful of M&M's out of the bowl on her

desk and popped them into his mouth. "Where's Mona? Since you don't want me, I guess I'm gonna have to hook up with your friend." He flashed a wide grin, which told her he wasn't really serious. At least she hoped so.

"You don't want Mona, so don't be playing games with my friend."

He shrugged. "I know, I told you, Mona is just cool to hang out with. We had so much fun the other night."

"Well, if you're angling for tonight, forget it. I have to work tomorrow and Mona has another audition." Olivia was so proud of her friend. She had wasted no time and had already made more progress than most aspiring actresses who had been roaming Los Angeles for years.

"Five bucks says she'll still go out."

Olivia laughed. She wasn't about to take that bet because Mona never met a party she didn't like, especially if someone else was footing the bill. She'd be more than thrilled to go with Kendall to one of his VIP spots. "Yeah, I'll pass." Olivia closed the folder she was reviewing, since obviously Kendall wasn't going to let her work. "So, have you heard back from the record producer?"

"Yes, as a matter of fact, I have."

"What? Why didn't you tell me?"

"I'm telling you now."

She tossed her pencil at him and he ducked just before it hit him. "You should've led the conversation with that."

"Yeah." Kendall flashed a big smile. "I'm going to meet with some of the executives on Monday. But get this. Not only were they impressed with the rap I did, they were loving some of the stuff I wrote. So don't be surprised if your boy ends up pennin' some tracks for Diddy."

"Wow, I am so happy for you."

"Thank you." He stood up, pleased that she was rooting for him. "I would hug you, but I don't want you to think I'm trying to do anything freaky." He stroked his chin. "I'm too handsome to go after women that don't want me."

She decided to ignore whatever that was supposed to mean. "I'm gonna get back to work because New York Fashion Week is coming up and I want to look at some new designers to suggest."

"I think you may have found your calling."

"Nah, I already found my calling." Dance would always be her passion. But since that didn't look like a dream she'd ever realize, she needed to cultivate her second love—fashion.

Kendall knew what she meant. "Let me see you bust a move," he said, pulling her by her arm up from the desk.

She promptly sat back down. "First of all, the kind of dance I do is *not* 'busting a move.' I do classical ballet."

He groaned in disgust. "Ewww."

She could not believe how narrow-minded he was. "You're a musician, yet you have no appreciation for the arts." She wagged a finger at him. "But before too much longer, I'm going to take you to the ballet."

"You must mean you are gonna take my body, because I'd have to be dead. That's the only way I'd go to the ballet."

She chuckled because on that she knew he was serious. "So, how much longer are you gonna work here?"

"The whole agreement with Dad was six months, so I gotta serve my time, unless, of course, the deal comes through with these execs."

Olivia nodded, then asked a question she'd been wanting answered—a topic she seldom broached with Kendall. "Are things any better with your mom?"

He shrugged, losing his smile. "I stopped trying to repair that relationship a long time ago. I mean, I love my mom and all, but she's got some serious issues."

Kendall turned into a totally different person when he talked about his mother. The jovial, comedic young man was replaced with a lost little boy, longing for his mother's love. It made Olivia feel sorry for him.

"I used to wonder why my dad put up with all that he did from my mom," Kendall continued, like he'd been wanting to open up about it. "But when I was fifteen, I found out that my grandfather put a clause in his will when he passed that if my dad ever leaves my mother, he loses everything—the company, the stock, the money."

"Wow, that's deep."

"What's so jacked up is my mom knows that and it gives her carte blanche to treat him any way she wants to and my dad just has to take it." Olivia could see the anger building in his eyes. "Sometimes it drives me crazy to see the way she treats him and he just lets it happen. I think he's keeping his eye on the bigger picture, probably stashing some money to the side. But for me, putting up with her is not worth any amount of money. Besides, when I settle down, it's going to be for love."

Olivia thought back over her life, over her struggles. Saying you could go without money was a lot easier when you'd always been swimming in it. "Money can make a world of difference."

"Money ain't everything."

"Spoken like someone who has it."

"No, seriously. You remember my homeboy Mark from the club?"

Olivia had to search her memory, but she remembered that they had met Mark the first time Kendall took them out. "Yeah, the one that looks like a muscular Will Smith. What about him?"

"Mark reminds me of my dad. Mark is messing with two chicks. One of them is a big-time Hollywood executive. She's rolling in the dough and everything. The other is a beautician from Compton. Now, all my other boys tell Mark that he needs to be with the executive. He rolls around town in her Range Rover, goes on exotic vacations on her time. She takes care of him, she treats him right. But when he's with Tasha—that's the beautician—there's this whole other side of him." Kendall started smiling. "He's happy all the time, smiling for no reason, singing corny songs. He has this inner joy. That's what I want. I want that inner joy."

As if that was the capstone to their conversation, he started to stroll away. He walked lightly, like talking about it was lifting his spirits.

*I wouldn't know anything about inner joy,* Olivia thought. She'd never seen her mother display any. She'd never experienced it for herself, even with Stephon. He had made her happy, but he'd never made her experience joy.

But now that she considered the idea, she was starting to feel something inside, and that was a direct result of the relationship she was developing with her brother.

Olivia's thoughts were interrupted when she saw Alyssa, the woman from PR, staring at her, almost as if she were trying to see through her.

"Hi," Alyssa finally said, approaching her.

"Hi."

"You know, when Shawn was talking about you and Kendall the other day, I thought she was running off at the mouth, but I think she may be onto something."

Olivia managed a laugh. "Trust me, there is nothing going on with us."

Alyssa crossed her arms. "Well, if there isn't, there should be, because you guys definitely have some chemistry." Alyssa continued smiling, but now it seemed forced. "Or maybe there's someone else you have your eye on?"

Olivia shook her head. "No, I'm focused on work. I'm not thinking about a man right now."

"No one around here has caught your eye? A pretty young thing like you?"

"No!" Okay, this woman was getting out of line.

"Dang, calm down." Alyssa smiled once again. "I was just saying I was surprised no one had snatched you up, especially since I think you should give Kendall a chance. You can tell he likes you."

"I'm here to work," Olivia forcefully reiterated.

Alyssa held up her arms. "I wasn't trying to be pushy." She glanced at her watch. "Let me get out of here. Enjoy the rest of your evening."

Olivia frowned as Alyssa walked off. Once again, she got an eerie feeling about Alyssa. She asked too many questions and seemed too concerned about Olivia's love life.

Olivia finally brushed off the thought. She had enough to worry about. She didn't need to add some weird-acting woman to her plate.

# Chapter 29

As Bernard reached the revolving door of his office building, he was stopped by a scraggly-haired man in dirty clothes. He was shocked when he recognized who it was.

"Jerry?" Bernard squinted to see if that was indeed his former employee. Jerry's eyes were puffy, like he'd been crying for days. He never was the most well-kept person, but Bernard had never seen him this bad. "Are you okay?"

"No. No, I'm not." Jerry frantically ran his fingers over his matted hair, then brushed down his dirty shirt as if trying to make himself presentable. "Mr. Wells, please. Please, I need my job back."

"Jerry, I am so sorry, I wish that I could help. But we told you that if you didn't show up, you were at risk of losing your job."

"But you know why I was missing work. My baby girl is very sick. And she's getting sicker. Can you understand how helpless I feel as a father?"

Bernard could easily understand. He understood it, but he just couldn't do a whole lot about it.

"Did the money help you any?"

"It did and bless you for it. That's how we've made it this far. But it's the insurance. Without it we can't continue the treatment for my daughter. I told your wife that and she said I should've thought about that when I wasn't showing up for work." Jerry fumbled as he pulled a picture out of his pocket. It was a five-by-seven photo of an adorable little girl about eight years old. Her long ponytails rested on her shoulders and she wore a huge grin, with one of her front teeth missing. "This is my baby. This is Terralyn." Jerry thrust the photo at Bernard.

"She's beautiful." Bernard handed the picture back. "But there's nothing I can do."

Jerry clasped his hands like he was praying and fell to his knees. "Mr. Wells, you know I was a good employee. And I only started messing up when my baby got sick. After losing my wife last year, Terralyn is all I have."

Bernard's heart went out to Jerry because of the desperation in his voice. "I understand that and I wish that there was something that I could do."

"What about money? Can you give me some more money?" Jerry pulled himself up off the ground.

Bernard knew that Adele would have a fit if she ever found

out he had given money to former employees, let alone was *still* giving them money. "I'm sorry, I can't. Have you tried any assistance programs?"

"I've tried everything!" Jerry screamed. He took a deep breath to compose himself.

"Look," Bernard said, taking $400 out of his wallet, "this is all I have. I gave you some severance money already when I really shouldn't have."

"And I used it for my rent and my baby's treatment."

As he handed Jerry the money, Bernard shook his head to reiterate that he could do nothing. Bernard had to agree with his wife. For the last year, Jerry had been a liability. While Bernard would've handled the firing differently, Jerry did need to go. "This is all I can do."

Jerry slowly took the money, defeat registering on his face.

"I'll be praying for you. But that's all I can do. Excuse me." Bernard stepped around Jerry and walked inside his building.

Bernard hated to be cold and his heart truly ached for Jerry, but he didn't want to start the bad habit of Jerry's coming to him whenever he needed money. That would be a never-ending cycle. All of this could have been cured, he thought miserably, if he had stood up to Adele at the time she had fired Jerry. Bernard stood by the elevator, sunk in gloom as he waited for it to arrive. Everything in his life, it seemed, was ruled by his wife's control of the company. He couldn't tell her about his daughter. He couldn't tell Kendall he had a sister.

He couldn't forget the day he had cast the love of his life out into the street because he was the same coward he had shown himself to be today.

Bernard eased his Rolls into the four-car garage, his mind still churning. Thoughts of Jerry had been gnawing at him all day. He didn't think Jerry would do anything crazy, but Bernard was still worried. He knew a person who was desperate could go crazy all of a sudden. If that happened, he would not be able to help feeling that he was to blame.

He tried to push all of those thoughts aside as he got out of his car. He felt so guilty about Jerry, and he'd be worked up all evening if he allowed himself to keep trying to figure out the what-ifs. Besides, he had the huge charity event tomorrow, so he had to get his mind ready for the conversation he planned to have with Adele on the drive home. That's when he was going to come clean about Olivia.

Bernard was greeted by silence when he entered the house. He glanced out back at the maid's quarters. Vianessa's car was not there. Even the gardener who usually worked late on Thursdays was nowhere to be seen.

"Hello?" he called out. He debated going to Adele's room and asking where everyone was. Ultimately, he decided against it and headed to his bedroom.

When Bernard opened the door, he stopped in his tracks. Lying across his bed, surrounded by rose petals, was his wife.

"What are you doing?" he asked, astonished by the incongruous sight.

She smiled. A genuine smile that he hadn't seen in a long time. "What does it look like?"

His eyes made his way down her body, taking in the candy-apple-red lace negligee, thigh-high stockings, and high-heeled, strappy shoes. He didn't know his wife owned anything like that, let alone wore it.

Her expression was a mixture of seduction and apprehension, as if she wasn't sure she was doing the right thing. "Happy anniversary."

Bernard grimaced and she lost her smile. That's what had been gnawing at him.

"You forgot, huh?" She sat up and scooted to the edge of the bed. "I knew you would." She looked dejected as she grabbed her sheer robe from the edge of the bed.

"I've just had a lot going on."

She stood and draped her arm through the robe. "You always do."

"Umm, what's this?" He pointed at her outfit.

"Just trying something different." She shrugged slightly. "I know things haven't been great for us for a long time, and, well, I just decided to try something different."

"Wow. You look nice." Bernard hadn't seen that much of her body in years. When they did make love, it was in the dark, under the covers. He was amazed at her spectacular body. Her stomach was flat, her legs toned, her breasts more plump than he remembered. He was surprised to feel himself begin to rise.

"Those expensive Pilates classes do pay off," she tried to joke when she caught him taking in her figure.

A part of Bernard wanted to reach out and touch her. He felt an excitement he hadn't felt in almost two decades.

"I'm sorry, this is all catching me by surprise," he finally admitted.

"Believe it or not, I have needs, too," she responded, her voice soft and gentle.

Bernard had never thought much about her needs. And if he was being honest, he didn't know what she needed. Sex? Love? All of the above?

He reached out to touch her, letting lust take over. She closed her eyes and released a small moan as his fingertips touched her chest. The noise made him draw back. There was no doubt what she needed. She needed love, something he'd been incapable of giving her since the day they met. Giving in to lust right now, when she was this vulnerable, couldn't be good.

She must have seen the uneasiness in his eyes and she smiled. "If it doesn't fit, don't force it."

Adele tightened the belt on her robe and headed toward the bedroom door. "I gave Vianessa the night off, but I'll have her come in tomorrow and clean up this mess."

Bernard couldn't be sure, but he thought he saw Adele's eyes glistening, as if she was on the verge of tears. He felt his BlackBerry vibrate on his hip. Instantly his mind shifted to a more comfortable place: the needs of the job.

"Hold on a minute, don't go. We need to talk, but I need to take this. It's my secretary and this might be about the missing shipment."

She nodded but didn't move.

"Hello."

"Mr. Wells," Nicole said, "sorry to disturb you at home, but just thought you might want to know Jerry Cooper's daughter died today. You know she had been sick, and, well . . ." Bernard knew what she wanted to say. *You guys fired him and that just made things worse.* But she finished with "I just thought you should know."

"I'm sorry to hear that. Thank you for telling me."

"What's wrong?" Adele said once he hung up.

"It's Jerry, you know, the one you . . . the one we had to let go? His daughter died today."

"That's awful. What happened?"

"She had been sick." Bernard couldn't help it, he had to add, "That's why he missed so many days. I know you think he was making excuses, but I told you his daughter had leukemia. It's really why I didn't want to fire him."

Adele paused, not showing any emotion. "I'll make sure the company sends the family some flowers." She frowned at Bernard one last time, then added, "Your gift is under the pillow. Happy thirtieth anniversary," before turning and walking out the room.

# Chapter 30

It had been a long, yet productive day and Olivia was looking forward to getting home and putting some finishing touches on her condo. She still couldn't believe that she had a home that she owned. It was hers. No one could evict her. No one could make her leave. It was hers and she had the signed paperwork to prove it. She smiled as she imagined how happy her mother must be right now.

Olivia looked upward. "Mama, I don't understand a lot of things about this whole situation, but I think this is what you meant when you said this is the life I was meant for," she whispered. She threw her purse over her shoulder and headed downstairs, where she was going to meet Kendall, who was going to give her a ride home. She emerged from the building and looked up and down the block. Bernard had offered to buy her a new car, but after he literally gave her a house, she couldn't accept a car, too. She wanted to at least be able to make a down payment herself. Besides, he'd given her the Benz to use at her disposal.

Mona had, of course, called her crazy, but since they still had drivers at their disposal—and could use Bernard's Benz whenever they needed transportation—she'd let it drop.

"So, you really just up and say, 'Screw my past, I'm starting this new life'?"

Hearing the voice from behind her, Olivia turned around and was stunned to see Stephon standing there, looking angry and relieved at the same time.

"Stephon, what are you doing in LA?"

"Just going crazy worrying about you." He looked different. Stubble had sprouted around his chin and he looked like he hadn't slept in weeks.

Her first instinct was to throw her arms around his neck, but then she remembered his pregnant girlfriend. "Sorry you wasted a trip," she said icily. "A call would've sufficed."

"Not when I don't have your number and Mona isn't answering her cell." Mona had told her that Stephon had called so much, she'd put a block on the phone and deleted his numerous messages without listening to them. "I can't believe I had to track you down to make sure you're okay."

Her frostiness hadn't melted. "I'm okay, so now you can go." She stepped away from him and looked down the street, willing Kendall to hurry up and silently cursing herself for not calling for the car service. She didn't want to be so cold to

Stephon, but seeing him had brought back to the surface the pain of knowing he'd fathered a child with someone.

Stephon got in her face. "No, you're going to hear me out. I love you and I can't let you walk out of my life like this. I didn't travel halfway across the country for you to blow me off. We've been together since the tenth grade. You owe me more than that."

Olivia didn't understand where this was all coming from. "Kendall, we broke up a long time ago."

"Yeah, but we both knew we'd always get back together."

"Well, that obviously isn't going to happen," she huffed. The nerve of him to think she would forget about everything. "How did you even find out where I was?"

He grabbed her arm. "I'm always going to find you." He loosened his grip when he realized he was scaring her. "I'm sorry. I just want us to go somewhere and talk."

"I don't want to talk to you. Go back to your pregnant girlfriend." She pushed him aside and started walking off, anything to get away from him.

He came right after her. "I told you, she's not my girlfriend." He grabbed her again and pulled her back. His grip wasn't as hard this time, but she wanted him to leave her alone nonetheless. "Please, Olivia. Just hear me out."

They both stopped as a fire-red Porsche sped up onto the curb.

"I'm going to need you to get your arm off her," Kendall said, barely giving the car time to stop as he jumped out the driver's side of the car.

Stephon looked back and forth between the two of them. "What's it to you?"

Kendall took a step toward him. His chest was heaving, his nostrils flaring, his anger evident. "I'm not going to repeat myself. Let her go."

Stephon dropped his hand, then stared at Olivia.

"Are you all right?" Kendall asked.

"Olivia, what's going on? You know this guy?"

Kendall eased Olivia behind him. "Yeah, she knows me, and you're gonna know me, too, if you put your hands on her again."

"Kendall, I got this. It wasn't like that at all." Olivia knew Stephon might be unfaithful, but he wasn't violent. Plus, the last thing she wanted was a confrontation in front of England Enterprises.

"No," Kendall said forcefully without breaking his glare.

She was touched by the gesture and briefly imagined if that was what it would've been like growing up with an overprotective brother.

Stephon noticed the expression on her face. "Really, Olivia? Is this your man now?"

"Stephon, just go."

"You are so foul!" he spat.

No, he didn't have the audacity to be upset. But Olivia wasn't worried anymore. Kendall was bigger and had about thirty pounds on Stephon. And while her ex was acting aggressive right now, he definitely wasn't a fighter.

"I can't believe you. You want to act all self-righteous with me and you're kickin' it with this dude."

She wanted to tell him that she wasn't "kickin' it," that this was her brother. But she didn't say anything. Let him think what he wanted. Payback served him right.

He glanced over at Kendall's Porsche. "So you come out here and snag you some rich dude and just kick me to the curb?"

"Good-bye, Stephon."

"You are not going to dismiss me." Stephon stepped closer to her. "I love you and you owe me more than that."

Kendall bucked up, once again blocking Stephon. "Dude, you must think I'm playing with you."

"I'm not scared of you, rich boy."

"If you were smart, you would be."

The whole scene was outrageous. She'd never seen Kendall so angry, and she couldn't believe that Stephon had the nerve to act so hurt.

Stephon huffed, then looked around at Olivia. "Please, baby, can we just go somewhere and talk? Just the two of us."

"I don't have anything to say to you," she said flatly. "We are done. When you got someone else pregnant, you made sure of that."

"You were the one that broke up with me," Stephon yelled. "We weren't even together, so how are you gonna hold that against me?"

He was getting loud and the passersby were starting to stare, so she lowered her voice. "Okay. We weren't together."

"So, does this mean you don't love me anymore?" he asked, ignoring Kendall.

"I will always love you, Stephon. But I've moved on to a different part of my life now."

Stephon turned up his lips and stared at Kendall. "I guess you have."

Just then two of the security guards appeared. "Mr. England, is there a problem out here?"

Kendall cocked his head at Stephon. "Is there?"

"Naw, I'm leaving," he said, finally admitting defeat. Yet he added one last barb for Olivia. "When your rich boyfriend gets tired of playing in the gutter, don't come running back to me."

She couldn't believe his nerve. "Don't worry. And enjoy your baby mama."

Kendall didn't give Stephon time to reply as he took her hand and led her to his car.

Inside, she fell back in the seat, finally releasing a stream of tears. She never in a million years thought that she and Stephon would end this way. But the scenario that had just unfolded let her know that her chapter with Stephon was officially closed.

More than that was over, she realized. Stephon was her past, and it held no comfort for her now. She'd gained more than a new brother and a father. She'd shown that, given a chance at last, she could make something of herself. No man could ever make her feel the way she did right now. Her mother's dying words had not been in vain. She thought, *I'm going to make Mama proud of me.*

# Chapter 31

Bernard was shocked when he saw Alyssa once again standing in the doorway to his office. "Alyssa, I thought I told you—"

She held up her hand to cut him off. "Don't worry, I know what you told me. I just came to say good-bye."

That made him bolt upright. He motioned for her to come in, which she did, closing the door behind her. "What do you mean, good-bye?"

She looked like she'd been crying. Her eyes were puffy and red. "I got another job."

"What? Where?"

"Tommy Hilfiger."

"Excuse me? You're going to work for the competition?"

Alyssa just stared at him, her eyes watering. "I tell you I'm leaving and all you're worried about is me going to work for the competition?"

He caught himself. "No, it's not like that."

"Whatever, Bernard. I got your message loud and clear. I wasted two years of my life. But you live and learn. I just know that I can't continue working here, knowing you're in the same building, pretending that I don't care. That's your MO, not mine."

"Alyssa, I'm sorry."

"Yeah, you told me that many times. And you know what, Bernard? You are sorry. You want to run these games like you're not seeing someone else, but I know differently."

He rolled his eyes in frustration. He needed to tell her the truth. "Alyssa, have a seat." He sat down next to her. "I told you, there is nobody else."

"And I believed you, until I saw you with Olivia. The way you were looking at her, you can't tell me you don't have feelings for her. Then I saw her driving your Benz, the same Benz I used to drive."

He gave a pained laugh. "It's not like that at all."

"What is it like then, Bernard?"

He took a deep breath. He hoped that he didn't regret these words, but he owed her an explanation. "Alyssa, Olivia is my daughter."

"What?" She leaned back in her seat in shock.

"Nobody knows. Not Adele, not Kendall. Just Olivia and I. I'm trying to figure out the right way to tell everyone."

"I didn't know you had a daughter."

He released a heavy sigh. "It's a very long story. But like I said, no one knows."

"Then why are you telling me?" she asked slowly.

"Because I don't want to hurt you any more than I have. I don't want you to think there's anyone else. There's not. It's just that right now, that's where my focus is."

Alyssa smiled, understanding at last. "So there's nobody else? I mean, except your wife?"

"No, I told you that."

She wiped the stray tears off her face, then reached over and hugged him. She quickly caught herself and pulled back. "I'm sorry."

"It's okay." He prayed that none of his nosy staffers were looking through the window.

"So, are you still going to leave?"

She hesitated, but then nodded. "Yeah, I have to." She stood up and gave him a warm smile. "But at least now I can go with no hate on my heart." She kissed him on his cheek. "If your situation ever changes, call me." And with that, she walked out the door.

# Chapter 32

Olivia and Kendall sat in the quiet of the sushi restaurant. She hadn't wanted to go home, just in case Stephon followed her. Granted, he'd never be able to get through the security guard, but nonetheless she didn't want him to know where she lived.

Kendall had understood and taken her to get something to eat. But he'd also told her that a driver would be picking her up from underground parking until further notice—whether she liked it or not. She hadn't argued with him.

"Thank you," she said, sipping her sake.

"For what?"

"For coming to my aid."

"It was my pleasure." He took a bite of his dragon roll. "I know I don't seem like the fighting type, but I will knock a fool out when they mess with people I care about."

She smiled at his rich-boy bravado. "So you care about me?"

He looked playfully offended. "Not in that way. Don't try to come on to me. I just see you in, like, a sisterly way."

"Ha-ha."

They laughed and talked some more until the conversation shifted. He turned serious. "I told my mom about you."

She froze. "Told her what?"

"Not like that," he said, narrowing his eyes at her. "We were just having one of those rare conversations where we weren't fighting. She asked about work and I told her the girl that I started with was making it bearable."

Olivia's whole body went tense. Between her aunt Betty, Bernard's inexplicable fear, and the brief encounter Olivia had had, she knew Adele Wells was no one to fool with.

Kendall didn't notice Olivia's reaction as he continued, "She was more happy to hear that I hadn't quit yet than anything else. So that's all she kept talking about."

Olivia's shoulders sank with relief.

Kendall half smiled. "It was actually cool to have a halfway decent conversation with her for a change."

Olivia shook her head. "I still have a hard time believing you guys don't have a good relationship. I would've imagined growing up that life was a dream for you."

He turned up his nose in horror. "Are you freakin' kidding me? Why would you think that?"

Olivia shrugged. "I mean, I know you have your issues with your mom, but you got the best of everything. You never had to want for anything."

"You keep saying that and I keep trying to tell you, more money, more problems."

He could say that all he wanted, but Olivia would never buy it. "I'm someone who grew up struggling, and it ain't no joke. I had to give up college because we couldn't afford it. There were many days when my mom didn't eat just so I could have the last of the beans. Can you imagine ending each day with a prayer that a stray bullet didn't come into your apartment?" Olivia got misty-eyed at the memory of her next-door neighbor whose three-year-old son had been shot and killed when two rival gangs started fighting in the hallway. "Yeah, you don't know problems until you know where I came from."

She half expected him to look at her in a condescending manner. But he didn't. He just nodded sympathetically. "Yeah, I imagine that must've been hard, but life for me hasn't been a walk in the park either. No, I didn't have to want for any material things. But I *wanted* for a loving home. I *wanted* someone who gave a damn about me."

It was her turn to be shocked. She knew he didn't get along with his mother, but could he really think his parents didn't care about him? "I'm sure your parents love you."

"My dad, I know he does. But my mom, I don't know what her problem is. She's just so bitter and mean. And she takes it out on me and I don't get it. When I was a little boy, I used to do all kinds of things to get her to notice me, pay me some attention. But she pawned me off on every nanny that she could."

Olivia suddenly realized that was an opening. She should try to see what he remembered about her mother. Maybe he could shed some insight on why her mother would have an affair with a married man. "How many nannies did you have?" she asked casually.

"Well, the first one I can really remember, I had her for a while." He stopped and smiled at what had to be pleasant thoughts. "The memories have faded over the years, but I remember loving that woman so much. I remember how much she loved me. I used to wish that I was her son. And when she left, a piece of me died, I think. They say kids are resilient, but I don't think I ever bounced back. No joke. I went through a slew of nannies after that, none of them lasted any more than six months. I was a little tyrant." He chuckled.

"What do you remember about her?" Olivia had to struggle so her voice didn't crack.

He was pensive, as though those early memories were all a jumble. "I don't know. I just remember she used to shower me with kisses like I was her own son. She had a little girl, and I remember we used to play together." He was entranced with this memory, and his tongue touched his lower lip. "Don't tell anyone, but I have a picture somewhere. I don't even remember her name, but I remember she used to love to play with me. I let her dress me up, put makeup on me, a wig, lipstick, the whole nine to take that picture. She was like my baby sister and I adored her." He laughed and a deep pang set into Olivia's heart.

"Whatever happened to them?" Olivia managed to say.

"I don't know. One day they just left. And we never heard from them again. For the longest, I begged my mom to tell me what happened, but all she would say is 'She's a snake and I don't let snakes stay in my house.'"

The derogatory words made Olivia wince.

"I remember thinking my mom had to be talking about someone else. I know I was just a kid, but the woman I knew was dang near a saint."

*Me, too,* Olivia wanted to say.

"I tried talking to my mom about it, but over the years, I learned that was one subject you simply didn't touch in my house." He sighed wistfully. "I often wonder about Nana—that's what I called her—and her daughter." He frowned, trying to recall something. "I don't even remember that little girl's name. I just know I used to call her Pinky because she loved wearing pink. Everything she owned was pink."

Olivia was mesmerized by the conversation. She didn't remember any of that. All she remembered was wearing whatever secondhand clothes her mother could scrounge up.

He looked down sadly. "I wonder whatever happened to them. What they're doing now, why they had to leave."

The look on his face told Olivia that he sincerely missed them. She wanted so desperately to tell him the truth, to open up about everything right then and there, but the words wouldn't come. How could she explain to him that she'd been around him for almost three months and hadn't revealed her true identity? Now, she understood why Bernard was having such a hard time coming clean.

Kendall shook away his nostalgic thoughts. "Look at me, putting a damper on the evening, getting all sad and stuff." He summoned the waiter for the check. "So, ol' dude was your ex or something?" he asked, once the waiter walked off.

Olivia nodded. "Since the tenth grade, like he said. We broke up when he went to college, but I think we both thought we'd get back together. But that was before he got someone else pregnant."

"Dang, that's foul."

"Not really. Because we weren't together at the time. What was foul was that he tried to convince me to come to New York with him, and I'm wondering how he planned to work that out with a pregnant girlfriend."

Kendall wasn't cutting Stephon any slack. "I'm sorry, the way he was manhandling you, you're better off without him."

"Stephon wouldn't hurt a fly. But I was trying to tell him I can't go back to him. I can't do any drama."

"Well, you don't need to go back. Any man that puts his hands on you doesn't deserve a second chance." Just talking about Stephon was getting Kendall riled up again. He caught himself. "Sorry, I don't mean to get worked up, but that boils my blood." He finally smiled. "I had a female friend one time who got beat up by her boyfriend. At least she got some serious revenge on him. She had the neighborhood drug dealer, who just so happened to be her cousin, pay him a visit. Needless to say, the drug dealer beat that dude up so bad." Kendall shook his head, recalling the memory. "I don't believe in revenge, but I had to give her props on that one. As far as I know, he never touched another woman again."

While she was amused by the story, Olivia was more intrigued by his last statement. "What do you mean, you don't believe in revenge?"

He frowned as if he didn't understand her question. "Just what I said. Revenge is a wasted energy. Life is too short to be worrying about getting this person back, or making that person pay. You know, I'm not a religious person or anything, but I believe in that stuff about 'Vengeance is mine, said the Lord.'"

"Wow, so you, like, know some Bible stuff?" she kidded.

He laughed. "What, you think I'm an atheist or something?"

"Nah, you just didn't strike me as the churchgoing type."

"I'm not. My family doesn't do the whole church thing, unless it serves their purpose. But just because my parents don't take me to find God doesn't mean He doesn't find me."

He ate the last of his tuna roll, then continued, "Speaking of family, what about you? You never talk about your family. Where's your mom, your dad?"

That made her lose her smile. This was why she tried to stay clear of anything other than general conversations. In all of their talks, she'd never gone into details about her mother because she was worried that would lead to questions about her father. And she didn't want to keep the lies building up. It was bad enough that she'd lied to Kendall about why they'd come to Los Angeles in the first place. She'd told him it was to help Mona break into acting.

"My mom died," Olivia said solemnly. "And my dad, well, I'd just rather not talk about him."

Kendall nodded in understanding.

They made more small talk, and by the end of the conversation she was more sure than ever that they had a serious connection. She felt awful being trapped in a lie. He really should know.

"All right, let's get out of here," he said. "That jerk should be long gone."

Olivia followed Kendall out to his car. They got in and headed back to her place.

Kendall popped in a CD. "Check out this new joint I wrote," he said, a huge grin on his face. "This is the one I gave to the Sony execs."

She listened intently as music filled the car and Kendall began rapping a tune that could very well be playing on the radio.

They had just taken the exit off the 405 and were turning onto the street in front of her condo when Olivia glanced out the window. Her mouth dropped as she looked on in horror and screamed, *"Kendall!"* as an oncoming SUV slammed into the driver's side of the car.

# Chapter 33

Olivia tried to focus. Her vision was blurred and she had no idea where she was. She just knew it was cold, freezing cold. She was about to sit up when a sharp pain flared in her temple. That's when she noticed the tubes connected to her body, the ticking machine, the hospital room.

"Nurse!" she said, fumbling for the call button.

"Yes?" the nurse said, racing into the room.

"Where am I?"

The nurse began checking Olivia's vitals. "You were in a bad car accident. You've been out of it for a few hours, but it looks like you're going to be okay."

"I don't feel like it," she said, rubbing her throbbing head.

"Like I said, it was pretty bad. What you're feeling is a concussion. But we have you all taken care of. You probably won't spend more than a day or two here." The nurse continued to busy herself. "But the doctor will be in to confirm all of that for you."

Olivia's hands immediately went to her legs. If her legs were damaged and she could no longer dance, she didn't know what she'd do. She breathed a sigh of relief as she stretched her toes and felt movement in both of her legs.

She suddenly remembered what had happened. "Oh, my God, Kendall. Where's Kendall?" she said frantically.

"Is that the young man in the car with you?"

She nodded, her heart racing. "Is . . . is he dead?"

"No, he's alive. He's just in pretty bad shape. He lost a lot of blood."

Olivia threw back the covers, trying to get out of bed. "I need to see him."

The nurse rushed to restrain her. "You need to rest."

Olivia was about to protest when a white-haired doctor walked into her room. "Hey, little lady. Are you causing problems in here?" he said, smiling.

Olivia was in no mood for pleasantries. "I need to go see about my brother." She tried to get up again. This time the doctor came forward to stop her. "Is that the young man in 127?" he asked the nurse, who nodded.

The doctor turned to Olivia. "Your brother is in surgery."

"Is he okay?"

"He is in critical condition, but hopefully, he'll pull through. He does need a blood transfusion because he lost a lot of blood." The doctor looked down at his clipboard. "Unfortunately, he's O-negative and we are extremely short on

O-negative blood donations, so we're waiting to hear back from the blood bank."

Her heart fluttered. "I'm O-negative. Can I donate?"

The doctor exchanged glances with the nurse, then checked his chart again. "Well, I don't see why not. Everything checked out on her, right?"

The nurse nodded. He handed her his clipboard and turned back to Olivia. "That's great. We'll run some tests, get you set up, and hopefully all of this will work out."

Olivia fell back on her bed. There was no hopefully in this case. It had to work out. She couldn't lose her brother, not after she'd just found him.

It was amazing, she reflected, that she was ready to not only give blood. She was willing to give him a kidney if it meant saving his life. She didn't understand the strong connection. She'd always desired a family. Now she felt that she *needed* a family. Her mother had always been enough—until Olivia knew she had more family members out there.

"You ready?" the nurse asked, walking back into the room.

"I am."

"It's a blessing you came in with him because with all the blood he lost, he really didn't have time to wait on a transfusion."

As the nurse chatted away, Olivia suddenly realized that Bernard had no idea what had happened. "I need to call our father."

"Oh, I think he's been notified." The nurse tied a rubber hose around Olivia's arm. "That's one of the hard parts about our job, calling family members. He said something about their being a few hours away, but they are on their way back right now."

Her heart sped up as the nurse went back to drawing her blood. The word hung in the air: *they.* Bernard and Adele. Together. If *they* were coming, that meant trouble wasn't far behind.

# Chapter 34

Bernard swung the car into the hospital parking lot, nearly running over a stop sign.

"Would you slow down?" Adele snapped, just as nervous as he was. She hadn't stopped fidgeting since they heard the news.

Bernard had gotten the call just as she was about to go onstage. She'd given him the side eye when he'd answered his phone, but his secretary had called four times back-to-back and Bernard knew it had to be some emergency.

And was it ever!

His heart had plummeted when Nicole told him the hospital was trying to get in touch with him because Kendall and Olivia had been in a horrible car accident.

"How can you be so calm?" Bernard asked, although he knew that the three glasses of wine she'd had at the event were probably helping. "Didn't you hear me when I said the hospital said he almost didn't make it?"

"*Almost!* You just checked five minutes ago. They said he's stable now. And of course, I'm worried. But us killing ourselves on the way won't do anyone any good. We don't need to end up in the hospital ourselves."

He ignored her, whipped into a handicapped parking space, and jumped out.

Once they had raced inside the sliding ER doors, the two of them were quickly led back to the emergency-room lobby, where a doctor immediately came out. After a brief introduction, he got right down to business.

"Your son had a major accident, lost a lot of blood. We were worried for a while because he needed a transfusion, and as I'm sure you're aware, his blood type is rare. Thankfully, a donor came through."

Both Bernard and Adele were immensely relieved.

"That is wonderful," Bernard said. When Kendall had hurt himself skateboarding when he was seventeen, it took days to get a transfusion because his O-negative blood type was so rare.

"Well, it was actually his sister. You'll be happy to know she's doing fine," the doctor said with a smile meant to convey how nice it was that they had such a close family.

*"Sister?"* Adele said as Bernard's heart sank.

The doctor looked confused. "Yeah, the woman that was riding in the car with him. She said she's his sister." He glanced down at his clipboard. "I think her name is . . . Olivia." He tapped the board when he found her name. "Olivia Dawson. By the way, we've checked her out and we're going to keep her overnight, but she should be able to go home tomorrow."

The color drained from Adele's face and she had to hold on to the wall to steady herself.

Bernard tried to cover up with a question. "Can we see our son?"

"Not yet. He's in recovery. If you can just have a seat in the lobby, we'll come out and get you." Bernard squeezed Adele's hand. "But your son and daughter are going to be fine," the doctor said before hurrying off.

Bernard wanted to say something, anything to keep his wife from exploding. But he could already see the wheels churning in her head, especially when she mumbled, "Olivia." She suddenly stood erect, then walked over to the nurses' station.

"What room is Olivia Dawson in?"

"Are you relatives?" the nurse asked.

"That's her father," Adele said, her tone icy as she pointed at Bernard.

"She's in Room 112."

"Thank you," Adele retorted, spinning off and heading down the hall.

Bernard took off after her. "Adele," he called.

His wife ignored him as her heels clicked determinedly down the hallway. He cursed as he followed her. Bernard had had every intention of telling Adele on the drive back from San Diego, but after the call from Nicole, his mind had been on nothing else but the accident.

"Adele, let me talk to you." Bernard tried to stop her before she eased open the door to 112.

Adele stepped into the room and stared at Olivia. "Oh, my God. You," she mumbled. "I do not believe this."

Olivia sat up in the bed, taken aback at the intrusion.

"What in the hell are you doing here?" Adele hissed.

"I'm trying to recover," Olivia said, confused, as she looked from Adele to Bernard.

Adele spun around to face her husband. "Is this some kind of sick joke?"

Bernard stepped forward. "Adele . . ."

She looked at him in dawning horror. "And you brought her in to work for you?"

"Adele, I . . . I wanted to tell you," he stammered.

She was in shock as she fully took in Olivia's appearance. "How dare you bring her back into our lives?"

"Can we not do this now?" Bernard said gently. "She just saved your son's life."

"Don't give me that crap. How long have you been lying to me? How long has she been back?"

Bernard so didn't want to do this, but he saw the look on Olivia's face and knew he had no choice. "She showed up three months ago," he sighed, "and I'm sorry I didn't tell you."

"So you just decided to do what you do best, lie about it."

He didn't respond.

"Mrs. Wells, I know this is a shock to you." Olivia was still a little sore, but felt much better and was anxious to get out of this place, which they told her she could do tomorrow.

Adele spun her head like she was in *The Exorcist*. "You don't know anything about me. If you did, you'd know that you shouldn't have dared come around my family."

"Adele, it's been twenty years," Bernard pleaded.

She snapped back toward him. "I'm sorry, I didn't know there was a statute of limitations on my pain."

"I know you're upset, but—"

"Have you been communicating with Lorraine all these years?"

"No, not at all," Bernard protested. "I just found out about Olivia because she appeared one day at the office."

"And I just found out I had a father," Olivia interjected. "I wanted to know if it was true."

Adele laughed. "And you expected to get the truth from him? He wouldn't know what the truth was if it ran him over with an eighteen-wheeler."

"I understand that you're upset."

Adele backed away, her hands up like he was the most vile person in the world. "You don't understand anything." She ran her hands over her hair. "Oh, my God. I can't believe you did this."

Bernard eased up behind his wife again. "Adele, please? Let's go outside and talk."

She stepped away, repelled by his closeness. "What kind of game have you been running? Does Kendall know? He told me about the new girl at work that he was close to. I never in a million years . . ." Adele spun back toward Olivia. "Does he know you're his sister?"

Bernard lowered his head in shame as Olivia bit down on her lip. “No, he doesn’t know,” she said.

“So you’ve been lying to everyone as well? Like father, like daughter.”

“Mrs. Wells, I’ve been trying to get Bernard to tell you guys,” Olivia said, exasperated.

Bernard knew his biggest nightmare had come true. What he had thought about himself the day before—that he was a coward—was true. That’s what had led to this mess. “Can we go outside and talk?” he repeated.

“Get away from me. Get away from me!” Adele cried. She was shaking, on the verge of eruption. “I need a drink.”

“Adele, that is the last thing you need.”

“Don’t tell me what I need! You have no clue what I need or what I want.” She bolted toward the door. “I need to escape from this horrible place before I lose my mind.”

After the door to the hospital room closed, Olivia let go a long sigh. She looked as if she wanted to hammer Bernard with *I told you so*s, but he guessed his misery was showing, so she only said, “Aren’t you going to go after her?”

He sighed heavily. “No, when she’s upset, it’s best to let her cool off. I know I should’ve told her.” He was mad at himself for embarrassing his daughter like this. “But it was going to be a disaster either way. And somehow I have the feeling that the storm is only starting to brew.”

# Chapter 35

This was the day Bernard had hoped would never come. Last night had been the worst night of his life. He'd tried to find Adele, with no luck. He hadn't wanted to leave the hospital, but he had to go look for her. He'd never found her, and she didn't come home. Kendall, who was recovering this morning, had woken up asking a ton of questions.

"I don't understand," he'd said this morning. "Does Mom know about the accident?" Bernard had seen Kendall briefly last night, but his son had been so sedated, he hadn't even known Bernard was there. That's why Bernard had left to try to find his wife.

"I told you she was here yesterday. She stayed by your side all night," Bernard lied.

"Well, where is she now?"

"I'm right here." Adele appeared in the doorway. Her usually immaculate hair was askew. Her eyes were bloodshot. Bernard didn't know if her disarray was from lack of sleep or alcohol.

"I'm sorry I wasn't here when you woke up." She stumbled into the room, paused, and tried to pull herself together. All eyes were on her.

"Mom, have you been drinking?" Kendall asked, struggling to sit up.

She held up her thumb and index finger. "Maybe just a teeny bit," she giggled. "I just came to check on you." She wobbled into the room. "How are you feeling?"

Kendall looked at her strangely. "I'm okay. Hurting some, but I'm okay. It's not as bad as it looks."

"That's good." She reached up to stroke his hair, but she knocked over the small pitcher of water that sat next to his bed. "Oops," she giggled.

"Maybe you should come back at another time," Bernard said, taking her arm.

She jerked away from him. "Maybe you should get your filthy hands off of me."

"Adele," Bernard hissed, as his brow furrowed and his nostrils flared. Yet he noticed that Adele looked like she was fighting back tears.

"Mom, what is wrong with you?"

She straightened her shoulders and brushed down her clothes. With a haughty air she said, "I am the noble Adele Wells. Whatsoever would make you think something's wrong?"

Kendall was watching this performance in awe. "I can't believe you came in here drunk."

She leaned over his bed and whispered loudly, "Ask your father why I've been drinking."

Kendall gently pushed her away in disgust. "I'm not asking Dad anything. Dad was here while you were off somewhere getting sauced."

Adele chuckled. "That's because Dad is so perfect," she said, her voice laced with sarcasm.

"Somebody has to be," Kendall snapped, extremely upset at Adele's behavior.

"Adele, please?" Bernard said.

She all but growled at him as he stepped toward her, stopping him in his tracks.

"See? Dad is always trying to appease you, and you're always so bitter and angry."

"Oh, I'm bitter and angry?" she said with a pained laugh. "As if I don't have reason to be bitter and angry?"

"Mom, you're straight trippin'," Kendall said, gritting his teeth in anger.

"Stop talking to me in that slang," she yelled.

Kendall continued to be baffled. "Mom, what in the world is wrong with you?"

She gave Bernard a withering look. "You want to know what's wrong with me, Son? I'm tired." She brushed loose strands of hair out of her face. "Tired of my husband, the esteemed Bernard Wells. Ha! Everyone thinks I'm the bitch. I'm the low-down, dirty one in this union, and Bernard, he's so . . . so perfect—"

"Don't do this," Bernard pleaded. "You're drunk. You don't want to do this. This isn't about you."

"It never is!" She no longer tried to keep her tears at bay, which caught Kendall by surprise.

He reached for her. "Mom, don't cry."

She pushed him away. "Don't! I am sick of this. I am sick of all these lies."

"What is your problem?" Kendall asked, frustrated.

"You want to know what my problem is? Your low-down, dirty daddy is my problem." She waved wildly. "The lies he's been telling for years." The door opened and Olivia, dressed as if she was about to leave, appeared in the doorway. "The lies he's *still* telling, like working with Miss USC here." Adele jabbed her thumb in Olivia's direction.

The expression on Olivia's face said she couldn't believe she had walked right into this madness. "I-I'm sorry. I'll come back later." Olivia turned to leave.

"No!" Adele shouted. "Come on in. We're all one big happy family."

Olivia glanced from Kendall to Bernard, then back to Adele. "Look, Mrs. Wells"—Olivia advanced tentatively into the room—"I understand that you're upset by what my mother did, but I had no control over that."

Kendall was even more confused. "What? You know her mother?" he asked Adele.

Adele cackled. "I thought I did." She swerved a little, losing her balance, but she grabbed the bed to keep from falling. "But I guess I didn't or I would've never let the tramp move into my house."

"Mom, what are you talking about?"

Adele grinned like a child revealing a juicy secret. "You mean, you worked together with her all this time and you didn't recognize your sister?"

Olivia's heart sank when she saw the expression on Kendall's face.

*"Sister?"*

"Adele, I can't believe you did that," Bernard mumbled.

She ignored her husband. "Take a good look at her." Adele pointed at Olivia. "You don't remember playing with her when you were little? I mean, how could you not know? She's the spitting image of your nana Lorraine. Or shall I say, the perfect blend of your former nana and *your father*."

Kendall looked to Olivia as if he desperately wanted her to confirm that his mother was drunk and talking crazy. "What is she talking about? Are . . ." He paused, studying her as if a memory was setting in. "Pinky? My Pinky?"

*"Your Pinky,"* Adele said nostalgically. "That's what you used to call her, like she was some little baby doll. Your nana's baby girl. Your playmate." Adele stopped smiling. "Your sister."

"You're my . . . my sister?"

"I . . . I wanted to tell you," Olivia stammered.

Adele's hand went to her mouth in feigned disbelief. "Oh, my. You mean my darling son didn't know that his father was sleeping with the help?" She stopped, her face filling with venom. "But it's not like Lorraine was the first whore that my husband took up with."

"Now, wait a minute." Olivia understood this woman was

hurting, but she wasn't going to sit by and let her disrespect her mother. "Do not talk about my mother like that."

"You don't get to tell me what to do, little girl," Adele said, jabbing a finger in Olivia's direction.

"Enough," Bernard repeated.

"No." Adele smiled like a madwoman. "You're into hiding inconvenient truths, but let's share another truth that wasn't so convenient." She turned to her son. "Do you want to know one of the other whores?"

"Adele!" Bernard's voice was full of panic.

"Don't worry, I'm not going to tell him about Alyssa." Adele leaned over and whispered to Kendall, "He thinks I don't know about his latest conquest. Little Miss Alyssa." She laughed. "But I know everything," she sang. Suddenly, Adele lost her smile. "No, that's not the other whore," she said as she stared sadly at Kendall. "That title belonged to your mother."

"What?" Kendall said.

"I can't believe you," Bernard whispered.

"Yep, your dad has always had a penchant for the ladies," Adele said, her voice filled with pain.

"Dad, wh-what is she talking about?" Kendall said.

"Your mother is not in her right frame of mind," Bernard said sternly. "She's drunk. Again."

She smiled through her tears at Kendall. "You want to know why I drink?" She leaned in and lowered her voice. "It helps ease the pain." She viciously wiped her eyes. "But right now I'm perfectly sane. Yes, a little tipsy, but sane nonetheless. I'm just tired of being the bad guy." She glared at her husband. "I'm tired of grinning and pretending while people lavish praise on your father and look at him all pathetic, like 'How can you stomach her?'" Tears gleamed on her angry face. She pointed back at Kendall. "I took in your bastard child once." Then she turned and pointed to Olivia. "Then you had the audacity to do it again!"

"Dad, what is she talking about?" Kendall shouted.

"Tell him!" Adele urged. "Tell him how you knocked up someone else and asked me to raise the product of that affair!"

Bernard remained silent. He felt as if smoke were literally coming from his ears.

*"You're not my mother?"* Kendall said in astonishment.

"I've tried to be," she said, sobbing. "In every shape of the word. But I look at you and I see her. I see your father's betrayal and it kills me. Every day. Yet I dealt with it the best I could."

Kendall rubbed his temples, trying to make sense of everything. "I don't understand. Dad, someone needs to tell me what's going on."

Olivia looked dumbfounded. Bernard could only imagine what she must be thinking.

"Who is my mother?" Kendall said, near hysteria.

Bernard didn't say a word as he stared at Adele with hate-filled eyes.

Adele tossed her hair over her shoulder and tried to compose herself. "Your mother was a stripper that your father knocked up. I didn't know anything about her until she showed up at the hospital on the same day I lost my child." Adele rocked from side to side as she recalled the story. Tears now trickled down her cheeks. "You weren't two months old when she dropped you at the foot of my hospital bed and said, 'Here, hope this makes you feel better.' Then she left." Adele released a sad laugh. "So, here I am grieving the loss of a child my husband and I had been trying to conceive for months, and this woman drops a kid at the foot of my sickbed. And I was just supposed to be okay with that?"

Kendall fell back against the pillows. *"You're not my mother?"*

"I had a son, too," she said, her chest heaving, "but God took my son and Bernard tried to pacify me with another one. And you wonder why I'm not into religion? Because who does that? What kind of God inflicts that kind of pain?"

Adele's bottom lip trembled as she glared at Bernard. Olivia stood off to the back. Bernard hadn't even noticed that Mona had eased into the room and was standing beside Olivia holding her hand.

A deafening silence filled the room, until Adele finally turned to Kendall. "I'm sorry. I love you. I do. As best as I know how." She touched his face, but he recoiled like he couldn't stand her touch.

She dropped her hand, brushed down her hair, then stood erect. "But if you're going to hate anybody, hate him." She pointed at Bernard. "God knows, I do." With that, she left the room and left all of them standing in stunned silence.

# Chapter 36

"So, you're just going to pack your things and go?"

Bernard stepped around his wife and walked over to the dresser to remove some more clothes without saying a word. Two days had passed since her blockbuster revelation. He'd stayed at a hotel the past two nights because he was scared of what he'd do if he saw her. Now that he'd calmed down, he'd come home to do the only thing he could do—leave.

His first instinct had been to run to Alyssa. But he knew that wasn't fair to her. He didn't want to give her false hopes. There was no future for them. Even if he did leave Adele for good—which now seemed his only choice—Alyssa was young and wanted a child. She wanted what he couldn't give. He'd hurt Lorraine by being selfish and holding on to her. He refused to do that to Alyssa. That had left him relegated to a hotel and feeling more alone than he'd ever before felt in his life.

Kendall had banned him from the hospital. Olivia wasn't welcome either, and that had torn her apart. Bernard didn't realize how close his two children had gotten, but when Mona had to literally drag Olivia out of the hospital room in tears, Bernard had seen the pain in her eyes. He'd made her lie to Kendall, and now Kendall hated them both.

"You are being so childish," Adele said.

He could no longer contain his anger as he spun toward her. "*I'm* being childish! After that stunt you pulled, you have the nerve to call me childish?"

"Don't get all self-righteous on me. That was long overdue. You lied to me from the very beginning."

He looked confused.

"That's right, I knew you were seeing someone when we met."

He was shocked. She'd never, in all their fights, let on that she knew there was someone else. "You knew about Lorraine?"

"Of course I didn't know who she was. Do you think I would've ever let that tramp come live in my house had I known? But I knew there was someone."

"And you pursued the relationship anyway?"

"Oh, please, I didn't have to work too hard. Once you got a taste of the good life, you dumped that other woman so fast, I just had to wait at the altar."

Bernard stared icily at his wife. At that moment he despised everything about her. He couldn't believe that not only had she just destroyed their son's life, but that his relationship with her had been a part of some calculated plan from the beginning.

"Don't look at me like that. You're the one who messed up here. And then you have the audacity to bring that damn woman back into our lives."

"That *damn* woman is my daughter!"

Adele's glare was a reflection of her pain, and Bernard softened his stance. He'd had a lot of time to think. As mad as he was at Adele, watching her that day had shown him just how much he'd hurt her.

"I'm sorry." His shoulders sank in defeat. "I know that it may be painful for you to accept, but I let you take Olivia from me once. I couldn't let her slip out of my life again. You made me choose once, but there was no choice this time. I was just trying to figure out how to tell you. How to tell you and not lose her in the process."

Adele wiped her eyes like she was determined not to cry. "I'm not trying to make you choose. You go right ahead and live happily ever after with both of your kids."

Bernard shook his head. "You know, Kendall always said he felt like you hated him, but I said, 'No, that's your mother. She doesn't hate you. She loves you. She may not show it, but she does love you.'"

"I do love him." She looked like she had aged years in the past two days. The tears she'd been holding back made their escape. "What did you expect from me, Bernard? You had no respect for my feelings. First, you lied to me about everything with Sandy," she said, referring to Kendall's birth mother, "then you ask me to keep the child."

"Sandy said she was going to put him in foster care. What

was I supposed to do?" Bernard said, feeling the echo of an old argument.

"I don't know. Maybe we could've talked about it. Maybe we could have asked her to hold off at least until I left the hospital. Whatever, but you should've considered my feelings! You asked me to do something of that magnitude without ever taking into account how I felt about losing my own son."

Bernard had no idea she had been so upset about losing the baby. She'd acted as if getting pregnant were an inconvenience, and she constantly complained about what the unborn baby was doing to her figure.

"I know you don't think it," she said, reading his mind, "but I loved my child, a child I carried for nine months, then had to deliver stillborn, and you never gave me time to grieve."

"I'm sorry," he muttered. He really was. His wife had exhibited that cold demeanor for so long, he forgot that a real live person with feelings existed underneath there. Bernard hesitated. "I know you don't believe this, but I never meant to hurt you."

She looked at him icily. "I would hate to see what you were capable of if you were trying."

Bernard contemplated trying to explain some more, but he had no words that would change what had happened. He knew he'd wronged Adele—from the day he'd said, "I do," he'd known their marriage was wrong.

"Why do you think I wanted a baby so bad?" she asked, her voice cracking.

Bernard remembered her abrupt shift. She had never talked

about kids, then all of a sudden, she became obsessed with getting pregnant. It had taken nine months and one miscarriage before she finally got a viable pregnancy.

"I don't know. It felt like something else to check off your to-do list."

She let out another pained laugh. "You just don't get it. I wanted a child, I wanted *your* child, because I thought, maybe, just maybe, if I gave you a child, you'd learn to love me."

He stiffened in shock. "I—"

She held up her hand to cut him off. "Enough with the lies. You never loved me. You loved this life." She extended her arms to motion around the bedroom. "You wanted to be Hampton England's son-in-law, not Adele England's husband." She gently sat down on the bed. "I knew that going in, but I'd hoped that I could change your mind. I thought that I could show you that loving me wasn't so bad. But you never gave us a chance."

Bernard was speechless. This was a side of his wife he'd never seen. "I'm sorry."

"Yeah, you said that." Silence filled the room before she finally stood. "It's probably best that you leave. It's long overdue." She headed to the door, then stopped and turned back to face Bernard. "I am sorry about what I did to Kendall. I don't know how I'll make it up to him, but I will."

Bernard was about to respond when his cell phone rang. He immediately checked the number, and his expression filled with concern.

"I'll let you get that," she said, easing out of the room. Bernard should've stopped her, continued trying to talk to her, but Olivia was calling and he needed to talk to her. She'd been avoiding his calls since they'd left the hospital.

"Hello."

"Bernard," she said, her voice frantic, "Kendall is missing."

"What do you mean, missing?"

"He's gone. He left the hospital."

Bernard's heart dropped. "Oh, my God," he muttered. If something happened to his son, he'd never forgive himself.

"Mona and I are out searching for him."

"Where could he be?"

"We have no idea. We were hoping that you could tell us. Do you have the phone numbers for any of his friends?"

Bernard felt sick in the pit of his stomach as he realized that he didn't even know the names of Kendall's friends, let alone their phone numbers. It dawned on Bernard that he knew nothing about his son's friends, his hangouts. His life.

"I don't, but let me see what I can find out. Should we call the police?"

"I don't think they're gonna do anything because it hasn't been long enough."

"Oh, they'll do something," Bernard said with authority.

"Well, you do what you have to. We'll keep you posted."

"Olivia?"

"Yes?"

"Thank you."

She let a few beats pass, then said, "This isn't for you," before hanging up the phone.

Bernard hated the disgust he heard in her voice, but he couldn't blame her. He took a deep breath and headed out the room to tell Adele that Kendall was missing. He hated that a flicker of wonder crossed his mind: Did she even care?

# Chapter 37

"Okay, you know I'll ride or die with you, wherever. And trust, I love rolling around in this drop-top Benz," Mona said, "but we've been at this for four hours now and I'm tired."

The two of them had gone to the hospital to check on Kendall, only to find his room empty. He'd still been a patient yesterday, but he'd refused to see them. He had given the nurse specific instructions that he didn't want any visitors, especially anyone claiming to be family.

Olivia knew that Kendall was mad at her, at everyone, but she hoped he just needed more time to sort through his feelings. However, when she and Mona had returned today and found out that Kendall had unexpectedly left, her worry turned up a few notches. Especially because the nurses had no idea where he had gone.

They'd driven to Kendall's house, his friend's recording studio, and the gym where he worked out. They were hoping someone had seen him. But each stop turned up nothing.

"I can't give up yet," Olivia said, turning down another street. LA was so big, and she had no idea where she was going. She just knew that she had to keep searching. "He's out here somewhere. He hasn't fully recovered. He could be out on the side of the road, bleeding to death."

"I doubt it's that dramatic." Mona's eyes narrowed to slits as she studied her friend. "Dang, you sound like you really care about him or something."

"I do." Olivia couldn't believe how much she cared. She knew he had to be hurting. When he'd ordered them all out of his room—screaming so loud the nurse had come in and cleared the room for him—Olivia's heart ached. She knew how it felt to find out your whole life had been a lie. She understood his pain. She wouldn't rest until she found him and explained how much she had wanted to tell him who she was.

"Okay, let's keep going then." Mona sat pensively as a new idea took shape in her mind. "Say, what's that guy's name at the club?"

"What club?"

"Remember? His friend that worked the door that night we went."

Olivia's fingers drummed the steering wheel. "What was his name? . . . Mike . . . Mark?"

"Mark! Yeah, Mark might know where he is." Mona glanced at her watch. "It's after eleven, so Mark is probably at the club. Do you remember how to get there?"

Olivia made a U-turn in the middle of the road. "No, but that's what the friendly navigation device on your phone is for. I know it's back this way. Look up the address while I head in that direction."

Mona found the address and directed Olivia.

Gradually, Olivia became aware that Mona's eyes were fixed on her. "What?"

"Can I ask you a question?" Mona said.

"Since when do you ask to ask me a question?"

"This is serious. I'm trying to understand this. We've been out here only a few months, yet you're acting like you've known Kendall for years. I mean, you should see the look on your face."

Olivia considered her words as she glanced at herself in the rearview mirror. Mona was right, she looked frantic. "I don't know." Olivia turned her attention back to the road. "I feel like I have known him for years. I keep saying it's like some kind of connection that I can't explain. I've never felt so drawn to anyone in my life."

Mona was intrigued by this idea. "I guess that's your DNA test right there."

"At first I thought it was merely my overwhelming desire to have a brother, a real, normal family. But then I realized the feeling goes deeper than that. I have these vague memories of him pushing me on a tricycle. Of him playing with me. They're memories that are starting to come back because we've been together. I think I can honestly say that I love him. And I don't want him not to be in my life."

"All that in three months? You don't think that you just want this so bad that you're making it more than it is?"

"No, I think he feels the same way. . . . Is this where I turn?"

Mona looked down at the GPS map on her phone. "No, it's the next light."

Olivia kept going. "Well, the way I'm feeling is definitely not made up." She smiled at Mona. Olivia was so grateful that Mona was making the journey with her. Mona had been there for her since middle school, and whatever she needed, Mona would move heaven and earth to get it for her. "I just want to thank you for helping me out with this."

"You know I wouldn't be anywhere else. I got your back." Mona pointed at the light. "This is your turn. Plus, I can't be mad at you. With my dysfunctional family, if I had something else to hang on to, I might be driving all over Southern California myself."

"I get the feeling that Kendall's family is a little dysfunctional itself."

Mona waved off the comment. "Girl, please. Rich folks ain't got no real problems."

"I don't know. That's what I used to think, and Kendall kept telling me otherwise. After that fiasco at the hospital, I'm thinking he might be right."

Mona nodded her head at the memory. "I guess rich folks can have some ghetto drama, too, because that was too much. But if I had to choose between rich-ghetto drama and poor-ghetto drama, I'm going with rich every time. At least I can buy some retail therapy to help me through my issues." Mona chuckled.

They entered the parking lot of the club and double-parked near the front door. A line of people were wrapped around the building, but Olivia and Mona quickly snaked through the line.

"Unh-unh, ain't no cutting," someone yelled.

Mona stopped and turned around to reply, but Olivia grabbed her hand and pulled her ahead. They had no time for a nightclub confrontation.

They spotted Mark working the door. "Hey, Mark," Mona said, waving over the people in front of her. "You remember us? We were with Kendall the first time we came here."

"Hey," he replied, immediately recognizing them. "If it isn't my two Southern belles." He motioned for them to come to the front and they did, much to the dismay and grumbling of the people in line.

"I was with Kendall, too," someone behind them shouted.

Mark ignored the people fussing as Olivia and Mona made their way to the front. He turned his nose up when he saw their outfits. "Umm, you do know we have a dress code?" he said, motioning toward their casual attire.

"No, no, we're not trying to get in the club," Olivia said. "We're trying to find Kendall."

He frowned, not liking the sound of that. "Okay, I need to know what in the world is going on." The guarded look on his face told Olivia he'd definitely heard from his friend.

"We've got to find him. He shouldn't have left the hospital yet. We're worried sick," Olivia said. "And there's some major family drama that might push him over the edge."

Thankfully, Mark didn't ask a bunch of questions. "Yeah,

he called, asking to come to my house, but I've been out all day. I told him to come by and get the key, but he said he was just gonna go to Tina's place."

"Who is Tina?" Mona said with a little more attitude than normal.

"That's his ex-girlfriend," Mark said.

"He still talks to her?" Mona said.

Mark shrugged, and Olivia realized that he wasn't giving up any more details than he had already. "I don't know. I'm just telling you what he said."

"Any idea where Tina lives?" Olivia said.

"Hey, can you guys take that reunion someone else?" someone from the line shouted. "Some of us are trying to get in the club."

Mark scowled as he scanned the line to see who had said that. "Keep talking and you're gonna be standing in line all night," he barked.

Whoever had mouthed off must have decided it was best to be quiet because he didn't say another word.

"Now, you know I can't get caught up in that, telling my boy's business," Mark said, turning his attention back to Olivia and Mona.

"Come on, Mark," Olivia pleaded. "This is serious. How would you feel if Kendall bled to death or something? He should have never left the hospital, and the stress of what he's dealing with can't be good."

Mark's eyebrows raised. "Was the accident really that bad?"

"It was worse. The accident was only one part. The

aftermath . . ." Olivia paused. "I don't know if he'll ever recover from that." Her heart sank even as she prayed that wasn't the case.

Mark sighed, then gave them the address.

"Thank you so much," Olivia said, typing the address into her phone.

"Yo, he said something about finding out you were his sister. Is that true?" Mark asked before they darted off.

Olivia nodded as a lump formed in her throat. "It is. I'm just hoping that not telling him that from the beginning hasn't done irreparable damage."

Mark didn't seem to think so. "Well, keep your head up, baby girl. Kendall can be stubborn, but he's a good guy. He'll come around."

Olivia fought back the tears that were welling up. "I really hope so." But she knew that getting through to Kendall was going to take a lot more than hope.

# Chapter 38

Olivia's heart beat in anticipation as she stood outside Apartment 809. Tina's place had been easy to find. Olivia said a silent prayer that he was still here—and that he would talk to her. After two more knocks, the door swung open.

"May I help you?"

Olivia was shocked at the sight of a girl standing there with bleach-blond hair, wearing a tight catsuit and smacking on a wad of gum. *This* was Kendall's ex?

"Yeah, I'm looking for my brother, Kendall."

Her eyes roamed up and down Olivia's body before she said, "Kendall ain't got no sisters."

Mona stepped up, pushing Olivia aside. "Look, Sheneneh, we know Kendall is here, so can you go get him?"

Tina wiggled her neck and held up a finger. "Oh, I don't

think so. You ain't about to come up in my crib—" She stopped when the door swung open farther.

Kendall stood there, looking tired and worn down. "What do you two want?"

Olivia's heart sank in relief, and before she could stop herself, she nearly knocked Tina over as she threw her arms around Kendall's neck. After a moment she realized that he wasn't hugging her back.

"Are you okay?" she asked, taking a step back and giving him the once-over.

He turned up his lip. "What do you think?" He turned away from her and limped back inside.

She walked into the small apartment behind him. Mona followed her. Tina looked like she didn't appreciate the intrusion.

"T, give me a moment," he said to her.

She rolled her eyes but walked into the back.

Mona looked at the girl in disgust. "So that's the kind of woman you're looking for?"

Kendall put his hand up, palm forward. "Not now, Mona."

Olivia could tell he was on the verge of going off, and Tina wasn't the point of their coming here.

"Mona, can I talk to Kendall privately?"

Mona glared at Kendall, then relented. "Fine. I need a cigarette anyway." She didn't bother to hide her anger. "I'll be right outside the door if you need me."

"What do y'all want?" Kendall snapped once Mona stepped back outside. "Why are you here?"

"I wanted to check on you." Olivia's voice was laced with concern. She glanced around the small apartment. It was quite nice—and didn't look like it belonged to the woman who'd opened the door.

"I don't need you to check on me."

Olivia inhaled sharply. She kept telling herself that he was not his usual self. "Kendall, I know this is rough on you."

"You don't know anything about me." He fell down into a recliner. He picked up a beer on the table next to him and took a swig.

"Yeah, I do." She wanted to ask if he should be drinking with all the medication in his system, but she knew he wouldn't want to hear any nagging from her.

"So, you know what it's like to have someone you love lie to you like this?" he said casually.

"Yeah, I do."

They exchanged stares for a moment, until he said, "Well, everyone I know and trusted has lied to me, including you."

That stung and she felt compelled to explain. "I wanted to tell you, but I didn't know how."

He looked at her like she was crazy. "How about all the times I told you about my life? Or maybe when you told me about your childhood?" His anger bubbled to the surface, and his voice was laced with sarcasm. "Or, here's a thought, how about you say, 'Hey, Kendall, the reason I'm not attracted to you is because I'm your friggin' sister!'" He grimaced as a memory flashed. "Oh, my God, and I tried to kiss you." He sat up and held his stomach like he was going to be sick.

"Kendall, please understand, I wanted to tell you so bad, but your dad wanted to tell you first."

"You mean, *our* dad?" He rubbed his leg like he was trying to ease some pain. "What was your plan the whole time? Use me to get to his money? Torture him by making him think you'd tell? Did you and your girl have a great laugh at my expense?" Kendall said, jutting his chin toward the front door.

Olivia could feel the hurt in his voice, and for the first time she thought about what her deception had meant to him. She'd never given it a second thought. She was so wrapped up in her own pain. She hadn't thought about how he'd feel about not only finding out his dad had cheated, but that the girl he'd grown close to over the last few months was a product of that affair.

"Kendall, I am so sorry."

"You know what? You, my dad, my fake mom, all of you can take your lies, your apologies, and go to hell."

"Kendall—"

"Get out and leave me alone!"

"But . . ."

He took out his wallet and pulled out two $100 bills and flung them at her. "Here, this is all the cash I have. Hit my dad up for the rest, since that's probably all you wanted in the first place. You're just like every other trick in my life—only after what you can get from me."

She couldn't believe the conversation had taken this turn. "I've never asked you for your money."

He ran his hands over his head. "Just go, Olivia. Leave me alone," he said, his voice cracking.

Olivia wanted to protest, convince him to hear her out, but she could see that now was not the time to try to talk to him. And her heart was breaking with each cruel word he tossed her way.

"Okay, fine. I just wanted to make sure you're okay."

"I'm fine. Now leave me the hell alone."

"I'll leave. We'll talk later."

"Or not," he coldly added. "Just go back to whatever rock you crawled from under. I don't want to have anything to do with you ever again."

Olivia felt her chest tightening as she struggled to open the door. As soon as she came out, Mona noticed her and ran to her side.

"Are you okay?"

"N-no," Olivia whimpered.

Mona grabbed her by the arm to hold her up. "Kendall, what did you do?"

"Don't start with me, Mona," he snapped. "Both of you can take your gold-digging asses back to Houston and leave me alone."

Mona dropped Olivia's arm. "Oh, I don't think so." Mona stepped toward him. She pointed her index finger in his face. "Now, I know you're going through some stuff, so I'm gonna give you a pass, but that's the last time you're ever coming at me or my girl like that."

"Come on, Mona," Olivia sniffed, pulling at her friend's arm.

Tina appeared in the door like she was taking up a role in a good action flick.

"Naw," Mona said, snatching her arm away. "He needs to be told about his little spoiled ass." She jabbed her finger in Olivia's direction. "All this girl ever wanted from you was your friendship and love. She never asked you or your daddy for a dime, even though I told her she should get whatever she could. Yes, she screwed up, but when your mind clears from its fog of self-pity, and you get past all that anger you got brewing inside, you'll realize that."

Mona stared at him, her cheeks flushed with anger. Kendall glared right back, but didn't say a word. Mona flashed a disgusted look at Tina, then said, "Come on, Olivia. Now we can go."

# Chapter 39

They had been riding in silence, and now Bernard wished his wife would say something, anything. When he'd gone to get Adele, telling her that Kendall was missing, she'd grabbed her purse and followed him out. She hadn't said much on the drive to the police station. Bernard had called in a favor to get a missing-person report filed. As they sat answering questions for the police, both of them realized there was so much they didn't know about their son. Adele had cried silently on the drive home until finally Bernard's cell phone rang, breaking the silence.

"Hey, any word?" he asked, answering on the first ring when he saw Olivia's name on the screen.

"He's at his ex-girlfriend Tina's house."

*Ex-girlfriend?* Another stab. Bernard had not known his son had a serious girlfriend. "Where does she live?"

"I don't think it's going to do any good." Olivia sighed. "We just left about an hour ago. He doesn't want to talk to anyone." Her voice was forlorn, and he could tell her visit had not gone well.

"I have to try."

Olivia gave him the address, which he punched into the navigation system. At least he had control over something in his life.

In another thirty minutes they arrived at Tina's Inglewood apartment. He half-expected Kendall not to answer the door and wasn't surprised when they saw movement behind the peephole. Yet the door didn't open.

"Kendall, please let me in," Adele said, the first words she'd uttered outside the police department since they'd begun their search.

"Go away!" he finally yelled through the door.

"I'm not leaving," she yelled back.

Kendall swung the door open. "What? The prim and proper Adele Wells is actually going to dare do something that might bring negative attention to herself?"

All the fire went out of her at once. "I deserve that," she said meekly.

He rolled his eyes and stumbled back inside. Each step looked like it was causing him major pain. They followed him in. The woman sitting on the sofa frowned at Bernard for his intrusion.

"Can you give me a minute?" Kendall said.

"Damn, this is Grand Central Station up in here," Tina mumbled as she grabbed her beer off the coffee table and headed into a back bedroom.

"What do you want?" Kendall asked after he heard her bedroom door close. "I can already guess that Olivia told you where I was."

"We need to talk to you," Adele said.

"Why, M—" He stopped himself. "I guess I can't say *Mom*."

"I will always be your mother," she said softly.

"Really? Because I think I'd be correct to say you've *never* been my mother."

Her eyes watered as she lowered her head.

"Son, please don't talk to your mother like that," Bernard said.

Kendall spun Bernard's way. "And you? Don't even get me started on you. You want to talk about me doing what's right and being an honorable person, and you're the biggest whore-monger out there." Kendall threw up his hands. "Just leave me alone. Both of you can go to hell."

Bernard stepped toward him, his lips pursed. "Son, I understand you're angry with both of us, but you will not disrespect me or your mother."

Kendall stared like he couldn't believe Bernard had the audacity to chastise him. But instead of arguing, Kendall blew a deep breath and began pacing the room. "What do all you guys want from me?" he shouted again. "How could you go all these years lying to me?" He stopped in Adele's face. "I spent all these years trying to understand what it was that made my mother hate me."

"It wasn't you," she said.

"I didn't know that!" he shouted. "All my life, I wanted to

know why you hated me. Hell, when I was a teen, I used to think I drove you to drink. That you hated me so much that you drank so you didn't have to be bothered with me."

"I don't hate you. I love you. I may not know how to show it, but I do."

Bernard had expected her to throw him under the bus, blame everything on him again. He was surprised when she didn't.

"Kendall, I haven't been a good mother, but that doesn't mean I didn't love you," she pleaded.

"Why did you even take me in?" he said, his voice strained.

"I loved you."

"Tell me the truth. For once in your miserable life, tell me the truth."

She lowered her gaze. "I wanted to make your father love me," she said sadly. "I had a child so he would love me. I took you in so he could love me."

"How'd that work out for you, Adele?"

She started crying again.

Kendall wasn't moved. "Why would you want someone who doesn't want you?"

She kept her gaze directed at the floor. Bernard had never seen her so defeated. "The heart wants what it wants," she managed to say.

"Oh, save that Hallmark bull for someone else. I know what happened anyway. You are used to getting your way. You were a spoiled little girl who was used to getting what she wants, and that includes my father."

Bernard knew he should step in, but his son was saying

things he'd wanted to say for years. After another minute of Kendall's tirade, Bernard could see Adele was on the verge of crumbling, so he spoke up. "Kendall—"

"No! All my life I have watched everyone run scared of both of you. If only they knew. You are two of the most miserable people I've ever seen in my life." Kendall waved a hand in finality. "And consider me gone because I'm no longer a part of your lives."

"You're our son and we love you," Bernard said.

"Whatever."

"I'm never giving up on you," Adele said.

Kendall was adamant. "Please. Both of you, go, and leave me alone."

Bernard felt that he needed to try to say something. "Kendall—"

"Go! I hate both of you and I never want to see you again."

His words made Adele flinch. Tears were openly flowing down her cheeks as Bernard took her arm and led her out the door. "Come on, Adele, let's give him some time."

"Yeah, give me some time," Kendall called after them. His voice was cracking and Bernard could hear the pain in his words.

Outside, Bernard expected Adele to assume her usual cold demeanor toward him, but she did something he'd never experienced. She collapsed in his arms and sobbed.

# Chapter 40

Bernard had dropped Adele off at home twenty minutes ago. He had no idea where he was going, but he knew that he couldn't abide Adele's presence. Yes, she'd apologized for the fiasco at the hospital, but he'd never be able to forgive her for what she'd done to his son, especially if his son never forgave him. She must have known that his barriers were back up because she asked no questions as she got out of the car and stumbled into the house. Bernard almost called out to her not to lose herself in alcohol, but he kept the car window up. He no longer had the stamina to deal with her issues.

Bernard drove for hours—from one side of Los Angeles to the other—and back again. Finally, he figured out what he needed to do.

Thirty minutes later, he was standing in front of Walter's apartment.

"Mr. Wells," Walter said, opening the door in shock. "What in the world are you doing here?"

"I'm sorry to just drop in like this, but I was wondering if I could talk to you."

"Of course, of course, come on back. I don't like you standing out front. It can get dangerous."

He led Bernard through the living room, where Walter's wife and five of his grandkids were sitting, watching a movie on television.

"Hello, everyone," Bernard said meekly as he passed through.

They all said hello tentatively, as if trying to figure out what was wrong.

"So, what's going on?" Walter asked once they were out back.

"I'm just having a hard time. I've made a mess of everything."

"Have a seat." Walter pointed to a raggedy patio chair and sat down across from Bernard. "Tell me what's going on."

Bernard swallowed hard, then decided to confess what was weighing on his heart. "It turns out, I have a daughter, one I hadn't seen since she was a little girl, and she recently came back into my life."

Walter didn't show any emotion. His eyes merely urged Bernard to continue.

"Not only that, but Kendall hates me now." Bernard inhaled deeply. "Adele is not his mother."

"Is that so?" Walter's expression remained neutral.

"I had an affair and Kendall is a product of that. Adele took him in and raised him as her own." In a rush the entire story spilled out. All of it. Even the parts no one else knew. It felt good to release the story after all these years. "I know you must think I'm some kind of lowlife," Bernard said when he was done.

"I don't think anything. It's not my place to judge. There's only one judge and jury that matters."

Bernard nodded, though he didn't really pay the idea much mind. "What am I gonna do?"

"Have you prayed?"

"Prayed for what? For them to forgive me?"

Walter smiled but shook his head. "For God to forgive you."

Bernard thought about the question. He had hoped Olivia would forgive him. He'd prayed for Kendall to forgive him. He'd never even thought to ask God for forgiveness.

Walter knew Bernard's answer by the expression on his face and said, "Well, that's first and foremost. Ask God's forgiveness and it is granted."

"Just like that?"

"Just like that. I mean, it needs to be heartfelt." Walter's demeanor was warm and genuine. And sincere. He made Bernard actually believe his words.

"Oh, I feel it. I feel horrible about what I've done, and I want to figure out a way to make it right."

"Well, the first step is to go to God with a humbled heart and ask for His forgiveness. Can you do that?"

Bernard nodded, though with more certainty this time. It was strange. He couldn't remember the last time someone had prayed for him. He couldn't remember the last time he'd prayed. When he was a little boy, his grandmother used to say things like "Prayer works." He didn't know if it was true, but right now he could only hope his grandmother had been right. He closed his eyes and bowed his head.

Walter started with an intense prayer, asking for guidance, direction, and compassion and for God to show His unchanging hand. Bernard was really into it until he heard Walter say, "Now, Lord, Your child Bernard will confess his sins and seek Your forgiveness with his own tongue."

Bernard's eyes popped open. "You want me to talk?"

"I want you to say what's in your heart," Walter replied without opening his eyes.

Bernard paused. What was he supposed to say when he hadn't held a conversation with the Lord in years?

"Just speak from the heart," Walter urged.

Bernard didn't know what came over him, but he just started talking, and for the second time that day—the second time in his life—he confessed *everything.*

After they'd closed out the prayer, Bernard had a question for Walter. "Am I forgiven?"

"If you confessed and believed it, you are."

"I did." Bernard stood awkwardly, not sure what to do next. "Now what?"

Walter smiled warmly. "Now you have to forgive yourself."

# Chapter 41

"Why are you staring at me?" Olivia asked Mona, who was leaning against the doorframe of Olivia's bedroom, her arms folded, a chastising look across her face.

"So, you're just gonna up and run. And go where?"

Olivia put some more folded clothes in a suitcase, then turned around again to her dresser. "Home."

Mona shook her head as if this were the most ridiculous thing she had ever witnessed. "You said yourself, you don't have a home anymore, at least not in Houston. Are you gonna stay with your aunt Betty at the senior citizens' center?"

Olivia threw down the outfit she had just taken out of the drawer. "What am I supposed to do, Mona? Stay here and moon around a newfound family that doesn't want me?"

Olivia knew Adele would make sure she was fired. Kendall hated her. She hated Bernard. This had all turned into one big nightmare. She wanted to leave while she still had some dignity.

"Girl, screw that. This time three months ago, you didn't even know these people. Now, I understand you've grown all close to Kendall, but just because he's shut you out—for the moment, I might add—doesn't mean you should pack your stuff and go running for the hills." Mona blew an exasperated breath. "You're living better than you've lived your entire life. You have a job you love and you're running. Why? Because Kendall is mad at you? He has a right to be mad at you. You lied to him."

Olivia looked at her friend in astonishment.

"Oh, don't give me that look, you did lie."

"But—"

"But nothing. You lied. His mama lied. His daddy lied. And y'all act like he's supposed to get over it because you said I'm sorry."

"Whose side are you on?"

"Of course I'm on your side. But you know I'm gonna be real with you. Give him a minute to get over it."

Olivia sighed dejectedly, then picked up the outfit that she had tossed down. "I know you booked that pilot and you don't want to leave, so stay. If you're worried about the condo, you can keep staying here. It's paid for. You'd just have to pay for upkeep."

"Girl, ain't nobody thinking about this condo. I'm worried about you."

Olivia fell down on her bed. How had she made such a mess of everything? "Mona, I came here for answers. And truthfully, in the beginning, I kinda wanted Bernard to pay. But Kendall was right, revenge is a wasted energy. I wasted all of this time."

"Come on, Olivia, you might have initially wanted revenge, but from the moment you got here, your interest in your family has all been genuine."

"I didn't count on growing to care about them, to love them."

Olivia could tell Mona was getting frustrated. She'd been trying to cheer Olivia up since they'd left Kendall's place yesterday. Of course, all of Mona's talking had only frustrated her since Olivia wanted to wallow in self-pity.

"How do you think Bernard will feel with you just up and leaving?"

Olivia said darkly, "I couldn't care less how he feels. All of this is his fault anyway."

"And you running won't make any of that better. Put on your big-girl panties, give him a piece of your mind, whatever. Don't run and hide."

"But he's the reason we're all hurting."

"Okay, so the man screwed up—a lot. So did you. But you know he has a good heart."

"He hurt my mom, his wife, Kendall, me. Everyone."

Mona grabbed her friend by the shoulder and looked her in the eyes. "And with all that hurting, don't you think it's time someone moved forward in trying to heal?"

This time Mona did get through to Olivia. She slowly nodded, realizing Mona was right. If Olivia left now, she would still be hurting. So, she would still leave—but not before paying one last visit to dear ol' dad to clear the air and begin her healing.

# Chapter 42

The instant he saw the envelope, Bernard's heart dropped. Something told him it wasn't going to be good.

"What's this?" he asked as he took the envelope from Olivia, who stood in front of his desk.

"It's my letter of resignation. And an IOU for all that you have given me. I'll pay you back. I just don't know when."

He didn't care about the money. Only one thing stuck out in his mind. She was leaving. "Where are you going?"

"I'm going back to Houston." She took a deep breath. "I wanted to be professional and submit my resignation."

"Why are you leaving?" He looked down and saw the letter was trembling in his hand.

"Me coming here has been just one big disaster."

"Please, Olivia, don't go. I mean, I'm not talking about our situation. You've laid the foundation for a good life here. They love you at the dance school. You have Angela ready to devote a whole division to you. You are so good at what you do. Do you really want to give all that up?"

"Everything was built on a lie. Kendall will never forgive me. I've created a big mess. I wanted answers. And honestly, a part of me wanted you to pay for hurting my mother."

"You have no idea how much I've paid already," Bernard said miserably. "I paid the minute I let your mother walk out of my life. I paid when I lost you. I'm paying now."

Olivia didn't have all the answers she wanted, but this had ended so badly that she thought maybe she didn't need to know the rest. Although she was still upset with Bernard, she didn't want to leave with a hate-filled heart.

"There's so much I still don't understand," she found herself saying. "I see the pain your wife is going through, and I don't understand how my mother could have played a role in that. It makes me wonder if I ever really knew her. I mean, what kind of woman was she to do what she did?" Olivia asked, bewildered. "I understand why your wife is angry. What I don't understand is why my mother would do it."

When Bernard had prayed yesterday, he'd felt a peace come over him. But he knew he still had one score he needed to settle. His path to healing wouldn't be complete until he told Olivia everything.

"Have a seat," Bernard said, motioning toward the chair in front of his desk. She looked at him in alarm, and he sighed. "Everything you know about your mother is the truth. She was a good woman. She was loving, kind, caring."

"If she was all those things, why would she live under your roof—with your wife—and carry on an affair with you? Why would she conceive a child with you? It's no wonder Adele hates her."

"I would be the first to admit that I haven't done right by my wife. I haven't done right by a lot of people, including you," he said sincerely. "But your mother was a good woman. I don't want you to think otherwise. That's why you need to know the truth. The whole truth."

"You told me already."

"No, I haven't told you everything." He pulled open his desk drawer, then reached in and removed a letter in a sealed envelope. He tore it open. "I hadn't shared this with you because this was my darkest hour." He held the paper out to her. "It was a dirty secret that I wanted to stay buried, but you need to see it. It's a letter from your mother."

With apprehension she gingerly took the letter. He stood up and walked over to the bar to give her time to read it.

*My dearest Bernard,*

*I'll never understand why things turned out the way they did. Me moving into your house was a big mistake. I let my heart lead me into doing something I had no business doing. I should have never come here, into your home, because while I could resist the temptation to resume our relationship, deep down inside, I knew that you could not. But I just so desperately needed to be near you, even if I couldn't have you. I know you have tried to repent for what happened when you came into my room that night. I applaud that you have remained faithful to Adele and kept your distance from me for this long, but it was tearing my heart apart to be here and not be able to have you. We were foolish to think this situation would ever work. I know I was desperate and destitute, but coming here was not the answer.*

*I know you feel awful about what happened last month. I see it in your eyes every time you refuse to look at me, when you make a hasty exit when I enter the room. Your son craves attention from you. You're all he has and you're retreating into a shell of self-recrimination.*

*I know the man that entered my room that night in a drunken stupor, who forced himself on me, who cried as he entered me, was not you. It was a combination of the alcohol, the pent-up frustration, and the denial of our love. So I want to let you know that I forgive you. I will not hold that against you. And I will take that secret to my grave because I know your heart and you would never hurt me. But my heart does hurt, every time I see you and know that I can't touch you. I can't have you. So for that reason I'm leaving. I will make up an excuse to Adele. It's going to break my heart to leave my precious Kendall, but I can no longer take the torture. No, I did not want you that way, but I can't lie and say that your touch didn't bring back memories that I will cherish forever.*

*I know now that since we can never be together, it's time for me to move on.*

*With all my love,*
*Lorraine*

Olivia looked up from the letter. "I don't understand. This sounds like you raped my mother."

Bernard set down his now-empty glass. He'd downed the bourbon in one gulp. "It wasn't rape."

She shook the letter his way. "This says you forced yourself on her. That's rape."

"I went to her one night after I had too much to drink. You don't understand the pain and torture that I was going through, that we both were going through because we wanted to be together so desperately."

"You forced yourself on her," Olivia repeated, stunned. She was learning more and more about this man, and she wasn't liking what she was discovering.

"I went into her room to talk, but seeing her in her nightgown, yes," he said, stopping himself, "I forced myself on her. I told myself even though she was saying no, she wanted me as much as I wanted her. But you see, she forgave me." He desperately pointed at the letter. "She knew that wasn't me. She forgave me."

Olivia was so upset. She needed to know how he could do something like that. She still had so many unanswered questions.

"I don't understand. If she left, then what happened? How did I come into the picture?"

"She didn't leave. Shortly after that, she found out she was pregnant and with nowhere to go, I convinced her to stay."

"What? So she continued living there?"

He nodded. "But I never touched her again. We kept our distance and we didn't continue our relationship. I wanted it, but I respected her decision. Don't you see? I didn't want to risk losing her. She wanted to leave so many times, but she had nowhere to go, and honestly, I convinced her that you would have the best possible life if she stayed right where she was."

Olivia was starting to understand. This version lined up much better with what she knew about her mother. "So you weren't having an affair while she lived there?"

"No, we were only together that one time, the time that resulted in your birth. Your mother was not to blame for that. She wasn't to blame for any of it."

Olivia didn't know how she felt. She was happy to know that her mother had not carried on an illicit affair under Adele's roof. But she *had* lived there, knowing that she had Bernard's child. She took the job knowing that she was in love with Bernard.

A cornucopia of emotions ran through Olivia's body. She felt relief at finally knowing her mother's story. But Bernard—the man she'd actually come to care about these past few months—was some kind of monster. She was about to reply when she saw Adele standing in the doorway, her hand covering her mouth in shock.

Olivia and Bernard both went perfectly still, trying to gauge how much Adele had heard.

"A rapist, too?" she said, slowly entering the office. "Why does that not surprise me?"

Olivia felt compelled to speak up. What did she have to lose? "Mrs. Wells, I understand you've been through some things."

Adele folded her arms and glared at Olivia. "You have no idea what I've been through." Adele directed her hate-filled gaze at her husband. "The pain I've endured."

Olivia ignored their exchange. They could work out their issues after she was gone. Right now she just wanted to say her piece and go back to her life before she knew about Bernard Wells.

"Mrs. Wells," Olivia continued, "I'm sorry about all that you've had to endure. I'm sorry about what my mother did to you. And if you heard this conversation"—it was Olivia's turn to cut her eyes at Bernard—"then you know she didn't carry on this long-term affair with your husband."

Adele chuckled like that was irrelevant. "One time or one hundred times. She was so in love with my husband, she stayed in my home. That woman lived under my roof with a child that I adored." She regarded Olivia as if recalling a fond memory. "Do you know you used to come sit on my bed and brush my hair? I used to dress you up in frilly little outfits and take you out everywhere with me. I thought you were the most precious little girl. You were the bright spot in my life." Adele shrugged painfully. "And all along they both knew that you were my husband's child." She pursed her lips, fed up. "Nope, your mother is not this saint you want her to be. I trusted her and she betrayed me."

"I understand that's how you feel, but that's not the woman that I knew," Olivia said gently. "The woman I knew was kind, loving, and compassionate. She may have done wrong when she was with you, but she spent her life trying to make it right."

Olivia felt sorry for Adele, but she had been so unfeeling, she hadn't realized, right in front of her eyes, how desperately in love her husband was with another woman all those years.

"I want to say one more thing," Olivia went on. "Regardless of what happened, that's not me. I can't carry my mother's sin. I'm not saying forgive my mother, but don't hold *me* responsible."

Adele's demeanor became stiff again. "You don't ever have to worry about me forgiving your mother. It didn't happen when she was alive, and it's not going to happen now that she's dead." Adele caught Bernard's surprised expression. "Yes, I know she died. You don't think I'd let your daughter just reappear and I don't then do my research?"

"Mrs. Wells—" Olivia tried to interject.

"And since you're an extension of your mother, I will never, ever accept you in my life. I have no control over what my husband chooses to do." Adele cut her eyes at him. "I've finally come to the realization that he couldn't care less about my feelings. So I hope that the two of you have a wonderful father-daughter relationship, but I won't be a part of it."

Adele tossed up her hands like the conversation was over.

"I just came to let you know that I filed for divorce this morning," she told Bernard. "And you know what that means for England Enterprises? I've instructed Nicole to notify the board. We have an emergency meeting tomorrow at ten a.m. Please bring all relevant files and information," she said, her tone coldly businesslike.

Olivia expected Bernard to protest, for things to get ugly, but he sighed wearily and said, "Fine, Adele."

She glared at him one last time and headed toward the door. She added, for Olivia's benefit, "And I hope that your emergence was worth him losing everything." She marched out the door and headed back down the hall.

Bernard couldn't let this end like that. He had to stand up for himself—and for Olivia. "Adele," he said, following her out the office. He stopped in his tracks when he saw Adele standing face-to-face with Jerry Cooper.

"What are you doing here? How did you get in the building?" Adele snapped.

The crazed look in Jerry's eyes made the hairs on the back of Bernard's neck stand up. In what felt like a slow-motion scene out of a movie, Bernard saw Jerry pull a small chrome handgun from under his coat. *"Jerry, nooooo . . ."* Bernard screamed. But before he could move, the sound of gunfire rang in the building. Employees started screaming as they scrambled toward the exits. Adele let out a guttural moan, then collapsed to the floor.

Bernard raced to her side. "Adele, oh, my God, Adele!" He

looked up at a stoic Jerry standing alone, just feet away, a five-by-seven photo of a little girl taped to his chest.

"You were right, Mr. Wells," Jerry said. "She deserved to die. Just like my baby."

Then Jerry pointed the handgun at his right temple and fired a single shot.

# Chapter 43

Olivia sat outside in the lobby of the emergency room, slowly rocking back and forth. She couldn't watch another person die, even if that person hated her.

They'd rushed Adele to the hospital while words like "critical condition" and "dire situation" were tossed around by the rescue-squad personnel.

Olivia had no idea who had done the shooting until she saw the news report on the television in the waiting room. The shooting at England Enterprises was breaking news. They'd flashed a photo of Jerry Cooper, saying he had died at the scene. Apparently, he was distraught over the death of his daughter and he blamed Adele. The reporter was talking to a family member who said Jerry had begun spiraling downhill when his wife died last year. His daughter was the only thing that had kept him going.

The news story was heartbreaking. Olivia had heard rumblings of Jerry's firing, but she had no idea something like this could ever happen as a result.

At that moment, Olivia missed her former lifestyle. The one before all the secrets were exposed. The one before all this mayhem.

She was jolted from her thoughts as Kendall came racing down the hallway.

"What happened?" he said frantically. "They said my mother has been shot." He was sweating like he'd run the entire way to the hospital.

Bernard walked into the waiting room just as Kendall approached. "Kendall!" he said, hugging his son tightly.

"Mom. I need to see Mom! Is she okay?"

Bernard put his hands on Kendall's shoulders. "Calm down, Son. They took your mother into surgery a while ago."

"How is she?"

Bernard winced, and Olivia knew right away the prognosis wasn't good.

"Your mother was shot in the chest. She was alive when they brought her in, but . . ." He swallowed the lump in his throat. "We have to keep our fingers crossed." He paused, then corrected himself. "We have to pray for her recovery."

"She has to make it," Kendall cried, clutching his father for dear life. "The last words I said to her were I hate her. I can't let her leave me like that."

Kendall sobbed and Olivia's heart broke.

A nurse appeared in the waiting room. "Mr. Wells, your wife is out of surgery."

"Is she okay?" Kendall asked.

The nurse's expression remained impassive. "The doctor will have to tell you how she's doing. I came to see if you wanted to come back with your wife."

Bernard looked to be unsure if he should leave Kendall.

"I got him," Olivia said, easing up behind her brother and wrapping her arms around his waist.

"I want to go," Kendall said.

"Just wait. I'll come right back," Bernard said. "I just want to see how she's doing."

Kendall reluctantly nodded as his father walked away. As soon as Bernard turned the corner, Kendall sank down in a chair and continued crying. Olivia sat next to him, rubbing his back. She didn't want to say anything. She just wanted to provide a comforting touch.

He mumbled softly, "Why did I have to be so ugly to her? If she dies, I'll never forgive myself."

"She's going to be okay," Olivia said, though she was not sure of that at all.

"Why did this have to happen?"

"I don't know. But you have to stay strong. She's gonna need you to be strong when you see her."

She allowed Kendall to cry without interruption for a few minutes. Finally, he took the Kleenex she offered him and blew his nose loudly. He used another one to wipe away his tears. She had never seen him look so wretched. "Do you know where I was when they caught up with me?" He sniffed, then continued without waiting for her to answer, "I went to go see my birth mother." He said it as if it were the worst thing he'd ever done.

"*Your birth mother?* How did you find her?"

"It was easy," Kendall said harshly. "She's a freakin' stripper."

"What?"

"Well, not technically. Not anymore. She still works at the club, though. What fifty-year-old woman works at a freakin' strip club?"

Kendall told her how Bernard had reluctantly given him Sandy's last known information. Kendall said he had tracked her down in less than three hours.

"What did she say?"

His eyes were red and puffy. "She was shocked at first," he said dully. "Then she asked me for some money."

Olivia gasped.

"I haven't seen this woman in twenty-five years and the first thing she does is ask me for money? When I told her I didn't have any, she wanted to know why I was bothering her."

"Why did you go see her?"

He shrugged. "I wanted to know about her. I wanted to know why she gave me up." He stared pointedly at Olivia. "I guess I wanted answers like you."

"Did you get your answers?"

"She said she gave me up, and I quote, 'Because I didn't want any damn kids.'" He shook his head. "The only reason she had me was because she thought I'd be a meal ticket, but that got old real fast, especially when she learned my mom was the one with the money and not my dad."

Olivia's heart went out to Kendall. She could see how painful that conversation had been.

"She said I needed to count my blessings that I had some rich folks to take me in. She even pointed to the back of the club and told me she lived in the room in the back and she was okay with it. She didn't need a kid cramping her style." He looked like he wished that Olivia could help him make sense of this strange encounter. "How could she be so cruel?"

It was amazing how people always thought the grass was greener on the other side. Olivia thought life had been so much better for Kendall simply because he had grown up with money. Kendall thought his birth mother would be so much warmer than the one he'd known all his life.

Both of them couldn't have been more wrong.

"My mom used to always say, sometimes we have to see a dark cloud to appreciate the bright ones," Olivia found herself saying.

"What does that mean?" Kendall asked crossly.

"I know you have issues with your mom, but maybe you needed to see your birth mother—the way she really is—so that you could appreciate Adele."

Hearing his mother's name brought back a rim of tears. "I need to tell my mom I'm sorry," he said, jumping up. "I need to let her know that I forgive her, and get her to forgive me."

"You'll have time."

He turned to face Olivia, his eyes desperately praying that her words would come true.

"I'm so sorry, Kendall," she felt compelled to add. "You may never forgive me for deceiving you, but I can't say that enough. I have been so happy these past months to find out I have such a nice brother."

She waited for him to respond, hoping that her apology didn't ignite his anger all over again.

Kendall didn't say a word as he reached out and pulled his sister into the tightest of embraces.

# Epilogue

They would never be one big happy family. But a near-death experience has a way of changing people, and Adele Wells had definitely changed for the better.

"So when is this thing going to start?" Adele asked, irritated.

"Patience, Mom, patience," Kendall said, planting a kiss on his mother's forehead.

She sighed and leaned back on the sofa of Kendall's spacious West Hollywood home. Olivia could tell Adele was a little uncomfortable being here with everyone, but she had showed up nonetheless. This occasion meant the world to Kendall, and Adele had put aside all of her issues to be here.

It had been over a year since Olivia had set foot in Los Angeles. Bernard had done what he should have done a long time ago: he'd moved out. Of course, he had waited until after he nursed Adele back to health. He'd told her all the while that he had no intention of leaving, but by the end she told him that she wanted him to go. Getting rid of Bernard had lightened the burden that Adele had carried for years, the one that had made her bitter and angry. Kendall had told Olivia recently that Adele had stopped drinking and was now dating a man twenty years her junior.

Bernard hadn't been so lucky in love. He'd tried to patch things up with Alyssa, but having her heart broken once was enough. Despite his pleas, she refused to give him another chance. She'd told him that while she would always love him, in her heart she knew he would never love her and she was tired of settling. Bernard wished that he could tell her she was wrong, but he knew she wasn't. His one true love had slipped through his fingers, and he was sure, he had told Olivia, that his punishment was to pay for that betrayal for the rest of his life.

Instead, Bernard had buried himself in trying to build a small company he'd taken over. While Adele might have changed, she could not permit him to keep running England Enterprises. She did let him keep one of the small companies he'd acquired, and over the past year he'd begun making a name for himself.

As expected, Olivia had promptly been served her walking papers for "intentional deception" in her hiring. But Olivia's talents had impressed her old supervisor, Angela Barrows, so much that she'd taken Olivia with her to her new job as a buyer for Macy's. Olivia's life had never been better. She'd made peace with her mother's past, and she had a newfound family.

Maybe, Olivia thought, she could get her happily ever, after all. At least where her family was concerned. She still had no love life. She had heard that Stephon had married his baby's mama, but that was okay with Olivia because she was confident that one day she'd find someone who would give her joy. After all, Kendall had found his, in the most unlikely of places. That's why they were all here today.

"Okay, everybody be quiet," Kendall said as he grabbed the remote and turned the volume up on the TV.

"Kendall, it's really not that big of a deal," Mona said, walking into the living room.

Kendall pulled her close to him and planted a deep kiss on her lips. "Are you kidding me? My baby is making her television debut. That's a big deal to me."

Mona grinned widely as Kendall directed everyone's attention to the television. Olivia was proud herself as a scene of Mona in an emergency room filled the screen. Olivia couldn't believe that her best friend had landed a recurring role on *Grey's Anatomy*. And Olivia had to admit, Mona had nailed it. Shonda Rhimes would be crazy not to make her a permanent character.

"So, is that why you summoned us here, for her five minutes of fame?" Adele asked.

Olivia tensed up, wondering if Mona would go off on the woman. This was Adele's first time really around Mona. Adele wasn't thrilled about Kendall's and Mona's relationship, but Adele was so happy that Kendall had forgiven her, she didn't really give him a hard time about it. Olivia hadn't been happy with the news either. But after a few minutes around them she realized that they were happy together. They helped one another find their inner joy.

"Now, Mrs. Wells," Mona said, sliding onto the sofa next to Adele, "you know everybody has to start somewhere. Next time it will be ten minutes, then twenty, till I'm the star of the show." Everyone chuckled, even Adele. "But you know something? Kendall has the big dinner with the new client at Sony, and I have no idea what to wear. I was hoping perhaps we could go shopping and you could help me pick out some things since your style is always so on point."

Adele smiled, then squeezed Mona's hand. "It would be my pleasure, Mona."

Olivia had to give it to her girl. Olivia never thought anyone could break down that wall Adele had built, but Mona was doing a fantastic job. Kendall hadn't become the superstar musician that he wanted to, but he'd found steady work producing hits for some top singers.

"Olivia, can you help me out in the kitchen? I'm gonna get the dessert for everyone," Mona said as she stood and headed out the living room.

Olivia followed her friend into the kitchen. She still couldn't believe this was now Mona's home. Well, she could believe it. After all, Mona had announced what she wanted in LA from the very beginning, and what Mona wanted, she usually got.

"Mona, I'm proud of you," Olivia said as Mona lifted a cheesecake out of the refrigerator.

Mona set the cake on the table. "Thanks, girl. But I owe it all to you." They hugged. "If you hadn't come here, I wouldn't have come with you." Mona stuck her hand out and wiggled her finger. "And I wouldn't be getting married next year."

Olivia still couldn't believe that. Her best friend was going to be her sister-in-law. That had been Kendall's Christmas gift to Mona.

They had celebrated Christmas a few days ago—with both Bernard and Adele. Olivia smiled to herself, remembering the big surprise her father had in store.

"Well, there's one more Christmas gift to open," Bernard had said when all the presents under the tree had been unwrapped. He handed Olivia an envelope.

"What is it?" she asked, taking it. She assumed it was a check, since that was Bernard's way of dealing with everything. Their relationship had been strained this past year, to say the least. There was so much that she had to forgive him for. But he was patient and told her to take all the time she needed. He'd be right there waiting.

Bernard didn't answer. Both he and Kendall stood there grinning as she tore the envelope open and pulled out a letter. Her heart dropped when she saw the letterhead.

"Read it out loud," Kendall said, excited.

"'Dear Miss Dawson, it is with extreme pleasure that we invite you into the 2014 incoming class of the Juilliard School.'" She looked up in awe. "What is this?"

Bernard and Kendall continued grinning.

"What does it look like? It's your Christmas gift," Kendall said.

"It looks like a letter of admission to Juilliard."

"It is. You're excellent at fashion, but I knew you said your heart was with dance, and I have learned that a person should follow their heart," Bernard said.

"But . . ."

"Keep reading," Kendall said.

She returned to the letter. "'Your tuition, books, and housing have been covered for the entire four years, and we look forward to having you as a Juilliard student.'"

"How?"

"My money is good for something," Bernard said.

"Like a whole new arts center," Adele mumbled sarcastically.

Kendall flashed a smile at his mother, then turned back to Olivia. "The Lorraine B. Dawson Center for the Arts."

"What?"

"I can't bring back your mother, but I want to honor her memory," Bernard said softly.

"Naturally, if they got a whole new arts endowment, they can't deny the daughter of the person the endowment is named after, can they?" Kendall said.

Olivia stood, staring at the letter in stunned disbelief.

"It's all legit," Kendall said.

Finally, she squealed with excitement. She was going to Juilliard! But as she jumped up and down, she noticed Adele out of the corner of her eye. Olivia calmed down, then turned to Adele. "Are you okay with this?"

"No, but it doesn't matter what I think." Adele casually shrugged. "That was a long time ago, anyway. I'm letting bygones be bygones. Not worth my energy to be upset about it."

Her response was a long way from that of the nasty woman Olivia had met a long time ago, and that's all Olivia could ask for now.

She focused her attention on Bernard. She knew he couldn't be doing so well with trying to get a new company off the ground. "How . . . ?"

He knew immediately what she was referring to. "A long time ago, I promised your mother that I would build a nest egg for us." A look of pain crossed his face at the opportunity he had missed. "Well, I never did anything with that nest egg, and over time it grew into a lot of money." He shrugged helplessly. "So I thought, what better way to finally spend it?"

Olivia couldn't think of a better way either.

# A Note from the Author

Every book, every time, I swear that will be my last time doing a note from the author. But when the time came to send in my final corrections, I just couldn't send my book back without acknowledging the people who help me do what I do. But just to be clear, this isn't an acknowledgments page, so if your name isn't here, don't feel slighted. This is just a note from the author to thank a few people, say a few things, and let you know how eternally grateful I am to be living my dream.

And I *am* living my dream.

I'm making up stories for a living. (See, Ma, you always called it lying and didn't buy my "active imagination" argument, but it paid off. And these stories *are made up*. That's my story and I'm sticking to it. I don't care if it sounds just like something that so-and-so did. Any resemblances to actual characters or situations are purely coincidental. If you shared something with me and you now see it in my book, that's just a coincidence as well. Besides, if you don't tell anyone it's you, I won't either.) But I digress. The great thing about what I do is that, while fictional, my stories mirror the lives of so many people. I can't tell you the number of people who say they've learned to forgive, to love, to heal, to be open and honest, who renewed their relationship with God, who gave their marriage a second chance, etc., etc.—all because they were moved by something in one of my books.

That's some powerful stuff and it makes everything I do worthwhile.

But I wouldn't be able to do what I do if not for some important people who make my writing career possible. First and foremost, thank you, God, for blessing me with a talent to write.

Much thanks to the man who has been there from the very beginning, who nurtured and encouraged my dream when it was still a concept, Dr. Miron Billingsley. Thank you to my three lovely children, who bear with me when I'm writing and traveling.

And to my absolutely incredible support system, there are not enough words to show my gratitude for helping my writing career flourish by making my personal life flow as smoothly as possible. My mother, Nancy Blacknell, I am what I am because of you. This has been the most trying time of our lives, but your resilience shines and you'll be back to your old self in no time. My sister Tanisha Tate, who does whatever I need, whenever I need it, without complaint (okay, I take that back, you do complain, but you still do it, so thanks)!

As always, many, many thanks to my agent, Sara Camilli; my editor, Brigitte Smith; Melissa Gramstad, Louise Burke, the awesome people who design my covers (I've never met you, but you are the best!), and everyone else at Gallery Books. I've been so lucky to have found a publishing home I've loved from the beginning. Thanks for all your hard work!

## A Note from the Author

Thank you also to my extended support system: LaWonda Young, Jaimi Canady, Raquelle Lewis, Kim Wright, and Clemelia Richardson. You know that core group of people you should always keep in your life, the ones that will be there whether you're up or down, hot or not—you guys are my core. Thank you for always having my back.

To Pat Tucker Wilson, my sister in spirit, who has been an unbelievable support and a write-or-die friend, thank you for always being there. You know how much your friendship means.

To my writing twin, Victoria Christopher Murray, thanks for the inspiration, the friendship, and the never-ending support.

To Yolanda Gore and Kym Fisher, thank you. That's all I can say. A hundred times, thank you. Much love to Jason Frost as well.

Lots of love to my literary colleagues who always offer words of advice, encouragement, and are just trying to run this race with me . . . Nina Foxx, Tiffany Warren, Roy Glenn, Zane, La Jill Hunt, Angel Hunter, Renee Flagler, Dwan Abrams, Sadeqa Johnson, and Rhonda McKnight.

Once again, I have to say thanks to Reina and Regina King, Bobby Smith, Crystal Garrett, Roger Bobb, Shelby Stone, Queen Latifah, and all the fabulous folks at BET. Thank you soooooo much for making my movie dreams come true!

I know it may seem odd to some folks that I want to thank my social media family, but these folks have been there for me—even though many of them I've never personally met. They have reached through cyberspace to encourage, motivate, empower, inspire, and celebrate me. Thank you so much to Marcena, Bettie, Yasmin, Jetola, Julie, Sheryl, Noelle, Sheretta, Crystal, Sammi, Cindy, Kimberlee, Alicia, Marsha, Jonathan, Judy, Olivia, Juanita, Angela, Ashara, Nicole, Gwen, Denise, Kimyatta, Norlita, C. Mikki, Tanisha, Deborah, Romenia, Sonia, Kim, Beverly, Shannon, Antoinette, Gina, Carmen, Christina, Jamesina, Maurice, Lisa, Nedra, Donna, Nicki, Gee Gee, Dorothy, Paula, Tonia, Chevonne, Rochelle, Mia, Demetria, Sheila, Raquel, Loretta, Allyson, Keileigh, Makasha, Raine, Stacy, Jakki, Tameka, Cebrina, Margueritte, Tiffany, Tawni, Bernice, Dee, and Cecelia. (I know there are many more but I need to wrap up at some point!)

As always, much love goes to my wonderful, illustrious sorors, especially the Houston Metropolitan Chapters. And my sister moms in Jack & Jill.

And finally, thank you. Yeah, you holding this book. If it weren't for your support, I wouldn't be where I am today. If you're a new reader, thanks for checking me out. I hope you'll get hooked. If you're a previous reader, thanks for coming back. If you enjoy this story, I just ask one more thing . . . pass the word, not the book!

I know, I said I wasn't going to get caught up doing acknowledgments again, but when you have such wonderful people in your life, that's a promise that's just hard to keep.

Until the next book. . . . Thanks for the love.

*ReShonda*

Gallery Readers Group Guide

# a family affair

ReShonda Tate Billingsley

## INTRODUCTION

When Olivia Dawson's mother confesses on her deathbed that Olivia's father is the rich business owner Bernard Wells, Olivia and her best friend Mona head to Los Angeles to get some questions answered. When Olivia arrives, she finds a father who wants to keep her quiet, a brother she has vague and loving memories of, and the woman who banished her and her mother from Bernard's house years ago and who has spent her life denying Olivia's existence. Secrets can bind families together, or they can rip families apart. As startling revelations come to light, the patchwork family must learn to redefine love and to understand how lucky they can be.

## QUESTIONS AND TOPICS FOR DISCUSSION

1. Olivia's mother kept the existence of her father a secret. Do you agree with what she did? By the end of the story, do you think the secret Olivia's mother kept was for Olivia, her father, or herself?

2. Is it ever okay to keep a secret from a family member or a friend in order to protect them? Has a family member or friend ever kept a big secret from you? Did you understand why they kept the secret and how did you feel?

3. What would you do in Olivia's shoes when she walks into the England Enterprises building and meets Bernard for the first time?

4. Do you agree with Mona that "everything happens for a reason"?

5. Do you sympathize with Bernard's mistress Alyssa?

6. What do you think Walter's role in the story is?

7. Do you agree with Walter's belief that when he is going through trials in life "that's God working it out"?

8. Initially, what are your thoughts about Adele? Do they change by the end of the story, and if so, how?

9. What do you think of the revelation that Olivia learns from the letter her mother wrote to Bernard?

10. What do you think of Bernard turning to Walter for advice at the end of the novel? Has he changed? Is he redeemed?

## ENHANCE YOUR BOOK CLUB

1. Sketch some designs for England Enterprises. Share your fashion visions with the book club.

2. Bring some music to your book club meeting and create a sound track for *A Family Affair.*

3. See what Olivia is headed for in the Juilliard dance program: http://catalog.juilliard.edu/preview_program.php?catoid=13&poid=1266&returnto=1389. Select your ideal courses for her.